SHERLOCK HOLMES
AND THE
DUELLING DUKES

The Early Casebook of Sherlock Holmes

Book Six

Linda Stratmann

SAPERE
BOOKS

SHERLOCK HOLMES
AND THE
DUELLING DUKES

Published by Sapere Books.

24 Trafalgar Road, Ilkley, LS29 8HH
United Kingdom

saperebooks.com

ISBN: 978-0-85495-215-1

For Jon and Alison

From
Memoirs of a Medical Man
by A. Stamford FRCS

1924

CHAPTER ONE

'Stamford,' said Sherlock Holmes to me one day, in that casual manner he so often adopted when he was about to favour me with a challenging demand, 'would you be so kind as to enlighten me on the rules of cricket?'

We were in the students' common room at Barts Medical College at the time, making the most of our brief leisure by reading the newspapers. I was particularly cheerful that day, as I had completed my interim examinations, and felt confident of a good result. Holmes, during all the years I knew him, never took a formal examination, although his studies were immense and often a little peculiar. Once he had thoroughly explored the area that interested him, he liked to venture into the unknown with the intention of adding to the sum of human knowledge, and accordingly devised his own methods in the process.

It never failed to astonish me that Holmes, with such profound wisdom on so many subjects, should also have several extraordinary gaps in his understanding. His only explanation was that there were fields of study in which he had no interest and were of no relevance to his work. He therefore refused to accumulate unwanted material in his memory where it would occupy valuable space that could be better used for something else.

'Do you mean to take up cricket?' I asked, somewhat surprised since Holmes had never shown an inclination to take part in team sports of any kind.

'I do not,' he said, 'but I would like some acquaintance with the rules, and details of its nuances or subtleties, should there happen to be any.'

Holmes was a sportsman of considerable prowess, his preferences being boxing and fencing, combative pursuits where he had to rely solely on his own resources, man to man. My usual summertime exercise was cricket. Aficionados will not need to be told of the pleasures of that game, while others find it tedious and slow and can never be converted. Hoping to discover the reason for Holmes's sudden interest, I launched into a description of the batting pitch and positioning of the fielders and was moving on to the system of scoring when Holmes silenced me with a dismissive wave.

'Enough!' he cried. 'That is sufficient for me, and most probably for any reasonable man.'

This was disappointing, as I was about to emphasise the vital importance of the often neglected medium-pace bowler. 'But you should tell me why you have asked me this all of a sudden,' I said. 'Is it connected with one of those mysteries you like to solve?'

'No, but I have received a most unexpected invitation,' he said. 'Lord Redcar, the Duke of Charlbury, has a country estate in Oxfordshire, and proposes to hold a week-long entertainment in which a number of sporting competitions will take place. He invited his friend, the Marquess of Queensberry to be a general overseer of the sports, to ensure correct scoring and fair play.'

'A good choice,' I said. The young marquess was an enthusiastic and formidable sportsman in several disciplines and would undoubtedly be equal to keeping order in any company. I had already witnessed Holmes, as an amateur challenger in the boxing ring, winning a purse awarded by

Queensberry. My friend's skill and courage had made a deep impression on the marquess, who had invited him to lunch.

'Unfortunately,' Holmes continued, 'Queensberry took a bad tumble in a recent steeplechase, suffered a blow to the head, and was stretchered home unconscious. He came partly to his senses, and on being asked what should be done, all he was able to say was "send for Sherlock Holmes!"'

We were never to discover why Queensberry called for Holmes, since when he was fully recovered, he was unable to remember having done so. Little did we know that one day his words would reverberate around the world.

'You have been invited to take Queensberry's place?' I exclaimed.

'I have.' Holmes produced a folded letter from his pocket. 'Lord Redcar wrote to me himself.' I did not need to ask if Holmes would accept the invitation. He had not yet told me of his intention to become a professional consulting detective, but it was already obvious to me that to Holmes, solving mysteries was more than just an amateur exercise. It was an activity that consumed him and would always do so. He was still acquiring and improving the skills he needed to realise his ambition and was beginning to move up in society. The right connections would bring recommendations which would offer him challenges of the order and quality he craved.

'When is this event?' I asked.

Holmes named a week in the summer, those blissful days when academic labours are done, and students abandon their dreary rooms to disport themselves in fields and on rivers.

'And there will be cricket, of course,' I said.

'Cricket, fencing, sparring, running, archery, swimming — all manner of sports. The estate is extensive, and Lord Redcar has created an exercise room for pursuits of arms.'

'In such company you would not wish to reveal the sum of your knowledge of the English national sport,' I said with a smile.

'No, Stamford,' said Holmes with perfect seriousness, 'that I leave to you.'

I was of course delighted to be included. It also occurred to me that I could prove useful in treating those minor injuries such as strains, cuts and bruises which were so often the badges of honour amongst sportsmen.

'Have you ever met Lord Redcar?' I asked.

'No, I shall be travelling there on Saturday morning to meet him and discuss the arrangements, and will no doubt be questioned and examined to see if he approves. But he would be hard put to it to find another substitute, as there are an abundance of other sporting contests which are claiming attention.'

I was sure that Redcar would thoroughly approve of Holmes, who, while not of noble blood, had the presence and bearing of an aristocrat.

'Has he hosted such an event before?'

'Not on this scale, no. And unusually, it does not appear to coincide with the entertainment of a distinguished visitor, or a notable family event such as an engagement, or a son's majority.'

'Why now, do you think?'

'That,' said Holmes, thoughtfully, 'is what I would be interested to know.'

CHAPTER TWO

'The society papers are a mire of scandal and iniquity,' said Holmes, his nostrils flaring in distaste. 'I should read them more often.'

I must have looked a little shocked at this comment, for he smiled indulgently and went on, 'Villainy is not confined to the humbler classes. It exists everywhere; only the cost differs.'

I decided not to ask him if he anticipated any villainy at Lord Redcar's. There was, I suspected, a part of Holmes's character which always hoped to find it wherever he went.

We were on the train taking us to Charlbury station via Oxford. Lord Redcar had readily accepted Holmes's request to bring a companion to supervise the cricket, and we had received our tickets in a neat little envelope specially printed with his lordship's coat of arms, enclosing an elegantly penned note saying that a carriage would meet us at the station. I realised that I was about to enter a world for which I had no preparation, no experience. My origins are humble, my forebears, as far as I am aware, belonging to the class of respectable skilled artisans. I have never seen a reason for shame in this, although I have often encountered those who did and advised me not to mention it. I was about to be admitted to the ancestral home of nobility, as an invited guest, and by the front door.

Holmes, as I have often observed, was at ease in any society; he was able to adopt the style and manners of any class when it was necessary for his enquiries. His initial efforts at disguise, which I can recall with some amusement, had not been successful. I had recognised him at once, observing that his height and characteristic gait marked him out for anyone who knew him, whatever his costume. I like to think that although initially mortified by these comments, Holmes had made use of them to improve his skills. In time, he was able to make subtle changes in his voice and mannerisms, such that even I, who was so often in his company, would fail to know him.

'Have you learned any more about our host?' I asked.

'The general history of the nobility is open for all to see,' said Holmes. 'Their movements and family events are well chronicled in the respectable public press. What lies beneath those bland words is often more interesting. Lord Redcar is aged fifty-five and has been married twice. He has a daughter by his first wife and was a widower for many years when he took to marriage once again. It is much commented upon that his second wife is very young and beautiful.'

Whether or not Holmes approved of the situation was not apparent from his tone. I decided not to pursue that subject. 'Is he a great sportsman?'

'His principal interest is fencing,' said Holmes. 'He studies with a master who favours the Italian school, and I am told that he pursues the sport with considerable —' and here Holmes paused, as if carefully choosing his next word — 'enthusiasm.'

I have never taken up the sword, and Holmes noticed from my expression that elaboration was required.

'In brief,' he explained, 'the Italian school, which has been less fashionable in recent years, is noted for the vigour and directness of its attack, the French for elegance and subtlety.'

'Which is superior?' I asked. 'I mean, if a proponent of the Italian school engaged with one of the French, which one would prevail?'

'That question has led to quarrels and even duels for some years past,' said Holmes. 'The general opinion, with which I concur, is that the French school is superior, but in an extended contest an Italian master of strength and endurance may wear down a more agile opponent.'

I tried to imagine such a scene and was left with the impression that while it would be thrilling to watch, I would not wish to be anything other than a spectator.

The difference between my situation in life and that of Lord Redcar became even more apparent when we alighted from the train and boarded the carriage waiting for us outside the station. I have travelled in a London four-wheeler, and very occasionally a hansom. At the end of a busy day, a vehicle for hire carries some of the evidence of its multiple occupants and its own well-worn and decaying interior. It smells stale with a hint of tobacco, old garments, and bad air, rather like the odour of an unwashed corpse presented at the medical college for dissection. A carriage owned and maintained by a lord is a very different affair, polished and bright, with subtle ventilation allowing a waft of country breezes.

My nervousness may have got the better of me, and I must have given this away in my manner and movement. I was examining my fingernails for cleanliness when Holmes chuckled and said, 'The cutlery is used from the outer part of the setting, moving inward for each course.'

That wasn't precisely what I was thinking about, but he did gauge the general reason for my discomfort.

Holmes rarely missed an opportunity to explore the depths of criminality, and our wanderings were often enhanced by his descriptions of the hideous crimes that had taken place along our route. Thus far he had been silent on the subject, from which I guessed that the inhabitants of rural Oxfordshire were either extremely law-abiding or committed crimes so dull and unimaginative that Holmes did not think them worthy of his attention. Our progress along the leafy lanes in sunny summer weather was extremely pleasant, and I was almost wishing it were a longer journey, when Holmes spoke at last.

'The peace of the countryside often conceals a violent, bloodstained history,' he began. 'When King Charles I was forced to flee London, he established his court in Oxford. The city was besieged several times, battles were fought, and there were numerous raids and skirmishes. One action which is notorious hereabouts occurred in 1646, when a troop of Royalists was attacked by Parliamentarian forces. The Royalists were heavily outnumbered and forced to retreat. They took refuge at a roadside inn, located on this very way, which was soon surrounded. Demands for surrender were refused, and the commanding officer of the parliamentary forces, a Colonel Keogh, who was known more for his recklessness than good sense, ordered that the inn be set ablaze to flush them out. The Royalists who escaped the flames were slaughtered. The others, as well as the innkeeper and his family and servants, perished in the fire.'

'How shocking!' I exclaimed.

'More than two hundred and thirty years after the event, it remains the subject of long-held resentment, and the families allied to the opposing sides regularly engage in violent conflict.'

'Really?'

'Although nowadays it tends to involve a football.'

Some minutes later we saw a small roadside inn, its walls clothed in luxuriant creepers. A colourfully painted sign read 'Traveller's Rest'. A young woman in a spotless white apron was busy watering the flowers bordering the path which led to this island of tranquil refreshment.

'That inviting hostelry is built on the site of the former inn and stands as its memorial,' said Holmes. 'It is said that on a stormy night, one can hear Colonel Keogh demanding surrender.'

We continued on our way, with pastureland to our right and a high stone wall to the left, behind which we could see the upper portions of tall trees.

The carriage slowed and we turned away from the road into the approach to a set of iron gates, which were opened for us by a man who emerged from an ancient gatehouse. Proceeding along a driveway, I saw an encouragingly extensive stretch of grassland, certainly enough for a cricket match, and more distantly a densely wooded grove of trees. A sparkle of reflected sunlight suggested the presence of a small body of water. I was not sure what to expect of the house — something rather grand, like a small palace, I suppose, but it came into view in a more modest way, very stern and solid and venerable. Its broad stone-faced front was three storeys high, and topped by tall chimneys, with the edge of a wall hinting at outhouses and stabling lying just out of sight.

'It dates from the sixteenth century,' said Holmes.

'Then it must have been here when the inn was burned down,' I said. If the house had been besieged, there was no sign of it, and I wondered what story it could tell if the old walls had been able to speak.

We alighted and were met almost at once by a stockily built fellow in country clothes. He sported a greying moustache and short hair, cut like a brush. I assumed he must be Lord Redcar's estate manager but was soon proved wrong. 'Welcome to Charlbury Park, gentlemen,' he exclaimed, heartily. 'I am Montague Redcar. We are very informal here, so please make yourselves at home. I trust you have had a pleasant journey?'

'Very pleasant indeed,' said Holmes. He sounded sincere, but whether it was the glories of the peaceful countryside in summer or viewing the site of a historic massacre that had prompted his appreciation was unclear.

Lord Redcar ushered us into a stone-flagged entrance hall, made dark by old panelling. 'We have a very simple way of life on the estate,' he said. 'It is designed to make us comfortable with the least possible trouble. My butler Xavier manages all the arrangements, my housekeeper Mrs Pescott manages Xavier, I instruct Mrs Pescott and my wife advises me. But when you have refreshed yourselves, we may proceed to view the fencing hall, and after luncheon I will show you the grounds and where the outdoor exercises will be held.'

'Might I ask,' said Holmes, 'in whose honour this event is to be held?'

'Oh,' said Lord Redcar, with a light chuckle and a careless gesture, 'call it a gentleman's whim. I am not as young as I was, and while I can still give a good account of myself against younger men, I perceive that a time may come when I might have to turn to less vigorous exercise. Do you fence, Mr Holmes?'

'I do.'

'Splendid! And you, Mr Stamford?'

'I, er, no — I am a cricketer and undertake a little light sparring to keep me active in the winter.'

'Never saw the point of cricket, myself,' said Lord Redcar dismissively. 'Too slow for my taste. But I leave all that to you.'

Once we had brushed the dust of travel from our garments, Lord Redcar conducted us to his fencing hall and gave us a tour, describing its amenities and contents with unconcealed pride. It was an extraordinary room to have in one's home. I think it must once have been intended for banqueting, as it had the long rectangular shape designed for a dining table and set of chairs which would easily accommodate twenty or more persons, and several sideboards in addition, with ample space remaining for a busy team of servers, but it contained none of these things. The wooden floor, unpolished to allow the fencers some purchase for their feet, was empty of furniture, apart from a large wooden chest standing in one corner. A long area extending down the centre and some three or four feet in width, was outlined on the floor in paint. This was the place of combat.

The perimeter of the room was rather more interesting, since it displayed an impressive collection of antiquated weapons. The walls were fitted with low wooden troughs in which rested the ends of what looked like old-fashioned lances, some eight feet tall, still with their iron heads. There was a row of them, standing stiffly to attention. I was told they were actually thrusting spears known as pikes, and had been carried into battle by foot soldiers during the Civil War, the years of bitter conflict that had culminated in the execution of King Charles I. There were swords in plenty, of all designs and sizes, much battered from use and clearly of great age. I realised of course that these were not to be used in the week's competitions but formed his lordship's personal collection of weapons of war, the martial origins of what later became the formally conducted sport of fencing. The display was further enhanced by items of armour, decorated breastplates, gorgets which protected the throat, and helmets.

Lord Redcar was especially proud of a prized pair of sabres which were displayed in a glass case. These were cut and thrust weapons, with long, curved, tapering blades and heavy knuckle guards, in fine condition and beautifully polished. 'Italian,' he said. He proceeded to give us a brief history of the sabre, from its inception as a weapon of war, to its adoption as a duelling sword much loved by students who enjoyed displaying their facial scars, and finally, in a modified form, only recently developed by an Italian master, for sport.

The fencing foils were quite different. They were displayed on narrow brackets, the blades slender, smooth, and shining, the tips enclosed in dark wrappings. Lord Redcar took one down for us to inspect. I was surprised at how light and flexible it was.

'Mr Stamford looks a little nervous of our proceedings,' said Redcar with a smile. 'Please be reassured, the foil is a weapon of contact only. We do not cut, but lunge, and score points by touching the man with the tip. But we cannot pierce our opponent. The end, which as you see, is bound in leather, is not sharp at all, but flat, like the head of a nail.'

I was not entirely reassured since it occurred to me that if a foil were to snap when the fencer lunged, it would still be highly dangerous.

Framed pictures continued the theme, engravings demonstrating fencing positions taken from works of the renowned masters of that art. I was reminded of boxing illustrations, the old bare-knuckle pugilists with arms outstretched towards their opponents, their upper bodies leaning back to avoid being struck in the face. These old-time fencers adopted the same position, swords extended forward, heads tilted back, weight on the rear foot. Even with that precaution it seemed inadvisable that they were not wearing protective masks, and I assumed that this was the practice before such things were invented.

'I don't suppose you might like to essay a few passes with the foils, Mr Holmes?' asked Lord Redcar, jovially.

'I would be delighted,' said Holmes, with a bow. It was pointless for me to protest.

Redcar rang for a servant. 'Xavier will stand as our director,' he said. 'He has eyes like a hawk, and is to be trusted completely.' He threw back the lid of the wooden chest. I was somewhat relieved to see it contained face masks, gauntlets, and padded jackets. 'I expect you will find something here to fit you.'

'I am glad to see there are face masks nowadays,' I said. 'Not like those fellows.' I nodded towards the portraits of the old-style combat.

'Masks were devised a hundred years ago,' said Lord Redcar, 'but many fencers disdained to wear them, thinking it was unmanly to protect themselves. A mask was seen as a sign of cowardice and lack of skill. Of course, it made the whole business rather slow and mannered.'

The butler, Xavier, appeared with remarkable alacrity. He was aged about forty, tall and rather thin. His face was hard and narrow, with expressionless grey eyes. When Lord Redcar directed him to call out the hits, he simply replied, 'Yes, my lord,' and assumed the place where he would command the best view.

Suitably arrayed, Redcar and Holmes chose their weapons and faced each other on the marked-out track.

I could not really describe the combat, as I am not knowledgeable enough. For Lord Redcar, it involved violent lunging while stamping the forward foot and uttering loud grunts. Holmes was silent, aloof, his feet moving smoothly, his sword arm deflecting his opponent's attacks with elegant turns of the wrist. Every so often, Xavier would declare a hit, and they would pause and take up their starting positions again. Eventually the combatants bowed to each other, removed their masks, and shook hands. 'Well done, young sir,' said his lordship. 'But I think Italy has conquered France!'

Holmes merely inclined his head in acknowledgement.

I dared to ask about the cricket, which Redcar seemed to have quite forgotten about, and he conducted us to a small room next to the fencing hall, where there was a store of equipment, all somewhat worn but just about usable. 'We can make an afternoon of it, I suppose,' he said. 'I wouldn't want it to go on longer than that. Who are the other team, Xavier?'

'The Charlbury Village Players, sir.'

Redcar gave a little laugh. 'Our gentlemen sportsmen should soon see them off.'

The requirements for archery were also stored there: bows, arrows, quivers, and leather gloves. The straw targets, being rather bulky, were kept in a barn.

'Fine sport, archery,' said Redcar grudgingly. 'Good for the eye and balance. Even ladies may practise it with some success. My daughter, Henrietta used to like it.' He contemplated this for a few moments, then gave a little sigh, but said no more on the subject.

As we left the room, I said to Holmes, 'You let him win, didn't you?'

'I'm not a complete fool,' he said.

CHAPTER THREE

Our next destination was a small library, where there was a collection of old volumes which appeared to be mostly works of reference, including the usual directories of Oxfordshire and histories of the county. Our host did not strike me as a great reader.

The purpose of our visit was to be shown a large, framed map of Charlbury Park, which we examined carefully. The manor with its accompanying outhouses, barns, and stables, lay to the eastern end of the estate, and there was a garden area marked out to the rear. The remainder of the estate consisted of the grassland and woods.

A small river, the Charle, trickled unobtrusively through the grounds, sometimes drifting through the trees and later opening out into a small, probably artificial lake, a kind of Serpentine in miniature, before proceeding on its leisurely way. It was one of the many tributaries which flowed into the wider Evenlode and ultimately joined the Thames.

'I was hoping to have swimming, which is possible when the river flows more strongly, but the recent fine weather has left the waters too low and muddy. My guests would not thank me if I asked them to plunge in,' said Lord Redcar.

'Do you have a list of guests?' asked Holmes.

'Ah, yes, I am sure we do. Xavier, do you have such a thing?'

'I do, my lord,' said Xavier. He opened a drawer in a small writing desk, from which he extracted some papers. 'I took the liberty of preparing some material to assist the gentlemen.'

'Ah, that is excellent,' said Lord Redcar. 'I fear that the list is not yet complete, as I am still waiting for a number to respond to my invitations, but it ought to be a merry throng.'

'There are also some notes of the proposed events, and a copy of the estate map,' said Xavier, handing us the papers.

The list of names, even including those who had been invited but had not yet accepted, was quite brief. 'I hope there will be sufficient men for cricket?' I said. 'A team requires eleven. We are several short of that number.'

'Ah, there you have me. I am not very knowledgeable about that game,' said Lord Redcar. 'In fact, I have never so much as watched it. I have been told it is an excellent cure for sleeplessness, so if I should ever suffer from that complaint, I might venture to do so. But if we cannot make a team, I would not object to its cancellation.'

Cricket is, in my opinion, the most subtle and delightful of English sports, something I hoped Lord Redcar would one day come to appreciate. 'If you have fewer than eleven men, it is always possible to have an enjoyable match with a smaller team,' I said, encouragingly.

'Good, good. Well, gentlemen, there is just time to view the field, and then we will have our luncheon. Xavier, you had better accompany us.'

Redcar led us through a handsome dining room where double doors opened onto a sunny terrace. It was bordered by a balustrade, and well decorated with urns that spilled over with cascades of colourful flowers. A small table was furnished with a jug of lemon water and a crystal glass, and under a parasol sat a young lady clad in a delicate white summer gown. Keeping her company was a maidservant of more mature years, occupied with needlework. The lady looked around and smiled at us as we arrived, her maid rising to make a little curtsey. Redcar made the introductions with undisguised pride.

'Gentlemen, my wife, Lady Redcar.'

I have never married, nor am I ever likely to. However, I have in my lifetime met many ladies who are able to command almost immediately a gentleman's loyalty and admiration, and I was far from immune to their charm. Such a lady was Margaret, Lady Redcar, who epitomised beauty and grace without a hint of artifice. If there are portraits of her which men may gaze upon, they might wonder if such loveliness could really exist, thinking perhaps that the artist had exaggerated her features. I can say now that no artist could ever do justice to the reality.

I wondered if Holmes might find this feminine vision interesting, but there was no change in his expression as he bowed and uttered the usual politenesses.

Lord Redcar took us on our tour of the parkland, and I decided on the best place to locate the cricket pitch. My main concern was to make use of the smoothest possible surface, otherwise the results of bowling would have been eccentric to say the least. It also seemed advisable to ensure that the sluggish waters of the River Charle lay well outside the playing area. I suggested laying a rope to mark the position of the boundary, although given the general skills of amateur cricketers I doubted we would see many hits travel that far. His lordship had no interest in these essentials, but thankfully Xavier paid them close attention and assured me that all would be attended to according to my wishes.

'I intend to begin our sports with a pleasant little run around the estate, just to see which men have kept themselves in trim, although there may be a few little surprises for them along the way,' said Lord Redcar with a chuckle. 'No cheating, mind.

They will have to collect paper tickets as they go, each with a number, to show they have run all the course. Part of the way will be through the woodland paths, which will provide some interesting challenges. They will receive a map showing the route they must follow, the course of the stream and the position of the bridges. I shall take part also; it will be an excellent exercise to warm the muscles.'

'I suppose you must know the woods very well,' said Holmes.

Redcar laughed. 'Indeed, I do. They were my playground as a child, the place of my imaginary adventures, where I pretended to be an explorer in the jungle, but I promise I shall not press my advantage.'

We didn't delve into the woods, which I found far from inviting. I could see even from a distance that they were composed of old established trees, clustered close and dark, suggesting the presence of roots and undergrowth likely to promote a stumble or two. Sprains and scratches were a real possibility, and I decided that I would bring some suitable medical supplies to deal with these minor accidents.

Holmes had been reading the list of the guests' names as we walked. 'I do not know Baron Brambilla,' he said. 'Is he a swordsman?'

'My fencing instructor,' said Redcar. 'And you will also see listed the Chevalier L'Épine, a master of the French school. I have no doubt that they will be eager to try their prowess against each other. And then there is Sir Jasper Grey, who boasts that he can match two men at once with a sword held in each hand, and beat them, too. We may be obliged to put that to the test.'

'It is a very illustrious company,' I said, trying to sound impressed rather than nervous.

'Oh, yes. In fact, we have been sent sporting royalty by the university. There is a prince of India who is a student there, and also Viscount Northam, who trains the rowing team. He can follow his bloodline back to King Charles I and beyond, and I have been told that he is so modest about his royal ancestry that he hardly ever mentions it. Oh, and I ought to say that my cousin Sir Hubert Winchip will also be here,' added Redcar in a more sombre tone. 'I do not expect him to take a great part in the sports. He did once, in his younger days, but not now. He has suffered losses and disappointments in recent years and has been afflicted with melancholy. His father, Ambrose, was my first cousin, and since his death Hubert has never been quite the same. I hope the sports and the company might cheer him.'

It wanted a quarter of an hour to luncheon, and we returned indoors, to be greeted by Mrs Pescott, the housekeeper. A woman in her middle years, she blended so well into the manor that she appeared to be a part of it, like a piece of practical furniture much valued for its years of service. She brought a thread of comforting light to the otherwise gloomy interiors, and a note of calm to her employer's occasionally quixotic humours.

Luncheon was a welcome prospect after our walk, and we repaired to the dining room where platters arrived laden with cold chicken, ham, eggs, slices of savoury pie, fresh salads, and bread. Lady Redcar was a waif-like presence at table, gazing at the food on her plate as if she could not recognise it, and making most of her meal from dry bread and sips of water. To do him credit, Lord Redcar paid her constant attention, asking how she was and if there was anything else she might like, but she smiled and reassured him that she might have a better appetite later on.

There was a little time before the carriage would come to take us to the station, and Lady Redcar suggested she would like to show the visitors the flower gardens.

'Are you at all interested in flower gardens, gentlemen?' asked Lord Redcar, dubiously.

'I would like nothing better than to view the flower gardens,' said Holmes, with an unexpected burst of enthusiasm for the subject.

Lady Redcar summoned her maid, and we accompanied her into the sunshine, while Lord Redcar said he had some letters to write and would join us shortly.

The gardens were laid out in a very orderly manner, and were overlooked by a pretty little cottage, dressed in flowering vines and bordered by a sea of wild blossoms. The warm air was laden with fragrance, yet Lady Redcar, whose guiding hand I was sure had orchestrated this delight, seemed distracted and hesitant as she told us the names and character of the various shrubs and herbs that flourished on either side of the pebbled pathways. Her maid, whose name was Molly, followed us a few paces behind, and after a while her mistress suggested she might like to sit on an ornamental settle in the shade of a sapling. We continued our tour and eventually, once the maid was too far distant to overhear our conversation, Lady Redcar turned to us. As her face peered out from beneath the lace of her parasol, there was no mistaking the expression of a lady who needed our assistance.

'Mr Holmes, Mr Stamford, have you decided to supervise my husband's sporting enterprise?' she asked.

'We have,' said Holmes. I merely bowed agreement.

'Then I must tell you something,' the lady continued. We waited. 'I believe that my husband is about to place himself in very great danger.'

CHAPTER FOUR

I hardly liked to ask the reasons for the danger to Lord Redcar, but I wondered if our host, who appeared to be in good health, suffered from an unseen condition which might imperil his life. I braced myself for the prospect of dealing with an emergency while far from any hope of prompt assistance.

Holmes had other thoughts. 'Is this to do with the swordplay?' he asked. 'Lady Redcar, please be reassured: fencing, if the rules are strictly adhered to, as I am sure they will be, is not a dangerous sport. Mr Xavier appears to know his business very well, and I am sure he will prevent any infringements. I will also, I promise you, do my best in that respect.'

These words did nothing to quell her concerns. 'It is not the fencing competition which troubles me, but the possibility of unsupervised conflict.'

Holmes explored a little further. 'I notice that the list of guests includes both an Italian and a French fencing master. Rivalries do exist between the different schools. It would be unwise of anyone to try and come between them. But if you would like me to prevent their meeting in private to test their differences, I promise to do so.'

'It is not they who concern me.' It was now very apparent that Lady Redcar was addressing a fear she was finding it hard to express. She walked on a little further, and we followed. Then she turned and faced us again. 'Before I say any more, please tell me if you are acquainted with Sir Jasper Grey, Duke of Garthorn, who has also been invited.'

'I do not know him, but I know his name, since it appears in the sporting journals,' said Holmes. 'Chiefly concerning fencing.'

'I have not met him, neither do I wish to. If you have read of him, you will be able to judge whether or not he is an accomplished fencer.'

'He is reputed to be one of the finest there is.'

'Then it is worse than I had feared,' she murmured.

I could see that Holmes was impatient to know more, but unwilling to press for revelations the lady was struggling to divulge. 'Lady Redcar,' he began gently, 'kindly allow us to assist you in any way we can to alleviate your concerns. Only direct us and we are at your service.'

She permitted herself the ghost of a smile. 'I have been told that Sir Jasper Grey is sometimes referred to under another name. He has been called "the worst man in England".'

'That is not a title to be envied,' said Holmes. 'I will not enquire as to what brand of iniquity he practises. And your husband has invited him here? I find that extraordinary. Perhaps he has not been warned about Grey?'

'Oh,' said Lady Redcar regretfully, 'he knows that gentleman's reputation all too well.'

Holmes evinced astonishment. 'Yet despite that, he invites him to his home? I can understand your concern.'

'I have already taken steps to prevent any unpleasantness. My mother will come to stay and be my constant companion during the sporting competitions. You see the little cottage yonder? We call it Garden Cottage. We will have rooms there and my maid will attend us. Our housekeeper Mrs Pescott will ensure we have everything we need for a very pleasant interlude. As the lady of the manor, I will on occasion join our guests to dine in the main house, but that is only out of politeness, and I will not stay long. I shall be quite safe.'

'I am relieved to hear it,' said Holmes. 'Nevertheless, I feel it is a serious error to have invited such a man.'

Lady Redcar paused and allowed a milky frown to briefly mar her delicate brow. 'Mr Holmes, Sir Jasper Grey's notorious reputation is the very reason why he was invited. In fact, I think it is the reason for this entire event.'

We stared at her. Even Holmes was silent. Lady Redcar looked around at the maid, who was sitting contentedly in the shade with a little folded paper fan. However, she moved still further distant before she spoke again. We walked with her, all attention.

'I believe that for some little while, my husband has entertained the notion of challenging Sir Jasper Grey to a duel.'

We were somewhat taken aback by this statement, and I think that both of us were obliged to wonder if Lady Redcar was mistaken. It was Holmes who spoke first. 'With swords or pistols?' he enquired.

'Swords, naturally. I do not think Montague has a pistol in the house. But he has many volumes about swordplay in his study and has been reading them very assiduously of late. He has also engaged his fencing master, Baron Brambilla, for further lessons, and practised more often. And I have seen him standing in a contemplative manner before a portrait he has of Lord Cardigan, the seventh earl.'

That gentleman, who had died a few years previously after a long and tumultuous career, was especially notorious for his leadership in the Charge of the Light Brigade at the Crimea. This was an action which was referred to as courageous or foolhardy or possibly both, depending on the individual.

'Why Lord Cardigan?' I asked.

'Many years ago, he fought a duel with another officer, using pistols, and shot and seriously wounded his adversary. He was arrested and tried before a jury of his peers, but his position in society protected him; even the queen spoke out in his favour. Despite the facts of the matter being well known, and not denied, he was acquitted on a claim which many feel was contrived for the purpose. My husband has often spoken about this, and warmly approves the verdict. He believes that while injuring one's opponent even in a fairly fought duel is considered to be a crime, such an act should even now stand a chance of being excused or treated leniently. Many noble gentlemen still believe that seeking justice by combat is their ancient right.'

'A duel, whether with pistols or swords is always the result of a personal insult, a matter of preserving one's honour,' said Holmes. 'Has Sir Jasper Grey insulted your husband?'

Lady Redcar glanced at her maid once again and turned aside to examine the blossoms on a burgeoning shrub, touching the petals with her fingertips. 'My husband has a daughter by his first wife,' she said. 'Henrietta is aged twenty-two and last year she was married to Sir Walter Kingsley, a baronet, who has an establishment just outside Oxford. Montague dotes on her; I believe he would do anything for her. Some weeks ago, Henrietta and her husband were at a ball. Sir Jasper Grey was there. Neither of them had met him before. It was a warm night, and she went out onto a terrace to take a breath of cooling air. Grey followed her. Finding her alone, he approached her in a manner she found insulting, frightening even. His words, his actions — she could not bring herself to describe them. Fortunately, she was able to escape back indoors, and she made sure to avoid him for the rest of the evening. But later she overheard comments from other guests and learned of the man's reputation.'

'Has she not told her husband what occurred?' asked Holmes. 'If anyone should defend her, it is he.'

'Sadly, she has not. Her husband, I am sorry to say, is a jealous man. Although she has never given him any cause to doubt her, she is afraid that if he knew about the incident, he might come to believe that she had given Grey some encouragement, or worse still, that she welcomed his approaches and agreed to an assignation. When I last saw her, she told me of the encounter, and was adamant that she was repulsed by Grey's behaviour. My only advice to her was not to attend any event in future where Grey might be present. That might be hard to determine, of course, and she dares not make enquiries or even mention his name in case her words will suffer another interpretation.'

'Does Lord Redcar know what occurred?' I asked.

'I did suggest to her that for the time being she ought not to mention it to anyone else, in case word spread, but I found that she had already told Montague. He has said nothing to me, but he is aware that I have spoken to Henrietta and must suspect that I have learned of what occurred. Since then, I have observed the changes in his behaviour that I have mentioned. He is planning something.'

'You are sure he is contemplating a duel?' asked Holmes.

'Something of the sort, yes.'

'Not just a competition with sporting swords? To humiliate his enemy with a defeat?'

'If I thought that, I would not be so concerned. No, Montague is a man of tradition. I think he means to injure or even kill. He still believes in the privilege of nobility.'

I turned to Holmes. 'Do you think Lord Redcar can overcome Grey in combat?'

'I believe Grey is a much younger man, by some twenty years, but then one must never dismiss the experience that comes with age,' said Holmes.

'I am only relieved that he did not issue a formal challenge at once,' said Lady Redcar. 'He can be very impetuous. However, I think that while making his plans, he has received wiser counsel.'

'Wiser counsel?' asked Holmes. 'You must mean the butler?'

'Yes. In a formally conducted duel, Xavier would have been his second. I am sure Montague must have asked him and received sound advice not to precipitate a combat which would endanger his life. But they have been in close consultation, following which this gathering of sportsmen was announced. I think Montague is hoping that Grey will suffer some injury this week, which would be suitable revenge. In fact —' Her lips trembled and for a moment, she was unable to go on.

'You think he might be arranging for something to take place that would have all the appearance of an accident?' asked Holmes.

'That is my fear, yes,' she exclaimed. 'A fencing encounter with some error in the weapons used, perhaps. I can only guess at his plans. I don't know. But whatever happens, the outcome will be disastrous. Either Grey will see through the plan and injure or even kill my husband, or if Montague should by some good fortune prevail, he might find that his subterfuge does not assist him, and he will be arrested and charged with a crime.' Her face was suffused with distress, and she uttered a little gasp, pressing her hand to her forehead.

'Are you well, Lady Redcar?' I asked, anxiously, offering my arm. 'May I help you to a seat?'

'No — thank you,' she said, with a shake of the head. 'It is merely the heat of the sun and thinking of the dangers to my husband.'

'Would you like me to try and dissuade your husband from pursuing this course?' asked Holmes.

'Nothing will dissuade him. But you are in a special position here, supervising the sports. You may be able to learn the details of what he is planning, and step in to avoid it. I beg you, do not reveal my warning; he might suspect that I have discovered his plan and am attempting to frustrate it. Act only on what you yourself can see or hear.'

Understandably we gave our solemn assurances as gentlemen to do all in our power to protect Lord Redcar from Sir Jasper Grey, and himself.

It would soon be time to be borne back to the railway station for our return journey. I took the opportunity to speak to Mrs Pescott and obtained a through appreciation of the medicines and dressings she had available. There was a good supply in a box in the scullery, and she was experienced in their use. This meant that I would only need to bring a few things to augment them. The science of antiseptics was then in its early stages, and some medical men still refused to believe in their value, but I had seen for myself their use in surgery, and decided to prepare a lotion with which I could clean and purify any injuries.

Lord Redcar thanked us warmly before we left, and Xavier handed Holmes a notebook. 'You might find this useful, sir,' he said.

Holmes studied the notebook as we travelled. The butler's handwriting was extraordinarily neat. In fact, it was the writing on Lord Redcar's correspondence, and it contained a complete and perfect plan for the sporting events and how they were to be arranged. 'Meticulous,' said Holmes. 'It is only left for me to prevent accidents and murder.'

'I suppose,' I said, 'you wouldn't think of warning Sir Jasper Grey of Lord Redcar's intentions?'

'Most inadvisable,' said Holmes. 'Lady Redcar may be mistaken in her conjecture, but even if she is correct, Grey may not be a man who plays by the rules. We would only be giving him an advantage. All we can do is keep a close watch on them both. We shall divide the tasks between us. Swimming will not now occur, so I will supervise boxing, archery, and fencing, and watch Lord Redcar. You will oversee cricket and running and keep a close watch on Sir Jasper Grey.'

I didn't like the sound of that, but I knew better than to argue.

CHAPTER FIVE

Holmes once observed to me that when setting out on a venture, it was important to plan wisely, but with the strict understanding that plans had the unfortunate habit of going badly awry. He was always alert to the possibility of the unpredictable. Three days before the sports were to begin, we received a letter from Lord Redcar to say that two of the guests whom he had been sure would agree to take part had abruptly changed their minds, on finding it suddenly imperative to be elsewhere. Both gentlemen were known for their devotion to sparring, so this had seriously depleted the numbers available for that sport. His lordship had been making enquiries amongst his friends, hoping to find replacements, but without result. I could see that he might be able to augment the numbers in the cricket team from the male servants, but putting them in a roped ring with gentlemen might be considered a step too far.

It was something of a poser, but then I recalled that my friend, classics scholar George Luckhurst, who attended the same sparring classes as I, might be available. 'Luckhurst has some relatives with a place in Buckinghamshire,' I told Holmes, 'and I know he was going down there for the summer. If Lord Redcar agrees, I'll send him a telegram. He might come.'

In fact, I was sure that Luckhurst would come, as he had complained to me at some length about being obliged to entertain a distant cousin who did nothing but insult everything Greek and deplore his choice of occupation, while making poorly veiled hints and threats about a will. If my friend was really unlucky, there would also be a parade of single ladies arriving at the house with the anticipation that an engagement would be forthcoming by autumn. Luckhurst was an assistant keeper in the British Museum, his modest salary augmented by an annuity bequeathed by a great aunt. He therefore enjoyed as much income as he required without being beholden to anyone, and his studies left him no time to entertain ladies. While he found Buckinghamshire delightful, and there were some country houses with interesting collections he liked to visit, he did not relish being derided across the table at every mealtime, and my telegram was the perfect excuse to make an early escape.

I wondered if we should inform Luckhurst of our secret mission at Charlbury Park, as another pair of eyes might prove useful, but Holmes determined not. Lady Redcar, he pointed out, had not given us permission to mention this delicate matter to another person.

Since our initial visit, Holmes had studied the history of the two rival fencing masters, who had over the last few years made a great deal of noise from the issue of challenges and throwing of insults, none of which had ever come to anything. He was inclined to believe that nothing would ever ensue, since each time the two agreed on the time and place for a contest to determine whose swordsmanship was superior, one or other of them had some pressing reason which rendered him unable to attend. It was rumoured in the fencing fraternity that they had come to a temporary truce while in England, but there was an appointment to settle the matter once and for all in Paris next month. There, so I had been told, duelling in a public street with unabated swords was not so much a misdemeanour as a spectator sport, and a large crowd was expected.

Of Sir Jasper Grey there was little more to learn, other than his life of adventure with ladies, the mention of which in any gathering elicited either grunts of disgust or snorts of what might have been envy.

Holmes and I arrived at Charlbury Park early on the first day of the sports, and Luckhurst joined us shortly afterwards. Mrs Pescott was going about her business in her usual discreet way, Xavier was an island of calm and Lord Redcar was running from place to place, like a small charge about to explode.

Mrs Pescott conducted us to our accommodation. The upper floor of the manor house was mainly composed of servants' rooms, and the first floor was divided into a number of bedrooms with the usual offices. There were not enough bedrooms for us all to have our own, but I was happy to have a bed made up in the dressing room that adjoined Holmes's room. Lady Redcar would be retiring to the garden cottage, which enabled Redcar's cousin Winchip to share his lordship's suite. This meant there would be room for all. Our suite was well appointed in old-fashioned style, with a bedstead and wardrobe of carved oak, and a dressing table with a porcelain jug and basin for shaving water. All was very tidily kept and freshly swept, polished, and aired. I was sure we would be extremely comfortable.

We introduced Luckhurst to Lord Redcar, who fortunately took to him at once. Assuming that my friend's interest in Greek and Roman antiquities conferred an expertise in seventeenth-century English weaponry, he invited him on a tour of the exhibits. Luckhurst told me later that it was not hard to pretend the knowledge he did not have simply by admiring everything he saw and agreeing with Lord Redcar's description. While this was proceeding, we had the opportunity to speak to Xavier, who gave us a very thorough briefing as to the events, and any changes that had been made in the last week. Luckhurst would be taking the place in the running race originally assigned to one of the gentlemen who had not attended, and the other place was left vacant should the other man have a change of heart and arrive.

The first day was to begin with an interlude of peace before 'battle commenced', as Lord Redcar cheerfully put it. Our host and combatants were to gather in the drawing room for refreshments. Here, the required introductions would be made, and those who had not previously met could make their judgements on the enemy. A suitably light luncheon would be followed by a short interlude for the purpose of digestion, and then the first exercise, a run around the estate.

While we awaited the first arrivals, we were able to inspect the library. There was an edition of John Burke's *Peerage* which was more than forty years old, and his *Landed Gentry*, which was a little more recent. One volume which attracted my attention was a history of the county of Oxfordshire and I glanced through it, hoping to discover more about the dreadful siege at the nearby inn. I found it described in a few pages and understood why Charlbury Manor had avoided being burned by Parliamentarian forces. A member of the Royalist troupe, William Gilmartin, and his son Robert, a mere youth, had been amongst the few who were able to make an escape from the blazing inn. They had reached the gates of Charlbury Park, hoping to find refuge. The estate was then owned by an Oxfordshire lawyer called Maxstead, who happened to be a staunch Parliamentarian, and whose daughter was betrothed to the bellicose Colonel Keogh. Despite their desperate pleas for admission, the Gilmartins had found the gates firmly shut against them. William was discovered and killed, reputedly by Keogh himself. Robert had tried to escape by plunging into the river Charle where it entered the estate grounds through a dangerously restricted culvert, hoping to find a place to hide. Unfortunately, access to the grounds by that route was prevented by a set of iron bars. Weighed down by his clothing and armour, he had foundered and drowned. Although most of the books in the library did not appear to have been recently disturbed, a slim strip of paper fell from between the pages I was reading and fluttered to the ground. I picked it up and returned it to its place, wondering who had also been studying this violent history.

The first guest to join us in the drawing room was Lord Redcar's personal fencing master, Baron Vincenzo Brambilla. He was not above medium height, aged about forty-five, with wavy dark hair and a moustache carefully trained to add ferocity to his features. He moved with great assurance and addressed us with well-polished courtesy.

Lord Redcar introduced us, Holmes as an accomplished sportsman, and me as a cricketer and medical attendant. Drinks were being served with impeccable skill from a silver bowl of fruit punch by the butler, Xavier. Given that it was morning, and the punchbowl exuded a heady air of herbs and juniper, suggestive of gin as an important ingredient, both Holmes and I selected a lemon water instead, although Brambilla was happy with something a little stronger. I was looking at the oil paintings with which the room was well provided. One was of a rather pleasant-looking young woman, and I was standing before it, wondering what relation she might be to Redcar, when Brambilla came to my side. 'You are admiring Lady Kingsley?' he asked.

'I — yes, it is a very fine portrait,' I said, realising that this was Redcar's married daughter.

'I know what you are thinking,' he said, glancing at Lord Redcar, who was conducting an energetic conversation with Holmes. 'How could such a pearl have sprung from that rough and unattractive shell? And having done so, why should she have thrown herself away on Kingsley? I often wonder that, but I suppose wealth and position are great inducements.' He sighed. 'If I was a younger man, and possessed of an English title, and a bachelor, I would have captured that sweet lady for myself.' He beckoned to me. 'Come and see.' We moved on to another portrait, a rather older one, judging by the style of gown worn by the lady depicted. Her small, almost doll-like face peered timidly from a froth of flounces and lace, her form gathered into a pink silk bodice which sat atop a hooped skirt so laden with ribbon that I wondered how she had been able to move. 'The mother,' said Brambilla, 'the first Lady Redcar. I knew her, but only in her final years. She was never in robust health, but I am told that the birth of her daughter used the last of her strength and she faded away. I think Redcar took to the sword to give him an occupation to distract him from his grief.'

At that moment a footman announced the arrival of the Frenchman, the Chevalier L'Épine. He was younger than the Italian by about ten years, taller and more slender, with auburn curls and the thinnest moustache I have ever seen.

I felt some apprehension as to what these two might do when they confronted each other. Would they abide by their promise not to fight on English soil? Were either of them carrying weapons we knew nothing about? My imagination conjured images of pocket pistols and stiletto daggers. In the event, when they saw each other, they paused, gave curt bows, and then remained resolutely at a distance.

Holmes, I noticed, was studying them with great care. He had recently been making observations of the characteristic gait of certain occupations and had said that he could tell at once if a man had been in the military, even if he was not in uniform. I asked if he was able to tell the man's service and regiment, and he gave me a strange look. I gathered that the answer was 'not yet'.

More carriages were coming to the door, and the next one brought the announcement I had been dreading. Having heard so much about the deplorable Sir Jasper Grey, I was rather hoping to encounter a figure of respectable, modest appearance whose reputation for unrepentant villainy had been vastly inflated. These hopes were soon dashed when the door opened to admit a towering tree of a man, horribly handsome and stylishly dressed, whose easy manners and grace of motion gave him the appearance of a panther about to seize its prey. I hoped that I might be able to creep beneath his gaze and be dismissed as a person of no consequence.

The next arrival was Lord Redcar's cousin, Sir Hubert Winchip. He appeared to be between forty and fifty years of age. Of Lord Redcar's height, he was noticeably greater in girth. It was obvious to me from his slow, laboured gait that his sporting days, however successful they might once have been, lay firmly in the past. If he currently undertook any exercise, I thought his expertise must be shooting, or possibly riding where the horse would have to do most of the work. He and Redcar greeted each other warmly, asked after each other's wellbeing, and agreed that men of more mature years were easily able to teach the younger competitors 'a few things'. When offered a drink, Winchip looked askance at the small size of the punch cups, asked for two and eased himself into an armchair with a loud, wheezing grunt.

I determined to watch Winchip carefully, in case he should need deterring from any challenge inadvisable for a man of his physique. If that failed, I would be nearby to provide prompt medical treatment. It was not unusual to see men of such a build, after many years of idleness and self-indulgence, having decided to recapture their youth with unaccustomed exertion, being admitted to the anatomy room at Barts. In my pre-student occupation as a surgical attendant and dresser, I was instructed in artificial respiration, although it has to be said that in those days it was a very imperfect art. Once a man's heart has stopped, it is almost impossible to make it start again.

A far better prospect in the competitions was the next arrival, Viscount Northam, whose accent alone proclaimed him to come from that level of society that usually regarded mine as paid staff. Northam, who was in his thirties and at the peak of fitness, had the strength, eye and coordination of a seasoned all-round sportsman. He was quick to deny that the royal blood in his veins gave him any advantages. 'We are all equals here,' he announced, generously, his confidence noticeably faltering as his eyes lit upon Sir Hubert.

The name on the list that most interested me was that of Prince Albert Victor Rampal Singh. Redcar had told us that he was the eldest son of a maharajah who had made his home in London and was very active in public affairs, especially relating to improvements in education. The young prince, in his early twenties, was studying law at Oxford University, where he also kept his cricketing skills well-polished, and gave a good account of himself on the athletics track. I had never met anyone remotely like him and had some rather foolish idea that he might arrive on an elephant, wearing a jewelled turban. In fact, he arrived by carriage and was dressed in the English manner. On being introduced with his full name, he smiled and said he would be more than happy if we simply addressed him as 'Rampal'.

It appeared that our numbers were now complete, and Lord Redcar, clasping a cup of punch, turned to address us. 'Gentlemen,' he said, 'I bid you welcome. I trust that we shall have a fine time of it. You will shortly be provided with a programme of sporting events and a map of the estate.' He was about to continue when we heard a repeated clangour of the front doorbell, followed by a loud thumping on the woodwork, which reverberated down the hallway.

'Are you expecting anyone else?' asked Holmes, as the bell jangled once more.

Redcar was going to investigate when voices in the hallway, one loud and male, the other quietly feminine, showed that the impatient visitor had been admitted. Moments later, the door of the drawing room was flung open. Mrs Pescott stood to one side to allow the new arrival to enter. Had she tried to stand in his way, she might have been trampled.

The man who stormed in like an angry bull was aged about thirty, his face so red it looked as though it had been boiled. He stopped as soon as he saw Sir Jasper Grey, who was lounging in an easy chair, sipping his drink and looking remarkably unconcerned. 'That is the scoundrel!' the newcomer said, pointing a finger which shook with emotion. 'Do you entertain him, Redcar? Shame on you!'

Clearly, he was not the only man present who wanted to kill Sir Jasper.

CHAPTER SIX

The easy atmosphere we had so far enjoyed had vanished. Wisely, none of the guests decided to move or speak, and all eyes were on our host.

'Whatever is the matter, Kingsley?' demanded Lord Redcar.

His son-in-law turned on him in a fury. Even his lordship recoiled at such a powerful glare. 'Do you not know? Has my wife not told you of the words which passed between her and this blackguard? If not, then it is all the worse for her!'

'Kingsley,' protested Lord Redcar, 'you must be mistaken if you think my daughter is at fault. I beg you to treat her kindly.'

'I chastise her as is my right!' rapped the irate husband. 'She is mine to deal with, and I have her safe at home where this man cannot get at her.'

Redcar, giving up any attempt at placating Kingsley, turned to Sir Jasper, who had not moved from his comfortable position and appeared to be the calmest man in the room. 'What do you say to this, Grey? Is there any truth in it?'

Grey sipped his drink. 'It is a great deal of fuss and bother over nothing at all. Can a gentleman not pay a compliment to a lady?'

'Not if she is my wife!' thundered Kingsley. 'And I have yet to be convinced that she did not by some word, some glance, encourage your foul attentions!'

This scene, played out in front of an assembled company, had now gone beyond any pretence of delicacy. There were shocked expressions all around the room. I saw Xavier whisper some words to Lord Redcar, who nodded.

'Kingsley, this is not the place to air such suspicions,' said his lordship. 'Kindly consider that you may be labouring under a misapprehension. I cannot speak for Grey, but I am sure that my dear girl would never behave in the manner you describe. I suggest that you return home, talk to Henrietta in a quiet and calm manner and restore the harmony of your household.'

'Oh, no,' exclaimed Kingsley with a derisive laugh. 'I intend to stay here and keep a watch on this creature, in case he has some intrigue planned.'

Grey merely smiled, which only further angered his accuser.

By now, both the Italian and French fencing masters, as well as Viscount Northam and Prince Rampal, had decided that the weather being extremely fine, they should take a stroll on the terrace, and Luckhurst decided to keep them company. Winchip did not join them, as he appeared to be dozing, despite the disturbance. Holmes and I bowed to his lordship, ready to make our way outside, but Redcar held up his hands in protest. 'No, gentlemen, remain if you please.' It wasn't clear if he required us as witnesses, seconds or simply protection, but we stayed. Kingsley was a young man with a thick neck, both taller and stronger than Redcar. Who knew what he might do in a rage? I wondered briefly if the three of us would be enough to subdue him, but then of course one of the three was Holmes.

'Now then, Kingsley,' said Redcar, 'perhaps you might enlighten me as to what has provoked these accusations? I do not wish to have my other guests concerned, but you may speak freely in front of this company.'

Kingsley grunted and paced about the room. 'Who are these persons?' he demanded, gesturing insolently at Holmes and me.

'Mr Holmes and Mr Stamford are my trusted associates. They are friends of the Marquess of Queensberry, who has asked them to supervise my sporting week to ensure fair play,' said Redcar in a tone which did not admit of any objection.

Kingsley snarled but was obliged to accept the situation. It was brought home to me that trotting out the name of a celebrated nobleman was often enough to control an altercation.

'It would assist matters considerably if we were all to be seated,' said Holmes.

'I agree,' said Redcar, and sat down. We followed suit, as did Kingsley after a brief hesitation. Grey did not move, and Winchip continued to snore. Xavier offered Kingsley a cup of punch, which he seized and swallowed in one gulp.

'Some weeks ago,' said Kingsley, 'Henrietta and I attended the Countess of Eastleigh's ball. It was a warm night, and Henrietta, saying she felt a little faint, went out onto the terrace to take the air. At the time, I thought nothing of it. Wives have their weaknesses, you know. Yesterday I received a letter in which I learned, to my horror, that this scoundrel had been seen pursuing my wife onto the terrace. Or should I say joining her there? The letter was from an individual who, judging from its contents, I have no doubt was a guest at that ball, and saw and heard what transpired. I was informed that this reprobate, a man without principle or shame, had uttered words to my wife which should never have been offered to a lady.'

'Word, words, words,' said Grey, with a shrug.

'And did this honourable informant, whom I presume you are unable to name, tell you what Lady Kingsley replied?' asked Holmes.

'I have been told that Henrietta did not appear to be repulsed by what was said, as any decent woman should be, but made a reply which suggested to the observer that she received his vulgar expressions with approval. She then returned to the ballroom. She made no mention of this incident to me. Had she done so, I would have acted appropriately. But she did not. Her failure to do so speaks louder than any words. And now my worst fear is upon me. Has my wife abandoned all appearance of propriety and decency? Is she planning an intrigue with this scoundrel?'

'I can assure you there is no such intrigue,' said Grey.

'Sir, you are not a true gentleman, and your words are worthless to me!' said Kingsley. He set his cup aside and passed a handkerchief over his brow, which was running with sweat. Xavier refilled the punch cup, the contents of which Kingsley dispatched as quickly as the first. 'Naturally I arranged to have Henrietta locked securely in her room, where she is safe in the charge of my housekeeper. And her maid, whom I suspect of being involved in some way, perhaps by the passing of notes, has been dismissed. I travelled at once to Garthorn Hall to confront Grey with his abominable behaviour, and there I learned that he was here. And so, after a wretched night in the foulest of inns, I came here, hoping to discover the truth — that my wife has fallen under the influence, the wiles of this creature!'

I saw Grey's face change, losing its expression of casual and insolent humour, his eyes narrowing into a frown. 'You have locked her up?' he said, biting at the words in distaste.

'Yes, and I think I know what is best for my wife. So now, we will have the truth, or else if you disdain the truth, we may settle the matter as men. If you are not a coward, sir, kindly step outside with me, and I will prove the truth I speak in the sight of these gentlemen and the Almighty. Do you dare?'

Grey set his cup aside and uncoiled his long body from the easy chair, stretching to his full height. Kingsley was not a short man, but Grey was easily some six inches taller, and broader too. A smile played around his lips. 'With pleasure,' he said. 'Swords or pistols?'

Holmes was the first to step between the two men, and Redcar joined him. 'Gentlemen,' said Holmes, before Lord Redcar could speak. 'We cannot allow this. If you must prove yourselves, you must do so in sportsmanship, but our gathering here does not permit open combat. You may try to score hits with the foil, or in the sparring ring with gloves, but that is as far as it can go.' I thought Lord Redcar was a little disappointed with this statement. He could hardly contradict Holmes, but I felt he would have liked to see Kingsley and Grey fight it out, and would have been content with any outcome. I have to confess; I might have liked to see it too.

Kingsley's mood was rapidly dissolving into misery and self-pity. He applied the handkerchief to his forehead once more, and then announced that he would feel better if he splashed some water on his face, and abruptly left the drawing room.

Redcar turned to Sir Jasper Grey, who had seated himself again. 'I will not ask you to repeat the words you spoke to my daughter,' said his lordship. 'I do not wish to hear them. But you must tell me what her reply was. I will go and see her and speak to her in due course, so you should choose your words with care, as I know that she will tell me the truth.'

'I made some light conversation suited to a lady,' said Grey, casually, as if dealing with furious husbands was a common occurrence for him. 'She appeared upset, and I asked if she was well. She may have formed a certain impression, but I can't help that. She told me it was too warm in the ballroom, and she had come for a breath of cool air. I asked if I could assist her, and she said she was feeling well again and returned indoors. I have not seen her or had any communication with her since then. If she is too afraid of her husband to have told him what passed, that is hardly my fault.'

'Is Kingsley often like this?' asked Holmes.

'He has a strong nature,' said Redcar, gloomily.

'If I might make an observation,' I began.

'Ah, yes, of course. You are a medical man, and your opinion must be heard,' said Redcar.

'I think he might steady himself if he was to stay here for a short while, perhaps for an afternoon, and enjoy a walk in the fresh air. He should be encouraged to drink only mineral water, which would be preferable to alcoholic beverages which can stimulate the emotions. Then, when he has calmed his nerves, he may come to understand that his wisest course of action would be to go home in a better frame of mind and make peace with his wife.'

'Do you know, you may have something there,' said Redcar. 'Perhaps I had best not send him home while he is still upset. I know what I shall do,' he continued, brightening. 'I shall persuade Kingsley to go out with us on our little run this afternoon. It would be just the thing.' He turned to Xavier. 'Could you put Sir Walter into the schedule? He can go in the place after Luckhurst. So, our numbered field is complete. Let Mrs Pescott know we have another man for luncheon, possibly even tea. Is his carriage outside?'

'It is not, sir,' said Xavier. 'I think that, being in haste, he came by the railway and hired a conveyance at the station.'

'In that case, discover when he means to leave, and have a carriage ready.'

Xavier departed, and when we turned around, we found that Grey had left the room.

'I hope there is no chance of those two actually coming to blows?' I said. 'Of course, if they do, we have all the arrangements for sparring.'

'I would not advise it,' said Holmes. 'Sparring is a scientific art, unsuited to the enactment of revenge. Any fisticuffs might prove to be an unwholesome sight.'

'Well, Kingsley ought to be useful in the ring. I would match them if I could trust Grey to fight fairly, but I do not,' said Redcar. 'Fortunately, I have no duelling pistols to tempt them.'

'Do you believe what Grey has told us about his conversation with Lady Kingsley?' asked Holmes.

'Not a word of it,' said Redcar firmly. He glanced at his watch. 'There is so much still to do, and I could manage without these complications!' He sighed and hurried away.

'I fear,' said Holmes, 'that Lord Redcar has not been diverted from his intention to punish Grey for the insult to his daughter. But he is unlikely to do anything while Sir Walter Kingsley is here, since if any harm was to come to Grey, it would follow that our host's kinsman would be suspected of criminal action. There are abundant witnesses, and royal blood makes for compelling evidence. But the threat is far from over. It only rests, waiting for opportunity.'

There was a snorting noise which was the sound of Winchip waking up. He inspected the punch bowl and finding it empty, went away in search of refreshment.

I expressed my hopes that Winchip would not overstrain himself.

'He is an unhappy man,' said Holmes. 'He undertook to court a lady about three years ago, but it ended in failure, and he has since abandoned all hope of marriage.'

'How do you know that?'

'I observed the style of his clothes, which were then much favoured by swaggering young gentlemen of a romantic frame of mind. There are signs around the buttonhole that he was once given to the wearing of fresh flowers there. His garments have been somewhat neglected since, given no more than a cursory brushing. They no longer fit him well, which suggests he has gained weight.'

The other guests, seeing that the tumult was over, were now returning to the drawing room.

'Kingsley is certainly a hot-headed fellow!' said Northam.

'I have encountered him before,' said Rampal. 'He can be poor company, even when he holds his temper. When Her Majesty was proclaimed Empress of India last January, he saw it as an opportunity to make some highly insulting remarks in the presence of my family. It was a gathering of the highest calibre, and my mother was extremely annoyed. My father retained his composure for her sake, but it required effort.'

'That does not surprise me,' said Brambilla. 'Kingsley dislikes all nationalities except the English and makes no secret of it.'

'He does not dislike the French,' said L'Épine. 'No; he hates us with a passion.' His fist clenched, as if grasping the hilt of a sword.

'His poor wife,' said Luckhurst. 'I was introduced to her once, before they were married, and she seemed like a jolly sort. How can she endure him? Why would she take such a husband?'

'That kind of gentleman, I am sorry to say, knows how to be engaging when he courts, especially when there is a tidy settlement,' said Brambilla. 'Nothing is too much for him to do for the comfort and entertainment of the lady. No gift is too precious. Unhappily, once the match is made, he shows his real self.'

'I heard a curious thing,' said Rampal. 'I don't know if it is true, but I can see why many people believe it. When I told my friends that I was coming here, they asked me if Kingsley would be present and naturally, I said he would not. In fact, had I known he would be here, I would have refused the invitation. I was told that there was a rumour in Oxfordshire that Kingsley is descended from Colonel Keogh, a man who ordered an atrocity during the Civil War, in which many innocent civilians were killed. I have not studied that history, but it is supposed that Keogh was disgraced and changed his name. Is there any truth in it? Or is it just a matter of comparing the characters of the two men and making a not entirely unwarranted assumption?'

'Perhaps Burke's might answer that,' I suggested. 'There is a copy in the library here.'

'I asked one of the history professors,' said Rampal, 'and he said that many of the pedigrees sent to Burke by leading families — and published by him without being questioned — are deliberate invention. When the professor examines material relating to periods with which he is familiar, he often finds the claims to be not only false but impossible.'

'A man may lay claim to ancestry which he does not deserve,' said Northam, 'but he may also erase from his record any persons of whom he had reasons to be ashamed. I do not count myself amongst them, of course. A king who has lost his head is still an anointed king, after all. But Sir Walter Kingsley is no Royalist. I was introduced to him once and for reasons I can only guess at, he was quite insolent.'

'How many men would have good reason to play with the truth?' said Brambilla. 'Perhaps all of us in this room? I am sure that my ancestors must include some scoundrels and brigands I would prefer not to acknowledge.'

'*Sans doute*,' murmured L'Épine.

'L'Épine, you must allow me the privilege of insulting my own forebears, but that privilege may not be exercised by another man,' said Brambilla.

'Gentlemen,' said Holmes, evenly, as the two fencing masters glowered at each other, 'I beg you to display your rivalry in the spirit of fair sportsmanship. We have already had more drama enacted here than one might see on the popular stage, and Lord Redcar would surely not approve.'

'The time will come, sir!' said Brambilla.

'And then the victor will be named,' said L'Épine.

I could only hope that a pleasant run in the country would restore good humour to us all, but Holmes's eyes were alert for trouble, like a cook watching a pot of simmering broth which was in constant danger of boiling over.

CHAPTER SEVEN

With the hour of luncheon approaching, the gentlemen were gathered in the drawing room once more, but recent events meant that the tone of the gathering was far from convivial. Lord Redcar decided to address us all.

'I would like to remind you before luncheon is served, that there will be ladies present, and I expect — indeed, demand — appropriate behaviour and language.'

There was general assent, but Kingsley, who was still in a foul mood, rose and said that he had no intention of sitting at a table with Sir Jasper Grey.

'In that case,' said Redcar, who was having difficulty controlling his patience, 'I advise you to go to the breakfast parlour, where you will be brought a tray.' I was not sure if Kingsley expected to be given precedence over Grey, but failing to see his enemy vanquished, he left the room in a worse mood than before. Soon afterwards, Xavier came to invite us to the dining room, and was informed of where Kingsley was cooling his heels.

Lady Redcar joined us for luncheon, her husband taking her by the hand and making sure she was comfortably settled. Her mother, Mrs Fenton, was introduced to us, and sat beside her daughter. She was a good-looking woman with a youthful figure, though she must have been approaching fifty. Her abundant hair was almost precisely the same shade of gold as her daughter's. While she was dressed as a lady, it was apparent once she spoke that she had not been born as such. To her credit, she made no attempt to conceal an accent that originated far north of the Home Counties. I later learned that she was the widow of a man who had built a sizeable fortune in trade and had been prepared to part with a large portion of that fortune in order to be able to boast that his daughter was a duchess. He had lived just long enough to see his ambition realised.

There was a little talk of sports but in deference to the ladies, who it was assumed had no interest in manly pursuits, the conversation was soon directed to other subjects. Having exhausted all possible variations on the weather, Lord Redcar happened to ask Luckhurst how he was acquainted with us and was told that he had met Holmes at college. Luckhurst then launched into an account of Holmes's college days, in particular his friend's penchant for solving puzzles. The story of Holmes's marvellous solution to the mystery of the missing cummerbund had the table in roars of laughter. 'You should be a detective!' exclaimed Lord Redcar, chuckling, and Holmes modestly replied that it was not the first time he had been told this.

Having been deputed to watch over Sir Jasper Grey, I did as instructed, but it was not an edifying task. True to his reputation, he cast lingering glances at both the ladies. Naturally he admired Lady Redcar, but with his lordship at table, he was careful not to overstep the mark. Mrs Fenton, having no husband present, was made the object of most of his attention. All the gentlemen were pleased to look upon Lady Redcar, but they had the decency to make their admiration less obvious, with no hint that they saw her as anything other than a beautiful treasure, quite beyond any hope of acquisition. She bore their glances with a distant politeness, neither blushing nor showing offence, although I noticed that she averted her eyes from Grey entirely. He addressed no words to her, but maintained an air of easy charm, and spoke politely to Mrs

Fenton mainly on the subject of art and music, to both of which she appeared to be partial.

The two fencing masters were seated on opposite sides of the table and made no conversation but stared poniards at each other. From time to time, I noticed them mutter something I was unable to hear in their own languages. I had a little French which Luckhurst had encouraged me to acquire in case I should ever think of studying ophthalmology with some of the leading specialists in Paris, but at this point in my career it was not sufficient to follow a conversation.

'I hope there will not be trouble between those two,' Luckhurst said to us, later. 'I was told they were champion fencers, and we should have a fine competition of it, but now I think we will be hard put to it to keep them from each other's throats.'

Luckhurst, as well as his expertise in Latin and Ancient Greek, had an extraordinary facility with modern languages, and spoke French and Italian with ease. 'What were they saying?' I asked.

'It was not complimentary,' said Luckhurst. 'L'Épine compared Brambilla to a lumbering pig, and Brambilla thinks L'Épine is a talentless gadfly.'

'They may not appreciate that you understand them so well,' said Holmes. 'I suggest you do not enlighten them but let us know if they reveal anything of note. I would not wish them to besmirch the sports with unmannerly fighting.'

After luncheon there was a digestive interlude in the drawing room. Kingsley did not join us; he was still sulking in the breakfast parlour. Winchip, whom Lord Redcar thought might be able to exercise some placatory effect, went to talk to him.

After favouring us with some brief observations about the delights of the estate, Lady Redcar and her mother left the gentlemen to talk more freely. Lord Redcar went to consult with his butler about the afternoon's exercise, leaving the sportsmen free to indulge in manly conversation about Lady Redcar to the effect that she was a great beauty and Lord Redcar was a deuced lucky fellow. Grey said nothing, but his eyes gave him away. Northam was the most outspoken but pleaded in mitigation that as a descendant of the Merry Monarch, he could hardly help himself. The comments, however, were reasonably respectful, for which I was somewhat grateful. I did not feel I was in any position to remonstrate with such illustrious company had I been offended. Not that I am an innocent creature. Medical students, many of whom have sweethearts or even mistresses, sometimes indulge in vulgar talk, mainly to promote their own reputations. How much of it was true I had no idea and never felt any inclination to discover.

The subject of Lady Redcar lapsed at once when Winchip and Kingsley joined us. The aggrieved husband sat in a corner like a surly thundercloud, as far from Grey as was possible. The discomfort in the room was palpable.

Fortunately, Lord Redcar soon arrived to make an announcement, and we all fell silent. 'And so, gentlemen, the sports will begin! Play hard and play fair, that is all I ask. This afternoon, we are to take part in a steeplechase. Kindly adopt your sporting costumes and assemble on the terrace, ready to depart at two o'clock, where you will receive your instructions.'

Not all of us leapt up with enthusiasm. I did take the opportunity to make some light remark to Winchip to the effect that I hoped the run would not be too strenuous, but that I would be on hand to see that all the rules were adhered to. He gave a grunt of acknowledgement and patted his ample chest as if to demonstrate his robustness, saying he had been a champion on the athletics field in his youth.

Kingsley looked at his watch, a solid timepiece on a heavy gold chain, and thrust it away impatiently.

'Kingsley,' said Redcar, 'I know you have not come prepared, but I might be able to find something that will fit you. We have some attire in the fencing hall you might like to try.'

'I am in no mood for games,' said Kingsley, 'and that fencing garb would choke me. I'll go as I am.'

Redcar decided not to remonstrate with him, but merely patted him on the shoulder. 'We will speak later,' he said.

Once the sportsmen were suitably attired in knickerbockers and exercise shirts, they gathered on the terrace. Redcar and Kingsley arrived together in earnest conversation, and I hoped that between them his lordship and Winchip had been able to restore their troubled relative to a calmer frame of mind.

Winchip glanced around. Noticing that Grey was out of earshot and performing some muscle-stretching callisthenics, he confided to me that he had seen through Grey's little game.

'Game?' I queried, in the hope of further observations.

'The man has a soiled reputation, and I can't imagine why Redcar has invited him here, unless it is to make an example of him in the fencing hall and send him away in shame. I am only glad that Mrs Fenton is here to keep watch over Lady Redcar, but do you see what the scoundrel is doing? He has been flattering the old chaperone, worming his way into her good opinion, in the hope of gaining some time alone with her daughter.'

I admit that I had not realised this at the time. Having never moved in elevated society, I had been unable to observe these little nuances of behaviour which are better known in the noble classes. With every passing moment, I was becoming increasingly aware that what ought to have been a pleasant interlude of friendly and healthful exercise, had been revealed as a quagmire of dangerous possibilities.

CHAPTER EIGHT

It is a common feature of attempts to solve a mystery that one has to delve into the past and discover what occurred, often having nothing more than the often fallible and sometimes mendacious accounts of others to rely upon. Even the most apparently trustworthy documents can harbour falsehoods.

In recording these adventures, I rely not only on my memory, which despite my advanced years is, I maintain, as fresh as ever it was, but also on some records of my exploits with Holmes which I made at the time, if only to read them over for my own amusement. Holmes was careful to record the results of his interviews and observations. He either pencilled them into his notebook, or when that was not possible, consigned them to his prodigious and unfailing memory.

A detailed minute-by-minute account of the location of the main suspects during the commission of a murder is a luxury we were only able to obtain once, and that was on the afternoon of Lord Redcar's steeplechase.

The steeplechase for men on foot, as distinct from the equestrian variety, was then a recent novelty. It was much enjoyed by careless students who liked to hurl themselves over or even through obstacles as they ran across open country, and the muddier they made themselves, the better. Lord Redcar, or rather his butler, Xavier, had devised a course which did not leave the estate grounds and made the most of the natural obstacles, such as fallen trees and the winding path of the little stream. Athletic runners and gentlemen with long legs might take the stream at a jump in places, while others might prefer to wade. A few, at the cost of a longer route, would be obliged to find where stepping stones provided a less risky way across, or even the occasional timber or stone bridge.

Each man was provided with a map of the route, and a number. At various points on the course, a post or a tree was decorated with a string of paper tickets, each with the number of a runner, and he had to collect his own as he passed. The starting point was the terrace, where Xavier stood, armed with a notebook, pencil, and watch, despatching each runner in number order at five-minute intervals. The time of each man's departure was recorded, as was the time of his return, breathless and dusty, with the tickets he had collected along the way offered for inspection to show that he had run the full course. Xavier would then calculate the times taken to run the course, and points would be awarded for first, second and third places. I am not sure anyone cared a great deal about the points other than for their personal pride, but Lord Redcar had hinted that at the end of the week, the man with the most points would receive a case of his best wine.

Sensibly, the faster runners were to set out first. These were Northam — who some of us were already calling 'King Jack', although not in his hearing — and Prince Rampal, who while modest about his ability, was reputed to be fleet of foot. There followed L'Épine, Grey and Brambilla. Luckhurst and Kingsley came next, not because of their potential running speed but because they had taken the places of the two men who had dropped out, and Redcar did not want to upset the ticket numbers. The undoubtedly slowest man, Winchip, was next, and finally Lord Redcar took up the rear in order to see to any stragglers.

I did not take part, but I had made myself familiar with the route and its challenges and kept my eyes open for any signs of cheating. Most of the run would be visible from the house. The one area that was almost impossible to police was the denser section of woodland, where the route offered ample opportunities for tripping over unseen obstacles, spraining an ankle, getting tangled in low-hanging branches, falling into the stream, taking a wrong turn, or losing one's way entirely. In view of the kind of injuries that might be suffered, I was anxious that even small scratches should be well cleansed without delay. I had therefore brought with me some dressings of the kind used in surgery to prevent suppuration, and my antiseptic lotion.

I was sure Kingsley did not intend to go faster than a trot. He departed in his day wear, with a grim expression and no great sense of competitiveness. I hoped that on the way he would have the time and solitude for contemplation. I was relieved to note that his place in the running meant he was unlikely to be able to catch up with Grey and cause a disturbance.

As the runners returned one by one to enjoy cooling drinks and a seat in the shade, it was obvious who the best athletes were. Some had the nimbleness and energy of youth, like Luckhurst and Rampal, while others had the fortitude of hard training. Northam looked fresh and cheerful, and joked that he had half a mind to run the course a second time to set an example. The river being somewhat reduced in the hot weather meant that no-one had had any difficulty in crossing it when needed. The only injury was on Northam, who had torn his shirtsleeve on a branch and scraped his arm. I offered to dress the wound, but he said it was nothing, and reassured me that he had not shed any royal blood.

When all the men were back at the house apart from Kingsley, Winchip, and Lord Redcar, all of whom I had observed taking the woodland path, I became somewhat anxious. These three were slower than the others, and I expected them to take longer, but as time moved on, and they had not yet emerged from the trees, Holmes and I decided to go and look for them. Xavier kept watch from the terrace, and we hurried over to the woodland.

As we drew nearer, the first harbingers of the woodland proper were widely scattered trees, some of them venerable and twisted into curious shapes, and sawn-off stumps, one of which bore a flag placed to guide runners to the correct path into the woodland trail. The pathway was dry underfoot. There were no footprints and little disturbance in the packed earth that formed a track. However, Holmes indicated the freshly broken twigs that showed where the runners had passed. Sheltered from the bright sunlight we were cooler, although the air was heavy with the smell of the trees and all that lived in them. Slight movements high above our heads suggested that the runners had attracted the interest of birds and squirrels, while smaller creatures skittered away nervously into the undergrowth.

We decided to go by the route as shown on the map, but I saw Holmes glance rapidly about in case there were any signs that someone had lost his way. On finding the first tree where the paper tickets had been affixed, we saw that all had been collected, and moved on to the next, calling out for the missing men. We were nearing the third festoon of papers, when to our relief we heard a voice in response and approached the sound. In a small clearing we found Winchip sitting dejectedly on a fallen bough, with Lord Redcar beside him. Neither man looked injured. 'I only need a moment's rest,' insisted Winchip, although he was perspiring heavily. His sporting clothes, which were made for a much lighter man, probably his younger self, were stained with sweat. I checked to make sure his shirt was not too tight around the neck. It was, so I adjusted it to ease his breathing.

'Now then, old chap,' said Redcar, 'I think you and I had better stroll back to the house, where there are some nice cold drinks waiting. What about it?'

Winchip reluctantly agreed and heaved himself to his feet.

'And don't worry about anything else,' added his lordship. 'I'll see you are all right. I promise.'

'Have you seen Kingsley?' asked Holmes.

'He has gone home,' said Redcar. 'At least, he told me he was intending to when we set out. I offered to order the carriage to take him to the station, but he said not to bother; he'd walk up and hire a trap at the inn. I think he wanted time to be alone with his thoughts.'

'He must have covered a good part of the course,' said Holmes.

'Yes, well, if he took the way through the trees but didn't circle back to the manor, he would reach the road leading to the main gate. He's been here before, and he had a map. And it's sensible to come this way — far pleasanter in the shade of the trees. Here, help me with Winchip, there's a good fellow. Stamford, you wouldn't mind looking him over when we get indoors?'

Of course, we were obliged to agree, and travelled back the way we had come. I found Winchip surprisingly robust, just suffering a little from the unusual exertion, and a sit down and a drink soon saw him recovered. Nevertheless, I hinted that prolonged bouts of exertion might not suit him, advice he greeted with extreme ill-grace.

Lord Redcar was quite obviously relieved that Kingsley had gone home and appeared to think no more of the matter. Holmes was not so confident that this was the whole story and studied the map. 'If Kingsley has left the estate on foot, bound for the Traveller's Rest, he must have done so by the main gate. It is only a short walk from there. Let us see if the gatekeeper saw him leave. But first we should see which of the numbered papers Kingsley took from the course. He did take some of them but may have tired of the game thereafter. The main thing is to satisfy myself that he did not have an accident further on in the woods and is lying there injured. Since Redcar and Winchip did not complete the course, they would not have come across him.'

There was time before dinner, in the late afternoon light to go out to the woodland. I was grateful for the map, and following this, we saw that the only papers with Kingsley's number remaining uncollected were those posted on the open grassland, after the runners had emerged from the wood. The first of these was a prominent log seat, on which Kingsley's, Winchip's and Lord Redcar's tickets remained.

'So, it appears he did as Lord Redcar suggested and headed for the front gate,' said Holmes. 'The line of the trees in that location would have concealed him from anyone watching from the house.'

We sought out the gatekeeper, a grizzled retainer called Gorringe. He was a hard-handed man, sinewy and darkened by the sun and wind, like old leather that had been tanned and made stronger with time. He was also the estate's general handyman and gardener. We found him tending to a small vegetable patch behind his cottage.

'Mr Gorringe,' said Holmes, 'I understand that Lord Redcar's son-in-law Sir Walter Kingsley, who was here earlier, has left for home. He said he would walk up to the inn and hire a trap to take him to the station. Did you happen to see him leave?'

'Walking, was he?' said Gorringe, putting down his watering can. 'No, I haven't seen anyone either leave or arrive on foot. It's all been horse-drawn wagons today.'

'Oh?' said Holmes, hoping for elaboration.

'Yes, they come from the village with deliveries for the kitchens. They go down the drive, then round to the back entrance to unload and out again.'

'Is it possible that Kingsley could have asked one of them for a ride to the station?' I asked. 'Do they go that way?'

'He might have done,' said Gorringe, although he didn't sound convinced. 'They do go past the station on the way. I wouldn't expect a gentleman to do that, but he might have been in a hurry.'

'You must have seen the wagons leave,' said Holmes.

'I did, and I can't say I noticed they had a passenger, but then they have covers that can be unrolled to protect the produce from hot sun and rain and to shelter the driver. So, if they had obliged him, being a gentleman, he might have taken the seat by the driver, and I might not have seen him.'

That was all Gorringe could tell us. Holmes remained troubled, but regrettably, there was nothing we could do. The conflict involving Sir Walter Kingsley and his wife was a family concern, and one in which we had no business to interfere. I rather hoped that when Kingsley returned home, he would release his wife from captivity, throw himself on his knees before her and beg forgiveness. From what I had seen of the man, this seemed unlikely.

It seemed too much to hope that Lord Redcar would shortly receive a note from his daughter or son-in-law assuring him that all was well. Kingsley, however, had not struck me as a writer of heartening correspondence, and whatever he permitted his wife to write might not have been informative. Holmes thought the best we could wish for was a threatening letter to Sir Jasper Grey from Kingsley's solicitor, which would at least inform us that the irate husband had reached home. In the event, we heard nothing.

CHAPTER NINE

At afternoon tea, Lord Redcar announced that the winner of the steeplechase, based on the time taken to complete the course, was Prince Rampal, with Luckhurst second and Viscount Northam third. He suggested that any guest who wished to take the opportunity of engaging in fencing practice that afternoon should feel free to do so, as the next day would be the first full day of competition. He added very briefly that Sir Walter Kingsley was no longer at Charlbury Park, having decided to return home. I had no doubt that the visitors were delighted by this news, but no-one chose to express an opinion in the hearing of the absent gentleman's relatives.

Northam, who had expected to win the steeplechase, looked highly offended at the result, and asked to see Xavier's notes in case there had been an error. He spent several minutes examining the record but was obliged with some reluctance to accept that as written it was not at fault. He helped himself to tea, pastries and fruit from a table laid out in the drawing room, and slumped in a chair, with the expression of a man who had been unfairly dealt with according to his merits but could not prove it.

I did have the opportunity to speak with Prince Rampal later that afternoon, when complimenting him on his victory and mentioning Northam's ill-humour on being assigned third place. 'Does it not annoy you that Northam makes such frequent mention of his royal connections when it has to be said that in his case, the blood is a lot thinner than yours, the connection far more distant?'

Rampal smiled. 'Let him have his say, if it pleases him. I don't begrudge it. I respect my honoured parents above all things, and my sister is a jewel amongst women, but sometimes, a little distance is desirable.'

Neither I nor Rampal had any experience in fencing, and did not plan to engage in the sport, although we agreed that we would not be averse to observing the combat.

'Lord Redcar's assembly may be divided into men of experience, men who have dabbled in the sport and hope for instruction, men like ourselves who have never fenced but are curious to see it, and Sir Hubert Winchip, who is a hard man to please,' observed Rampal. 'But I have been told that in the French style it is a sport of great skill and subtlety, and a lady of expertise may triumph over a man.'

'I wonder if Lady Kingsley fenced?' I said. 'I know she liked archery.'

'Have you ever been introduced?' asked Rampal.

'No.'

'I met her once, very briefly. I do not think she would remember me.'

'Does her portrait do her justice?'

'It is a good likeness, yes. She has that look in her eye which I find very engaging. It says, "beware my wrath". She reminds me of my mother.'

We went to see the fencing practice sessions, during which Holmes was able to point out to us the differences between the two Italian practitioners, Lord Redcar and Brambilla, and all the others who favoured the French school. Most of the action was performed too fast for me to appreciate the finer details, although I did notice that Sir Jasper Grey seemed equally at home with the sword held in his right or left hand.

Holmes, while supervising the competition and not therefore taking part, decided to undertake some personal practice with the foil. He took a great deal of time selecting his weapon and uniform. In fact, he appeared to be examining very closely every such item available before he found the ones he preferred.

Lord Redcar was eager to spread the spirit of joviality over dinner, but it was hard work for him. Politeness was key, until the ladies left us to our brandy and cigars.

Next morning, Lady Redcar and Mrs Fenton did not appear at the breakfast table. Everyone was too polite to ask the reason for the ladies' non-appearance, but Lord Redcar filled the silence by saying that his wife liked to rise late and intended to go for a carriage ride with her mother later that day. Sir Jasper was disappointed but made no comment. I was sure he understood the situation all too well.

After breakfast we were invited to the fencing hall, where the swordplay was to begin. All were expected to attend, even those not taking part in the competition. Lord Redcar, Brambilla, L'Épine and Grey had brought their own uniforms and foils, but there were ample supplies on hand for the less well-equipped novices. The combat did not, however, start at once. His lordship had a mischievous glint in his eye, which became even more mysterious when Xavier arrived carrying a bowl of apples.

My puzzlement and concern increased when the case holding the two sabres was unlocked and the weapons were brought out for us to admire. As Lord Redcar held one out for our inspection, partially unsheathing it to exhibit the shining steel, even I could see that these were not light sporting swords, but real weapons, kept sharp and bright and eminently suited to doing harm. The sabre, he told us, was formerly carried into battle by cavalrymen. A man on horseback advancing at speed and brandishing that sweeping blade must, I imagined, have been a terrifying sight. I wondered why he was showing them to us.

'Now, then,' he said, 'I am about to demonstrate a nice little trick, and any gentleman who can emulate it will gain three points in this round of our sports. Xavier, bring the apples.'

Xavier brought the bowl, and Lord Redcar drew one of the sabres and performed a number of energetic cuts in all directions. Some of the onlookers took a few cautious steps back. He then nodded at the butler, who took one of the apples and lofted it into the air. Redcar stood his ground and made a powerful blow with the sword. The apple fell to the floor, split in two. Xavier picked up the halves and displayed them to the assembled guests, showing the neatness of the cut. There was some polite applause.

'Very good,' said Brambilla. 'I think I might try that. My friend Monsieur L'Épine would not succeed, I think, as he might find the sabre a little heavy for his delicate wrist.'

There was some amusement at this comment, although the Frenchman did not share it.

Brambilla reached for the other sabre, but Lord Redcar shook his head. 'Oh, that was not the trick,' he said. 'I was merely testing the sharpness of the blade.' Xavier produced a cloth from his pocket and carefully cleaned away all traces of apple from the sword before returning it to Lord Redcar. 'Now, this is the trick. Watch carefully, gentlemen.'

Redcar nodded at Xavier, who took another apple from the bowl, placed it in the palm of his hand, and extended his arm. As it dawned upon us what Lord Redcar was about to do, there were deep intakes of breath all around.

'I say!' exclaimed Northam.

'I am not sure that is wise,' said Rampal, gently.

The rest of us said nothing, and the others fell silent, not daring to speak further. The only persons not showing any concern were Lord Redcar, who was full of bounding confidence, and Xavier, who stood stock-still with no change in his expression.

Redcar advanced on Xavier, raised the sabre, and just as I thought he might have been playing a joke on us, he cut. The apple split cleanly in half, and Xavier turned to us and made a little bow, holding up the two pieces of apple so we could see that the fruit was perfectly divided with a single blow. He then held up his hand, palm towards us, to show that he was uninjured.

'Your butler has not a nerve in his body,' said Rampal. 'If you don't mind, I feel I had better not attempt it.'

'As swordsman or holder of the apple?' asked Redcar, with a smile.

'Either,' said Rampal. 'I am rather attached to my hand and wish to remain so. And I would be mortified if by some accident I cut your excellent butler with such a blade.'

'Come now, gentlemen,' said Redcar, turning to the rest of the assembly, 'will none of you wield the sword? If you do, I should advise you that Xavier has now done his part and you must select one of the other gentlemen to hold the apple. He will then have the opportunity of returning the favour. If either man cuts the other, he has the right to demand reparation. And no cheating, mind. No cutting wide to avoid risk.'

There was a silence as we all looked at each other. 'Not me,' said Winchip.

'I think that a certain amount of practice must be had before such a thing can, or should be attempted,' said Brambilla. 'I am a master of the foil, which is quite another thing, and would hesitate to take such a risk.'

'And yet, I insist that before we continue our sports, one of you must take the challenge and be deemed champion of the sabre,' said Redcar. 'You may select me, or any other man present as your partner. Does no-one dare? What about you, Grey? You are a bold fellow. Do you dare?' At this, Redcar took up an apple and held it out to Grey.

Sir Jasper hesitated, then there was a slight movement of his hand, suggesting that he was about to reach out for the apple.

'I will take up the challenge,' announced Holmes, before Grey could make his decision known.

Lord Redcar stared at him. Holmes left no room for dispute but took the other sabre and drew it. He strode about, testing the weight and balance of the weapon. His actions were quite wild, and those men who had dared to stand their ground when Redcar held the sabre now stepped back in alarm. 'Have you, er, used a sabre before?' asked his lordship.

'No,' said Holmes, blithely, 'but how hard can it be? I have seen you perform the trick. Surely all I must do is copy what you have just done.'

'And your partner?' Redcar glanced around. 'Grey?'

Grey looked surprised and said, 'Like Brambilla, I think some practice might be desirable. L'Épine, what about you?'

The Frenchman shook his head. 'I, too, am a man of the foil, beside which this is an axe.'

There was a brief moment of silence, then Holmes said, 'If no-one else volunteers, I will proceed. 'Now, who will I choose as my second?' There was complete silence. 'No? Very well, Stamford, take an apple and assume the position.'

I saw Luckhurst open his mouth to protest. 'Arthur...' he whispered, urgently, but I frowned at him and shook my head. He saw that all remonstration was useless.

My readers might think I had a hard choice in this business. This was not the case. I had no choice at all. In situations of this kind, something at the back of my mind told me that Holmes had some plan to carry out, and all I had to do was trust him. I extended my hand, with the apple in the palm. I had the good sense at least to hold my hand very flat and straight, as Xavier had done, with the fingers curving back as far as they would go. It was like the boxers of old or the unmasked swordsmen leaning backwards to protect themselves as much as possible through posture. I shut my eyes and tried not to tremble. Perhaps, I thought, it was just a ruse meant to test me, or even to test Redcar's intentions. Holmes didn't mean to actually make the attempt, and his lordship would step in with a laugh and stop him in time, praising his nerve. Then I felt something strike the apple. I opened my eyes and saw the fruit fall apart in two pieces. My legs wobbled in a curious manner, and it was all I could do not to faint. I was, of course, uninjured.

There were exhalations of relief all around, and a ripple of applause. I dared not look Luckhurst in the eye.

'Your associate does not have the iron nerve of Mr Xavier,' said Northam, with a chuckle.

'And yet,' said Holmes, turning to him, 'who is the more courageous? The man who has faced danger before and knows that the risk to him is slight, or the man who has not and is afraid, yet steels himself to face the danger, despite his fears?' Holmes turned to me and offered me the blade. 'It is your turn, Stamford.'

Nothing could have induced me to take the sword, and I am sure he knew that. 'No, you are the victor, Holmes.'

There were, unsurprisingly, no more volunteers. The sabres were polished and returned to their case, and fencing proper began. The apples remained for refreshment only. I had to reassure Luckhurst that Holmes had known what he was doing, but he remained unconvinced and pointed out that lack of a hand was a serious obstacle to the career of a surgeon.

It became obvious on reflection that Holmes had been obliged to step in to prevent Redcar demonstrating on Grey, the one man whom he judged would have accepted his challenge. The sabre was sharp and weighty enough in the hands of an expert to sever a man's hand at the wrist, an injury that might easily have proved fatal, given the risk of haemorrhage and blood poisoning. Holmes had seen Redcar's plan in an instant, and only the speed of his intercession had avoided it.

'Is it true that you have not used a sabre before?' I asked him.

'It is, but I have practised singlestick, at which I flatter myself I am competent, and the exercises are the same,' said Holmes, nonchalantly.

Before the fencing began, Holmes once more inspected the equipment provided by the manor: the padded coats, gauntlets, masks, and foils. 'I would not put it past Redcar to tamper with something and place Grey in danger of accident,' he said, 'but in view of the numbers present, that would be hard to achieve. I will suggest to the men who have brought their own uniforms and swords that they do not keep them here, but in their rooms, and every item must be carefully inspected for possible wear or damage before the competitions begin. If

Grey finds that some of his property is missing or unfit for use, I shall be very suspicious indeed.'

The fencing men indulged in some practice, and then the contests proper began, with points awarded for hits. The day's sport ended with the leading men being Brambilla, L'Épine, and Grey. Northam, who expected to be better placed, was a stylist with great energy, but he lacked accuracy. Grey in action was both fast and accurate, constantly confusing his opponents as he changed hands between bouts, which caused him considerable amusement. Somehow, the more he smiled and the more assured he appeared, the more dangerous he seemed to be.

CHAPTER TEN

The following morning saw the arrival of the Charlbury village cricket team, burly fellows who were much bronzed by the sun. They mostly came by wagon, and some by pony and trap. Their first action, after unloading their equipment, was to make determined inroads into the refreshments provided. My first thought on seeing them was that Lord Redcar had overestimated the ability of our gentlemen, who liked to dabble in the occasional match, over hardy souls who probably played several times a week in the summer. I decided not to comment, but had I been a betting man, I would gladly have laid five pounds on victory for the village team. The captain, a blacksmith called Seeley, was impressively powerful, and I looked forward to seeing him at the crease. They had brought with them a visiting amateur who was to open the batting, and an umpire.

Mr Gorringe, who knew a great deal more than his master about cricket and had played a little in his youth, had done his best to provide a smooth batting pitch, and clearly marked out the creases with whitewash. A rope had been unrolled around the field to signify the boundary. Xavier had donned a light jacket to signify his status as Lord Redcar's umpire, and he and the village team's official entered into a consultation with serious expressions that would not have been out of place on a county ground.

To my surprise, Lord Redcar asked me to play and then appointed me as captain. Some effort had been made at the manor to gather a team of eleven, but in order to do so, the gentlemen's numbers had to be augmented by Mr Gorringe and a footman. A stableboy stood by in case of injury.

Charlbury village won the coin toss and decided to bat first. Without knowing the cricketing skills of Lord Redcar's Gentlemen, it was hard for me to appoint fielding positions, but I did the best I could. I decided to make Winchip wicket keeper, as he would not have much running to do, although when he adopted his crouching position behind the wicket, I felt some concern as to whether he would be able to stand upright again. Still, he seemed willing. Grey and Northam, both with large, capable hands were in the slips, where I hoped they would be able to take catches, and they were joined by Gorringe. Redcar, the two fencers, and the footman, I assigned midfield, where I supposed most of the fielding was to take place. Luckhurst and Rampal, as the lightest and fastest on their feet, covered the boundary.

Holmes, having already enjoyed, if that is the appropriate word, some instruction from Xavier, was sitting at a table, noting the scores. We were happy to rely on the umpires to see to fair play, but Holmes and I had other things on our minds. Cricket is not a violent sport and fatalities are rare, but an unmasked man facing a fast bowler does have to accept some risk. I wouldn't have put it past our host to arrange for the best bowler in the village to hurl dangerous missiles at the body of the man he hated.

It was a perfect day for cricket. The sun was smiling at us from a cloudless sky, and a soft breeze rippled through the treetops. There was the exhilarating scent of freshly trimmed grass, and the promise of tea and cakes to follow.

I decided to open the bowling, selecting the least worn ball from the pile provided and adding a little careful polish with a kerchief as I watched the visiting amateur batsman, who was partnered with Seeley, stride purposefully to the crease. He was more than six feet in height, with the kind of figure that suggested he enjoyed the good things in life, and a beard that reached to his chest. I am not a fast bowler, but I am quite accurate, and I began by testing his mettle with the toss of a well-placed ball. The uneven bounce seemed to cause him no difficulty, for he effortlessly performed the most powerful and perfectly timed cut I have ever witnessed. The sound of leather striking willow in the centre of the bat was so sweet that I could almost taste it. Next instant, the ball was scudding across the grass towards the boundary, where it popped into the air as it crossed the rope, bounced merrily on its way, and hurried towards the trees, where it vanished into the long grass.

In those days, the practice of applying a fixed score to a boundary shot, which I recall was then either three or four runs, had only recently come into use, which was just as well, since the batsmen would have been obliged to keep running until the ball was either found or declared lost. The umpires signalled three, and it was generally agreed to save time by using another ball. This time, I made my approach with a livelier pace. The ball bounced higher than before, and the batsman, who despite my efforts seemed to have unlimited time to make his shot, played off the back foot with a sweep that lifted the ball to the heavens. It soared like a bird, and this time it passed well over the boundary rope before it fell, landing with a splash in the ornamental lake. The umpires signalled four runs, and the batsman strolled up to the crease line and calmly prodded the pitch with his bat, while he waited for the bowling to resume.

Luckhurst, who was nearest, ran to the lakeside in the hope of retrieving the ball, but having reached it, he stood and stared. When he had not moved for a few moments, I called out to him, asking if he could see the ball, but he shook his head, turned, and beckoned to me. His anguished expression and frantic movements told me that something was very wrong.

I ran to him, and Holmes abruptly abandoned his scorecard and joined us. There was something dark tangled in the reeds by the lakeside, which had already attracted a small cloud of interested flies. It was a human corpse, and although it was wallowing face-down, I thought judging by its build and attire that it was the body of Sir Walter Kingsley. The umpires came to see what we had found, and after a brief consultation they determined that their best course of action was, regretfully, to suspend play. The cricketers gathered by the lakeside and united their efforts to draw the body from the water and lay it on the grass, face upwards.

It was undoubtedly Kingsley. He was wearing the same clothing as when he was last seen, although the outer coat and waistcoat were now unbuttoned, and there were smears of mud and river slime on his shirt. The gold watch chain was still in place and Holmes pointed out the fob, which was a seal with the dead man's initials.

Decomposition was already very noticeable, the face bloated and discoloured. From the stage of rigor, which had passed its peak, I estimated that he had been dead for more than a day. As I conducted my examination, several of the cricketers recoiled from both the sight and smell of the corpse. If any of them had previously underestimated my nerve and stomach, they may well have been revising their opinions.

'Drowning,' I said, as the movement of the body had caused froth to seep from the mouth and nostrils, 'but some event must have caused him to fall into the water and rendered him unable to climb out. The water is very shallow. A seizure of the heart or fainting, perhaps. Maybe he tripped and struck his head on a stone.'

'That is possible,' said Holmes, leaning over the corpse and searching carefully for injuries to the head and neck. 'No,' he declared at last. 'The skin is unbroken, and I would expect bruising and signs of fractures to have shown themselves by now, but I see neither.' He drew the watch from the corpse's inner pocket and examined it carefully. 'A superior timepiece, Vulliamy of London, undamaged, and unhelpfully, it is still ticking.'

I heard someone mutter, 'Which is more than Kingsley is doing,' and there was some stifled laughter.

Holmes ignored the tasteless gibe. 'Perhaps an expert might extract more information, but I doubt it. Hmm, what have we here?' On withdrawing the watch, he had revealed from a place usually hidden well inside the waistcoat, a key attached to the chain, which he examined without comment. He then studied the corpse's hands, searching for evidence that Kingsley had tried to save himself as he fell. Holmes started at what he saw. 'Look here, Stamford,' he exclaimed. There were cuts on both palms and several fingers, with slight bruising but no obvious scrapes. The bones were not fractured.

'An attack with something sharp?' I said. 'A knife, or dare I say it, a sword?' A further examination and clearing of dirt and debris revealed a cut in Kingsley's shirt just under the ribcage, from which the soaking waters had almost removed traces of blood. Underneath it there was a wound of matching size on the abdomen, a clean-edged incision with some unusually shaped bruises around it.

'This man has been stabbed,' said Holmes.

'Stabbed?' exclaimed Redcar incredulously. 'With what?'

'That remains to be seen,' said Holmes.

'Well, we can't leave him lying there,' said Redcar.

'I rather think, my lord, that the police would prefer us to do so,' said Xavier.

Redcar looked horrified at the mention of police and turned to Holmes, who nodded agreement. He was continuing to examine the body in a manner which would have made it obvious to any onlooker that he had carried out this action before. 'No other injuries that I can see,' he said. 'A scuff mark on one boot.'

'Never mind his boots!' exclaimed Redcar, with a frantic waving of his arms. 'Someone must inform Henrietta! My poor girl! I had better go to her.'

'If I might say something, my lord,' interrupted the Charlbury umpire, 'I am Constable Bennet of the Oxfordshire police. Although I am currently off duty for the duration of today's cricket, I think that as there is a suspicion of foul play, I should now take charge of the situation. Sir, if you don't mind,' he said to Holmes, who was about to explore the contents of the corpse's pockets, 'I must ask you to desist, and leave the collection of evidence to the police.' Holmes stopped what he was doing, but it was with extreme reluctance. Bennet turned to me. 'And you are?'

Prior to my acquaintance with Holmes, I had never been interviewed by a policeman, but since meeting him it had become a regular event. A calm demeanour, politeness and helpfulness are crucial to the encounter. At least that is what I try to convey. I explained that I was a student of surgery at Barts Medical College and had considerable experience of examining corpses. I then introduced Holmes as a fellow student of anatomy.

'In that case,' said Bennet, 'I would be interested to hear your opinion as to how long this man has been dead.'

'He was last seen alive two days ago, just after we had lunch,' I said. I turned to Xavier, who informed me that the runners had assembled for the steeplechase with the first man departing at two o'clock, and Kingsley had ambled away half an hour afterwards. 'I would think he quite probably met his death that afternoon,' I said. 'Certainly, on the same day. Fully clothed and with his lungs filled with water, he would have sunk below the surface, and the gases of decomposition have only now brought him into view.'

'I have seen a few bodies pulled from rivers in my time, as the waterways here can be very attractive to swimmers in warm weather,' said the constable. 'I think we may be confident that the deceased met his death well before the Charlbury players arrived. I suggest, however, that for the time being no-one leaves the estate without my knowledge, as everyone will have to be questioned. That is only my advice, of course. I do not have the authority to prevent anyone leaving, but the police would take a dim view of anyone deciding to leave without giving me notice. Mr Seeley,' he went on, nodding towards the Charlbury captain, 'I am deputing you to go to Charlbury Post Office and inform Oxfordshire police headquarters by telegram. I suggest you take the trap. Once that is done, please return without delay.'

Seeley departed without quibble.

I could see from Holmes's expression that he was frustrated at not being in control, but it dawned on me that both of us, merely by being present at the time of Kingsley's death, would be on the list of suspects. Luckhurst too, whom I had inadvertently involved in a case of murder. We would certainly all be interviewed as witnesses. Holmes's keen eyes were already scanning the scene for clues, and I knew he must be planning his investigation. He wanted to explore the grounds and woods, and the course of the stream, but he must have realised that any such action would only attract suspicion and the police would put a stop to his efforts.

'The police surgeon will want to examine the body where it is found. While we wait for him, it had better be covered with a sheet to protect it from insect life,' said the constable. 'I will remain here to guard it, and I will speak to the senior officers when they arrive. You gentlemen had all better go indoors. And stay together until you receive further instructions.'

Xavier spoke briefly to Constable Bennet, who nodded, gravely.

'Match abandoned, I'm afraid.'

Of course, that was inevitable, but I thought it was a great shame. I would very much have liked to see more of the visiting batsman.

We trooped back to the house and gathered in the drawing room. Redcar tried half-heartedly to suggest what might be done for his guests' comfort and refreshment; however, Xavier politely told his lordship that he would see to everything necessary. No-one was terribly keen on food, although before long Mrs Pescott and a maid appeared carrying jugs of lemonade and a tray of glasses.

Redcar, who had added something more substantial to his lemonade from the drinks' cabinet, came to sit by Holmes. 'You say Kingsley was stabbed?' he said. 'But I didn't see anything nearby that could have done that.'

'The weapon may have been thrown in the river,' said Holmes. 'The police will look for it. There is nothing we can do.'

'You are sure it was a stabbing? I mean, it couldn't have been caused by a stone or a branch or something of the sort?'

'No, it was a clean cut from something with a wide, double-edged blade. Not a fencing foil, or a sabre. Something with a crossguard that created bruising around the injury. Like this.' Holmes produced his notebook and made a sketch of a cut wider in the centre and tapering at each end, but with semi-circular bruising on either side. 'And the position of the cuts and bruises on his hands suggests he grasped the weapon, perhaps to defend himself, or as it was pulled out.'

'Might he have stabbed himself?' asked Redcar.

'I wouldn't rule it out at this point in time. We will know more when the police surgeon has examined the body.'

'Then it might have been a weapon from this house!' exclaimed his lordship. 'I had better look to see if anything is missing.' He made to rise from his seat, but Holmes held up a warning hand.

'I beg you, sir, not to do so,' said Holmes. 'At least, not until the police arrive and you may conduct them through the house and let them see your collection.'

'Ah,' said Redcar, sinking back into his chair. 'Yes, I see your point. How come we didn't see the body before?'

'The waters were rather turbid,' I said. 'It is not unusual for drowned bodies to sink and stay hidden, only coming to light when they float to the surface. We can't even determine where he fell in.'

'I don't suppose you can identify the key on Kingsley's watch chain?' asked Holmes. 'I thought at first it might be the key he had used to lock up Lady Kingsley, but it is clearly a house key of some kind.'

'I don't know,' said Redcar. 'A room in his club, perhaps?' He took a long drink from his glass. 'But what about the ladies? What will they be thinking? What shall we tell them? Oh, dear me!'

'Perhaps Mrs Pescott could speak to them,' I suggested.

'Yes, yes, they will have to be told sooner or later, I suppose,' said his lordship. 'Perhaps for the time being we will not mention the stabbing to them. We will just say Kingsley has been found in the water and leave them to conclude that he simply fell in. And there is Henrietta! What shall I do?'

We could say nothing other than comforting words. With the exception of the Charlbury cricket team, we were aware that someone in the house, probably in that very room, knew more than they were saying. One of them might well be a killer.

Very little was said about Kingsley after that. We waited for the police to arrive. Seeley returned, having sent the telegram. There was some talk of cricket.

Holmes addressed the visiting batsman. 'I am no cricketer,' he said, 'but I recognise a fine sportsman when I see one. You will go far, Mr ...?'

A broad smile formed under the huge beard. 'Grace. William G. Grace.'

CHAPTER ELEVEN

It was a long, wearisome wait, but eventually Inspector Marsh of the Oxfordshire Constabulary arrived, accompanied by a Sergeant Dowd and the police surgeon, Mr Armitage. Marsh, a capable-looking officer in his forties, had been briefed by Constable Bennet. He held a brief consultation with Lord Redcar, who returned to the drawing room looking even more dispirited than he had done before. Soon afterwards, Marsh joined our assembly, and we listened expectantly as he addressed us.

'For your information, gentlemen,' he began, 'the surgeon is currently examining the body, which has been formally identified by Lord Redcar as that of his son-in-law, Sir Walter Kingsley. I will receive an interim report, after which the remains will be removed to the mortuary for a full post-mortem. There will be an inquest, of course, and you will be notified of the time and place as soon as it has been determined.'

'Will the surgeon be able to tell you anything today?' asked Redcar plaintively. 'When did Kingsley die? How did he die? I am hoping it was just an unfortunate accident.'

Marsh, who looked well used to anxious relatives demanding more information than it was possible to know in so short a time, smiled sympathetically. 'We can hardly ever be precise in estimating time of death,' he said, 'but on an initial external examination, the surgeon believes that Mr Kingsley died the day before yesterday, quite possibly within a few hours of his last being seen alive. More than that is for the coroner to determine. Sergeant Dowd is going to be taking statements from the Charlbury village cricket team, none of whom, I understand, were at Charlbury Park during the crucial time. But I will need to question everyone who was.'

'Oh dear, does that include the ladies?' sighed Lord Redcar.

'Everyone.'

'They have not yet been told of the tragedy,' said his lordship. 'In fact, they do not receive gentlemen other than family. Might I send Mrs Pescott, my housekeeper, to tell them what has occurred, and prepare them for your visit?'

It was agreed that this would be done. The sergeant was ordered to stand duty at the cottage door but was told not to enter unless asked for. I could see that Redcar was very concerned that the ladies would be distressed by events. However, I felt I ought to mention to him that even in the gentle retreat of Garden Cottage, they might have received an impression that something was afoot and could be experiencing considerable alarm, which would only be made worse by lack of information. Revealing the true situation, dreadful as it was, would at least relieve any anxiety Lady Redcar might have had concerning her husband.

The questioning and the taking of statements was a long process, and Mrs Pescott and the other servants were kept constantly busy with refreshments. Inspector Marsh, on learning that the guests were assembled for a week of sports, had no difficulty in advising us all to remain at Charlbury Park for the time being. There were to be no sports, of course, although he conceded that games of cards were permissible.

Sir Jasper Grey commented that someone had better inspect the playing cards to ensure that the edges were not too sharp. 'You are quite sharp enough,' grunted Brambilla, and Grey merely laughed. Everyone declined to play cards for money, which I thought very wise.

The fencing hall had been placed out of bounds, and none of the visitors were allowed to return to their accommodation until their rooms had been searched. Marsh agreed, however, to personally pay a visit to the home of Sir Walter Kingsley and inform the widow of her new situation. He promised Lord Redcar that if she should request it, he would be willing to conduct Lady Kingsley to her father's house so she could be comforted by her family.

Lord Redcar had been struggling with the wish to have his daughter in his care, and the instinct of a father to protect her from any contact with Sir Jasper Grey, but he did not like to admit the reason for his hesitation to Inspector Marsh. In the end, he agreed that he would like his daughter to be brought to Charlbury Park, where she would join the other ladies in Garden Cottage.

We remained in the drawing room under the watchful eye of Constable Bennet, while the servants had been told to remain in their own part of the house unless carrying out necessary duties. One by one, we were taken to be interviewed in the library. Every time a man was returned to the drawing room, there was an unspoken appreciation amongst the others present that he had not been arrested.

Very little was said about Kingsley's death until Lord Redcar was called to be interviewed. After a desultory silence, Grey spoke up. 'Look, we all know Kingsley was murdered, and it must have been by one of us. Who do we think it was? Any wagers, gentlemen?' It was in terribly bad taste but the least we could have expected from such a man.

'I rather thought it was you,' said Northam, bluntly. 'You were the one he wanted to fight.'

'But we didn't fight,' said Grey. 'Come, now, we are here for a week of sports, and we can't go on until the murderer is caught. Spare us all, whoever you are, and confess now, so we can continue.'

'Do you think Redcar would want to resume the sports after the death of his relative, even if the culprit was found?' said L'Épine. 'It is a time of mourning.'

'From what little I have seen of Kingsley, his loss would be a cause for celebration,' said Grey.

There was some muttering at this sentiment, but no-one actually disagreed.

'I must plead innocence in the matter,' said Prince Rampal. 'A conviction for murder would be a severe impediment to a career in law, and I have no wish to disappoint my parents. But Sir Walter Kingsley's deficiencies of character have been his own downfall. He was simply accorded the *karma* he accumulated during his lifetime.'

I was not ashamed to admit my ignorance of this concept, and Rampal explained the principle by which Kingsley had received the results of his own bad actions. I contemplated this unusual explanation, which sounded quite attractive, although I still believed, as I am sure did Rampal, that a human hand had made the fatal blow.

'What do you have to say, Holmes?' asked Northam. 'You are a detective of sorts, are you not? Although this may be a little out of your league, as it seems not to be confined to finding missing articles of clothing.'

I opened my mouth to speak and closed it again.

'Perhaps,' said Holmes softly, 'it might be as well if I knew which of us present had known Sir Walter Kingsley before coming here and formed an opinion of him. I, for one, had not met him prior to his arrival, and neither had Stamford or Luckhurst.'

'And yet,' said Prince Rampal, 'he was a man of whom, it might be said, one could form an opinion on a very slight acquaintance.'

'To be followed by a strong desire to murder him soon afterwards,' said Grey with a smile.

'Oh, I protest!' said Winchip.

'Do you?' said Grey. 'And yet I only speak what we are all thinking. What about you, Winchip? You must have known him longer than any of us. You had the misfortune to count him as a relative.'

'That is true,' said Winchip, reluctantly. 'And I will admit that in the last year, I have seen my dear cousin Henrietta go from a cheerful and spirited young woman to a shadow of what she once was. I have often wished that Kingsley would take up hunting so he might fall from his horse and break his neck.'

'Our host might think the same,' said Luckhurst. 'One can see that his daughter means a great deal to him.'

There was a moment of reflective silence.

'Kingsley has insulted so many for no reason other than his own prejudices, that there must be a thousand men who would be stirred to revenge,' said Brambilla.

'That is very true,' said Northam, 'but on the day of his death, there were only a few out of those thousand who had the opportunity of taking it.'

At that moment, Lord Redcar, looking extremely harassed, returned to the room. 'Holmes, the inspector is asking to see you next,' he said, sinking wearily into a chair.

Holmes rose and left the room.

Xavier appeared. 'Gentlemen, in view of the unusual circumstances, it is determined that luncheon will be served as a buffet in this room. It will be brought to you directly.'

Xavier, I thought, was a rather clever fellow, and if he had had a reason to murder Kingsley, I judged him to be one of the few men capable of doing so while standing on the other side of the field in plain sight of everyone else. While I did what justice I could to my luncheon, I tried to devise a method of accomplishing this feat, but without success.

Holmes was questioned at some length, but it would be a while before I was able to ask him about his experience. He returned unflustered, made inroads into the lunch table, and ate with good appetite. I was called next.

Marsh had already established the reasons that had brought Holmes and me, and then Luckhurst, to Charlbury Park. It was clear that we resided very low on his list of murder suspects, and somewhat higher on his list of useful witnesses. He appreciated that none of us had ever met Sir Walter Kingsley before our arrival.

'From your observations, Mr Stamford, do you have anything to say about who might have had a motive to murder the deceased?'

'I think we all took a dislike to him,' I said, cautiously.

Marsh smiled. 'But to go from dislike to murder is a journey few men would make, is that what you are saying?'

'Yes, it is.'

He looked through his papers. 'As far as I can see, Kingsley actively scorned and often insulted anyone he considered inferior to himself, by class, race, or nationality.'

'It appears so,' I said, thinking of Brambilla, L'Épine and Prince Rampal.

'And he was not a kind husband.'

'So I have gathered.'

'Any man who cared for the happiness of Lady Kingsley would have wanted to protect her. Some might even have hoped she would find herself widowed so he could seek her hand.'

'Yes,' I agreed, thinking of Lord Redcar, Brambilla, Grey, and Winchip. 'But of course, there are ways to free her which do not involve committing murder.'

'Expensive, complicated ways, so I am told,' said Marsh. 'Your friend Mr Luckhurst said he had met Lady Kingsley once, before her marriage.'

'Yes, he has family not far from here, and they had a habit of introducing him to eligible young ladies.' I paused as the implications of this became clear. 'Oh, but I don't believe he had any romantic inclinations towards her.'

'I would tend to agree. But I have heard a rather odd little story, today. There is a rumour going about the county that Sir Walter Kingsley was descended from a Parliamentarian commander, a Colonel Keogh, who committed an outrage in this area during the late wars.'

'I was told this story but have no idea if there is any truth in it.'

'You may not know this,' said Marsh, 'but the Oxford playhouse performed a piece on the subject not long ago. It stirred up a lot of ill-feeling. A crowd decided to burn Keogh in effigy. Old grudges die hard.'

'I suppose they do.'

'Did you know that Viscount Northam is of royal descent?'

'He may have mentioned it once or twice, yes, but —'

Marsh nodded. 'I know, these grievances serve as any excuse to rouse up a mob with too much drink inside them, but I can't see a gentleman like the viscount taking any notice.'

'Neither can I.' To my relief, Marsh thanked me, and my interview was over.

At length, all the interviews were completed, and the Charlbury players were permitted to return home. The searches would take most of the rest of the day. I wondered if any of the remaining sportsmen had an appetite for those activities which they might reasonably be able to continue. At least we were no longer required to be confined to one room to stare at each other in unspoken distrust. Once we were released from that promise, Lord Redcar asked to see Holmes and myself in the library. I felt sure he was not about to discuss sport.

CHAPTER TWELVE

We followed our host to the library, where he sat down heavily at the table, and we made ourselves comfortable. A volume of Burke's *Peerage* had been taken from the shelves and lay open in front of him. He sighed and closed it, liberating a small puff of dust.

'Your friend Mr Luckhurst,' Lord Redcar began, 'he spoke very highly of your talent for solving mysteries. Tell me, Holmes, and be thoroughly honest, was that all the truth or merely exaggerated praise?'

'It is entirely true,' said Holmes.

'I can attest to the fact that Luckhurst did not overstate the case — in fact, rather the opposite,' I added.

'But you are not actually a policeman, or a detective, Mr Holmes?' asked Redcar.

'I am not,' said Holmes, 'but my college days, as mentioned by Luckhurst, have not been my only instances of solving mysteries. Whenever I come across them, I cannot resist applying my methods to their solution. Stamford here has been a witness to that. He has often assisted me. We cannot supply any further details of the cases I have solved, as for reasons I cannot disclose we are sworn to secrecy. But we have acted for families and organisations that are highly respected in society, and regarding serious crimes. The police do not generally approve of interfering amateurs, but I am sometimes tolerated because I am more successful than they and am content for them to take the credit.'

'I would welcome your informal observations,' said Redcar. 'Someone in this house is a murderer, and the police are playing their cards very close. No-one is permitted to leave, not even the ladies. The police have been inspecting the weapons in my collection and searching every room in the manor. They are now going through every outhouse, barn and stable, in case anything is concealed. I have asked the inspector for more information, but he only says he cannot discuss his work with me. Have you any idea how he might be thinking?'

'If he follows the usual methods of the police, he will be trying to discover as much as he can about Kingsley, who his associates are, and what enemies he might have had. And he will also be making enquiries about the suspects — that is, everyone who was present at the assumed time of death — learning what he can of them, and establishing what motive they might have had to murder Kingsley. He will be trying to discover where the stabbing took place to see if there are any clues, and who might have been in the immediate vicinity at the time, and the surgeon will be forming an opinion on the probable weapon used.'

'You have seen the wound, and you have seen what weapons we have here,' said Redcar. 'Every weapon in my collection has been examined and pronounced innocent. There is nothing missing, but still, they will not allow anyone other than their men into the fencing hall.'

'Yes, I expect swordplay will be out of bounds for some time,' said Holmes.

Redcar growled with annoyance.

'We will know more when the surgeon reports, but based on what I was able to see, I am sure that the weapon that killed Kingsley was neither a foil nor a sabre. The point of a pike might have made the stab wound but not the bruises around it. I rule that out. If someone had taken an antique sword or knife from your collection, then cleaned and replaced it, I am sure that would have left some noticeable signs of use. But no-one has been seen outside the fencing hall with a weapon of any kind. How might it have been concealed? I look forward to discovering in due course the dimensions and depth of the wound, which will also tell us what skills and what strength the killer possessed.'

'Are you sure that Kingsley was the man targeted?' asked Redcar.

'He was known to all of those present by sight, and he was the only man running the course who was not in sports clothes.'

'An intruder, perhaps?' I suggested. 'A madman who came with a weapon, bent on mischief, and killed the first person he encountered, then escaped?'

Holmes glanced at me, and I saw he was not convinced.

'What about the wagons with deliveries?' exclaimed Redcar, suddenly. 'The murderer could have arrived on one and then escaped the same way. And there is no better place to conceal a weapon.'

'But if Kingsley was the chosen victim,' said Holmes, 'who would have known he would be found here and arrive prepared to do murder? Kingsley was not invited; he came here on a whim.'

'Ah. I see what you mean,' sighed Redcar.

I almost suggested the madman again, who seemed to be the best solution, since he overcame all the objections, but I doubted that my theory would be well received.

'It must have been someone who did not expect Kingsley to be here, but nevertheless had a motive to do him mischief. On seeing him, he must have decided to take his chance,' said Redcar. He suddenly smacked his hands together. 'Of course, I have it! Grey went ahead of Kingsley in the steeplechase.

Kingsley could not have caught him up, but supposing Grey stayed back or even turned around and confronted him? A quarrel, a challenge, a duel, and Grey was already prepared with a weapon for such an eventuality. He must have brought something with him and concealed it about his person when he went out for the steeplechase. He ran poor Kingsley through and dropped the weapon in the river. That is what must have happened.'

'That will be hard to prove, unless we find a weapon that can be placed in the ownership of Grey,' said Holmes. 'And that might not be sufficient, unless he was actually seen with it that afternoon. Then he would undoubtedly claim that he was defending himself.'

'The man is a villain!' exclaimed Redcar, thumping his fist into his palm. 'I had hoped for some good fencing, but now I see I should never have invited him here.'

'I assume you are taking steps to ensure that your daughter does not encounter him when she is staying here.'

'I am.'

'Lady Redcar was understandably concerned about his presence, due to his notorious reputation.'

'I can assure you that the ladies will be safe and well looked after. Henrietta will be able to join my dear wife and her mother, and they will be attended by the maid, Molly, and Mrs Pescott. Only members of the family and female servants will be permitted to be in their company. If you gentlemen should happen to see any unauthorised persons sneaking about, you must tell me at once.'

'Of course,' said Holmes. 'I assume that those paying visits for professional reasons, such as police, medical men, and legal advisers will be permitted?'

'Under supervision,' said Redcar. 'If a royal prince turned up with a marriage proposal for Henrietta, I would probably turn him away.' He sighed. 'For the time being, at least.'

'I have just remembered something,' I said.

Holmes and Redcar both turned and stared at me.

'It may mean nothing, but when Viscount Northam returned from the run, his shirt was torn. I asked if he was injured, but he said it was nothing and wouldn't allow me to see it.'

'I can't imagine him as a cold-blooded killer,' said Redcar. 'I suppose I ought to mention that before Henrietta was courted by Kingsley, she was introduced to Northam at a garden fête. I rather liked the fellow and thought they might make a match, but it never advanced beyond a nodding acquaintance. Henrietta said she didn't care for him. I don't know why. I suggested to her that she might try to get to know him better, but she wouldn't and that was that.'

'Did you think that Viscount Northam might make an offer for your daughter?' asked Holmes.

'No, and I soon learned that his sights were set elsewhere. In fact, I believe there is an engagement to be announced very soon, something in the highest ranks of society. He doesn't wish to thin his royal blood.'

'Kingsley might have imagined from that brief acquaintance that there was an earlier attachment between your daughter and the viscount,' I suggested. 'He was the jealous type. He might have quarrelled with Northam over it.'

'Northam did mention that Kingsley had been insolent towards him at a brief first meeting,' added Holmes. 'That does smack of jealousy. Men of that kind will see something where nothing exists and allow the thought to rule them.'

Redcar frowned. 'There was a curious thing Kingsley said to me when I spoke to him last. He said he knew something about Northam, something to his detriment, and was just waiting for the right moment to reveal it.' He sighed. 'But now we will never know what it was. It might have all been his foolish fancy, and Northam would have pooh-poohed the whole thing.'

'My lord, you have spoken to us with great candour, which we appreciate,' said Holmes. 'I gather therefore that you do not suspect either Stamford or me as being involved in the crime.'

'That is true. I have every confidence in you both. And I can assure you that I am entirely innocent. I am only hoping that the police will discover something which will lead to a rapid solution. But if they are unsuccessful, I beg you to apply your insight and experience to the matter.'

Holmes bowed and we both agreed to do all that lay in our power to assist him.

Once Holmes and I were able to converse privately, he commented, 'It may be that Lord Redcar's ambition to injure or kill Sir Jasper Grey himself has been replaced by the hope that the law will do that office for him. All the same, I do not intend to relax my vigilance, and neither must you.'

Later that day, Inspector Marsh asked to see both Holmes and me in the drawing room.

'Gentlemen,' he said, 'I am satisfied from my enquiries that neither of you have previously been acquainted with any of Lord Redcar's guests, family, and servants, with the exception of your friend Mr Luckhurst, whose first visit to Charlbury Park this is. His lordship has shown me copies of the correspondence relating to your invitation to supervise the sporting events, at the recommendation of a mutual acquaintance, the Marquess of Queensberry, and the arrangement to bring Mr Luckhurst as a last-minute replacement for a guest who was unable to attend. I have made it my business to learn all I can about the gentlemen here, and I have to tell you I have received interesting statements from St Bartholomew's Medical College, concerning the valuable assistance you have given to the police on a number of somewhat sensitive investigations.'

'Does that mean you rule us out as suspects?' asked Holmes.

'I rule out no-one until I can name the culprit,' said Marsh.

I thought Holmes would be insulted, but instead he smiled. 'I commend you, Inspector. No-one is above suspicion. But if there is any assistance we can reasonably give, we will do so.'

He nodded. 'In that case, I would like to know anything you may wish to put before me.'

'And I would welcome the conclusions of your surgeon as to the weapon used to murder Sir Walter Kingsley.'

'Ah, there you find the difficulty,' said Marsh. 'We have thoroughly inspected all the weapons on the estate — there are rather a lot of them, as it happens — and there is nothing to indicate that any of those items were responsible. The murder weapon, which we believe to have been a sword or long knife of some sort, must have been brought here by his killer. Or even by Kingsley himself.

'The blade was straight and double-edged. There is no way of knowing how long it was, but it passed right through his body. Some force would have been required. The cuts on his hands suggest an attempt at defence, or he could well have made them by pulling the blade out himself before he collapsed. We do not think the wound was self-inflicted. He would have quickly weakened from shock and blood loss, and he either fell or was pushed into the river, where he drowned.

'My officers have made a thorough search with that information in mind and found no weapons on the estate that fit the description or look as though they have been used in the last two hundred years. They are now engaged in examining all possible places where a weapon might have been concealed or disposed of.'

'Have you found the location where the stabbing took place?'

'We have not.'

'Might I be permitted to make my own searches?'

The inspector hesitated.

'I have carried out searches of scenes of crime before,' said Holmes. 'If you doubt me, please consult Sergeant Lestrade of Scotland Yard, and Professor Russell of Barts.'

Marsh's face relaxed into a smile. 'Come with me, sirs. Additional eyes are always welcome.'

'I assume,' said Holmes as we made our way outside, 'that you have examined the record so carefully kept by the butler Mr Xavier?'

'I have, and I also found that his watch is an accurate timepiece. We know exactly who was out in the grounds or the woods during the time Kingsley was murdered. One of them is undoubtedly the killer. We just don't know which one.'

CHAPTER THIRTEEN

'Are you satisfied that Kingsley was the intended victim?' asked Holmes as we made our way to the woods. 'That appears to be the general opinion of most of us present.'

'On the simple question of motive, it is most likely,' said Marsh. 'I think everyone knew him by sight, and being dressed differently, even seen from a distance he could be distinguished from the other runners, so there could not have been a mistake. He was seen entering the woods, although not leaving them. It was only assumed he had gone home, since he had told Lord Redcar that was his intention.'

'I did not assume it,' said Holmes, drily. 'It was only one of several possibilities.' He consulted his map of the steeplechase route. 'After the runners left the wood, the next position of the set of numbered tickets was the log seat, which is much nearer the house. It is on slightly elevated ground and visible from a distance.'

'Yes,' agreed Marsh, 'his ticket was not collected from that location, and he was not seen near there.'

'There are four ticket locations in the woods,' Holmes continued. 'The positioning of the tickets was known only to the runners and Mr Xavier and any servants he employed to place them. Might I suggest that we commence examining the route from the point where the runners first entered the woods? And not only the route itself, but all surrounding areas. The route of the runners was mapped out, but that does not mean they all followed it. The times taken for the men to run the course show that no-one made a large deviation from the route, but there was still some opportunity to do so to a smaller degree. Such a delay could easily be explained away as an error.'

Inspector Marsh raised a dubious eyebrow but didn't object. I, of course, was familiar with Holmes's careful and meticulous methods by now. It is easy to base searches on assumptions, but Holmes started from first principles, his intention being to omit no possibility, however unlikely it might be.

'Judging by the missing tickets, Kingsley is believed to have passed through most of the route and fallen into the stream where it is close to leaving the woods for open ground,' said Marsh. 'No tickets were found on his person, but he might have held them in his hand and dropped them.' If he thought that argument might cause Holmes to modify the thoroughness of his intended search, he was disappointed.

Plunging into the woods once more, it was not long before we reached the stream, moving sluggishly along its way. The sides of its channel were a tangle of tree roots, revealing how sunken it was from its winter levels. There were stepping stones, flat and dry, but it would have been wrong to cross at that point, for the first ticket location was directly up ahead. Holmes, like a bloodhound on the trail, moved very deliberately along the way, looking in every direction, not only on the path itself, but to either side. He sniffed the air, earth and vegetation, looking for evidence of passing feet, anything to show who had gone that way. Last time we had followed the path we were looking for weary or injured men. This time we were looking for the place where a man had died.

The first ticket location, a string hanging from the bough of a tree, had no tickets attached. All had been collected. I thought there was nothing to learn there, but Holmes, after a careful search, made a sudden exclamation and retrieved a tiny scrap of torn paper from the ground, which he examined carefully. 'I think this is the same kind of paper used to make the tickets,' he said.

'It must have fallen when one of the runners tore away his ticket,' said Marsh, looking impatient at what he must have thought to be an unnecessary delay.

'Possibly,' said Holmes. 'It may be nothing.' Despite this, he put the scrap in an envelope, which he took from his pocket.

We walked on, seeing nothing of interest until we reached the second ticket location. A string had been fastened to a tree trunk with nails. There were no tickets remaining, but Holmes, now on the lookout for more torn paper, found three small scraps lodged under some fallen branches, where they must have been scattered by a breeze. Once again, he collected them and placed them in a second envelope. Marsh said nothing but shrugged.

We reached the point where we had found Lord Redcar and his cousin, and passed it by, still with no discoveries, but on finding a stone bridge, we stopped and looked around. There was a narrow, heavily shaded path crossing the main one by the bridge and snaking away in both directions, deep into the woods.

Holmes pointed. 'See there,' he said, indicating one of the paths that led away from the main route.

'I don't see anything,' said Marsh.

'The trees are denser there, harder to move through. But there are some signs of smaller branches and undergrowth being disturbed. Material on the ground that has been broken by footfall. Someone has been that way.' He proceeded in that direction with some care, then subjected a tree trunk and some tangled growth to his examination through his glass. 'Yes, there is a thread, something from a garment, here.' He produced some forceps from his pocket and removed a small thread snagged on a branch. 'Not the white running clothes. It would need to be placed under a microscope, but I feel sure it is from a garment of some kind.' He placed it into an envelope.

'It might have been left by Mr Xavier, or more likely one of the servants when they were placing the tickets,' I said.

'Or someone who simply lost his way,' said Marsh. 'Perhaps it was Kingsley. He was certainly alive at this point because he took the next two tickets.'

'Any sensible person would surely have taken the main path, where passage is far easier. It is clearly marked on the map,' said Holmes.

'A gentleman might wish to move away from the main path for reasons of nature,' said Marsh. 'Of course, we can't know when that thread was left,' he added, impatiently. 'Come along, gentlemen, I want you to see where we think the murder took place.'

I could see that Holmes wanted to linger for a more detailed search, but Marsh led the way, and we had no alternative but to follow. After a while the path widened, as did the stream. Then we reached the point where a twisted dead tree had been the third ticketing station, but it was on the other side of the stream. This was where the runners had to choose how to reach it.

'Do we know who jumped across and who had to double back to the stepping stones?' asked Holmes.

Inspector Marsh hummed a little and said he would confirm those details, which I assumed meant that he did not know. I thought that the more athletic men — that is, everyone except Sir Hubert Winchip — would all have been equal to leaping the narrow stream at that point.

Further on we reached another of the little bridges. A rather rickety affair of gnarled wood, it looked as though it had been there since the house was built, and the woodland had somehow arranged itself around it. A cord was tied around one railing for the tickets. All had been removed apart from those of Lord Redcar and Winchip. Holmes searched with great care, but there were no torn papers about.

'So we can see that his lordship and his cousin did not come this far,' said the inspector, 'but Kingsley did.' He glanced at Holmes, looking for agreement.

'It certainly appears so,' said Holmes. He paused for thought. 'Inspector, I am sure you are thinking as I do. At some location, Sir Walter Kingsley received a fatal stab wound with a double-edged weapon. He also entered the water. Was he pushed, or did he fall? I doubt that he was carried, as he was a heavy-set man, and a body is hard to move. Where did these two events take place? The stabbing and the entering the water? From what I saw of the body when it was recovered from the lake, there was nothing to offer us any certainty on either count, but since he was still alive when he fell, and subsequently drowned, I think these two events occurred very close to each other.'

'Did no-one show any signs of having been involved in a violent event when he returned?' asked Marsh. 'Did no-one have wet clothing or bloodstains?'

Holmes glanced at me, and my duty was plain. 'I ought to mention a small thing I have recalled. When Viscount Northam returned from the run, his shirt was torn. He told me he had caught it on a branch, but he wouldn't let me see if he was hurt.'

'My word, he may be our killer,' said Marsh. 'But I will question him and ask to see the tear and any injury, and he will not be able to say no to the police.'

We walked on and found the last of the ticket placements not far from the edge of the woodland, and in an area where the stream was wide and ran nearby. As before, Kingsley's ticket had been taken, and Redcar's and Winchip's remained.

'It stands to reason that the murder must have taken place close to here,' said Marsh. 'Kingsley was not seen to leave the wood and must have fallen into the water nearby. He was then carried downstream to the lake. If there were any spots of blood on the ground, we won't find them now. They will have been a meal for flies.'

'What was he carrying on his person?' asked Holmes.

'Nothing of any importance. A pocketbook, a handkerchief, some banknotes, cigars, that kind of thing. His watch and chain, with a seal and a key on it. Oh, and there was a letter, but it was too soaked in water to read.'

'Have any of the tickets with Kingsley's number been found?' asked Holmes. 'If they were not in his pockets, he might have dropped them.'

'We think he must have held the tickets in his hand and dropped them, and they are scattered about somewhere. Or they went into the water with him.'

'Does nothing strike you as strange?' asked Holmes.

Marsh looked puzzled, as so many men did when Holmes asked them that question. 'Well, if something strikes you as strange, let me know what it is; I would be interested to hear it.'

'The purpose of the runners collecting the numbered tickets was to hand them to Xavier when they returned to prove that they had completed the course.'

'Yes.'

'But Kingsley did not intend to complete the course. He went for a walk, probably to have some time alone to reflect on his situation, but he never meant to return to the house. Before setting out, he told Lord Redcar he had decided to go home. Once he emerged from the woodland path, his intention was to walk up to the inn and hire a trap to take him to the railway station. Why did he trouble himself to collect the tickets? And where are they?'

Marsh had no answer to either question.

The day was wearing on and it was growing too dark for further searches in the dense woodland, which would have to continue the next morning. One comfort was being told that we were all now permitted to return to our rooms for the night.

Marsh departed for his sad duty of informing Lady Kingsley that she was now a widow. I wished I could have been present at that interview. I would have made a close study of her expression when she learned that her husband was dead.

CHAPTER FOURTEEN

'Do you think Viscount Northam might be the killer?' I asked Holmes the next morning as we prepared to go to breakfast. The breakfasts at Charlbury Manor were hearty and plentiful, designed for sporting men with good appetites, but few of the visitors had been able to do them full justice.

'There are reasons to suspect him, and men have been hanged for less, although they are not usually viscounts,' said Holmes. 'You saw that the last time we entered the library, a copy of Burke's *Peerage* was lying open on the table?'

'Yes, although I didn't notice the page,' I said.

'I did, and I intend to consult it as soon as the coffee is served.'

In the library, Holmes extracted the volume from its place and laid it on the desk, then turned the pages to the one he sought. He smiled. 'As I thought, someone was looking up Northam's pedigree, since he refers to it so often.' He sat down, and there was some concentrated silence as he studied the entry.

Luckhurst came to join us, eager to know if our perambulations of the previous day had uncovered anything of note. I am a little ashamed to say that I took care to satisfy myself that the thread discovered by Holmes could not have come from my friend's garments, which I was pleased to confirm were of a quite different weave and colour. Not that I suspected him, of course, but any coincidence of material might have gone badly for him.

When Luckhurst arrived, Holmes gave me one of those warning looks I knew so well, and I realised I was not to describe our findings to anyone not involved in the investigation. Luckhurst is a sociable fellow and might have unthinkingly mentioned them in conversation. I didn't think Holmes would mind my stating what we had not found. 'I don't suppose you saw any of Kingsley's steeplechase tickets scattered about?' I asked. 'We have been looking for them. He might have dropped them somewhere.'

'I can't say I have.'

'What did you do with yours?'

'I put them in my pocket and showed them to Xavier. Of course, Kingsley was in a foul mood — muttering to himself about Redcar's childish games. Perhaps he simply tore them up. Just the sort of thing he would do.'

'Great Scott!' said Holmes, jumping to his feet. 'Of course, I have been a blind imbecile not to see it!'

'See what?' we chorused.

'I think I know the place where Kingsley was killed,' said Holmes. 'And it is not where Marsh thinks it is. Is the inspector here?'

Fortunately, Marsh had returned to Charlbury Park, with the news that he had brought the sad tidings to Lady Kingsley, who was making arrangements to travel to her family home on the following day. After a hurried conversation with Holmes, we accompanied the inspector to the woodlands. Luckhurst was eager to go with us, but Marsh made it very clear that he was not to be of our number.

'Do the police suspect me?' he protested to me.

'I don't think any of us are free from suspicion,' I said. 'But, of course, Holmes is always able to make himself the exception.'

'Ah, yes, I think I see. Well, I shall amuse myself in the library until you return.'

'What have you found, Holmes?' demanded Marsh as we set out.

'You recall the scraps of paper?' said Holmes.

'Yes, the remnants of the tickets. What of them?'

'They are highly significant, but I have only just realised it. Kingsley had no intention of returning to the house, so why would he even collect the tickets? He had no reason to.'

'But he did.'

'Not all of them. He was an angry man, and not in the best of moods to take part in Lord Redcar's sports, which he was heard to deride as childish. Suppose he took the woodland path: it was the best way to his destination and shaded from the hot sun — somewhere he could walk alone with his ruminations. On seeing a ticket, and remembering the rules imposed by Lord Redcar, he pulled it from the cord and tore it up to show his contempt for the game. He walked on, and finding the second ticket location he did the same. Wind and weather have scattered the pieces somewhat, but not all of them. It was those pieces we found.'

'But there were no pieces at the last two locations,' said Marsh.

'No, because Kingsley did not take them. The person who took them must have been his killer, who did so to draw attention away from the site of the murder. Now, what does that tell us?'

Marsh tried to think of an answer. I didn't, because I knew Holmes was about to answer his own question.

'The man who killed Kingsley knew the path and the rules of the game and where the tickets were placed,' said Holmes. 'Did he know that Kingsley intended to go home? The only person who we can be sure knew that was Lord Redcar, because Kingsley had told him just before he set out on the run. But

Kingsley might also have told his killer. The absence of the last two tickets on the day of the steeplechase suggested to us that Kingsley had indeed gone home, which is why no-one remarked on his absence.'

'Are you saying that Kingsley wasn't killed at the edge of the woods, but somewhere in the middle, between the second and third ticket location?' said Marsh.

'Precisely. We have not been able to search every inch of ground, but now we have a far smaller area where we can make a close search and hope to find some clue.'

Plunging once more into the woodland, we followed the path until we passed the second ticket station. 'The killer, we must assume, was known to Kingsley and would have had no difficulty in approaching close enough to stab him, without arousing suspicion of his intention. A knife would have been easily concealed, perhaps simply held behind his back. Kingsley stopped to confront this person. The faster runners had gone on ahead, and Redcar and Winchip behind them had paused to rest. The killer might not have known that, but could well have guessed they would be slower. That gave a few minutes during which any altercation would not be heard.'

'I think we are both of the opinion that he was killed near water and was pushed or fell in,' said Marsh. 'A strong man might have carried him, but it would not have been worth the effort.'

'I agree. Where the trees are so dense, it would not have been possible to easily reach the riverside from the path, especially carrying a body.'

The path eventually wound nearer to the river, and here we once again encountered the little stone bridge. This was a low affair, roughly built from blocks of the same material that formed the walls of the estate. An old, twisted tree dipped knotty branches towards the water. Stone slabs at either end of the bridge would have provided seats for the weary. This was where the paths crossed, the bridge being their meeting point. The less trodden ways wound away in both directions, promising only a tangled dark.

'It was here I found that thread,' said Holmes, 'and I think it may have been left by the killer, if he was hiding from view, waiting for Kingsley to appear. This wider area is a place to stop and talk. Perhaps that was all that was intended, but the weapon was there for use, as Kingsley could well have turned dangerous.' Holmes cast his gaze about, trying to imagine what had happened there and what signs it would have left. At length he knelt down and passed his glass back and forth, then pointed with an exclamation at the base of one of the stone slabs by the riverside. 'Look here, a smear of what appears to be black boot polish. And there was a fresh scuff mark on one of Kingsley's boots. I am sure it was not there when he arrived. No gentleman would have gone out with his boots in that condition. He must have staggered away from his attacker when stabbed, caught his foot on this stone and fallen into the water. The murder weapon must have been pulled from the wound before he fell in.'

'So where was he standing when stabbed?'

'Between the old tree and the stone. No further.'

'And the knife?'

'It may be near here, at the bottom of the river. Or the killer might have washed it in the water and taken it away with him.' Holmes studied the area round the aged tree with some care. 'Look here,' he said. 'Broken twigs — they have been crushed underfoot. This is where it happened.'

Marsh nodded. 'I'll have my men search the river between here and the edge of the woods for the weapon. It can't have gone far.'

Holmes was content that one of the paths leading away from the stone bridge had not been used recently, but in view of the evidence that someone had used the other, he determined to see where it went. Inspector Marsh made a brief protest, but this time Holmes would not be deterred. Since both Holmes and I were of slender proportions, we were able to pass along the way without too much difficulty, but Marsh, of larger build, declined to join us. The path was still defined but clearly little used, and it wound its way past stout trunks and outcrops of stone to the edge of the trees. We emerged, finding ourselves close by the entrance gate, and near to where the dingy and uninviting opening of the culvert brought the river Charle's grey waters into the estate. Holmes said nothing, and we made our way back to the inspector, having found nothing to advance us. Or at least, that was what I thought.

Back at the house we joined Luckhurst in the library, where he was reading Burke's *Peerage*.

'I suppose you won't say what you have found, if anything,' he muttered.

'I am sorry, but — I am sure you will know in time,' I said.

'At least Burke's is open for all to see,' he said. 'It seems that King Jack really is a royal.'

'It is a fortunate man who can be certain of his ancestry,' said Holmes, 'but on the basis of what we can see here, no-one can contradict him.'

I sat at the table to take a look. 'According to Burke's,' said Holmes, 'he is supposed to number in his forebears a son of

King Charles II, who therefore counts Charles I as his grandfather.'

'From what I have heard of the Merry Monarch, so can half of England,' said Luckhurst. 'But not a legitimate son, surely? I mean, he is not about to lay claim to the crown?'

'There were no living descendants of Charles II and his queen,' said Holmes. 'But he had a great many favourites amongst the ladies at court, and he was very generous to them, granting titles to their children.'

'Including that of Viscount Northam?'

'Yes. See here.' Holmes pointed out the entry. 'The peerage was first created in 1665. As Prince Rampal correctly observed, there is much in these volumes that might be disputed and require correction. Some histories are the result of rumour and supposition, or even invention. But I have followed the line to its commencement, where it is suggested that he is related to the Gilmartins. The first viscount was one Robert Fitzroy Gilmartin.'

'Oh, I have heard that name!' I exclaimed.

'Indeed, you read of the father and son, Royalists William and Robert, who died after the siege at the nearby inn in 1646. But there was a daughter, Annabel. It is believed that after the Restoration, she was presented at the court of King Charles II and bore a son, who was named Robert after her late brother, taking the name Fitzroy to indicate he was the son of a king.'

Holmes picked up a small paper slip which was nestling between the pages of the book. 'I wonder who placed this here.'

'There is a similar slip in the book of Oxfordshire history,' I said.

'Is there now?' said Holmes. I found the volume, and we compared the two paper slips. 'If I am not mistaken, these were cut from the same sheet,' Holmes went on. 'It's good-quality notepaper, and the thickness, the weave, and the colour — pale violet — appear to be identical, and of recent manufacture. I wonder if there are any others to be found?'

'You think someone has been researching here?'

'I do.'

I glanced around the room. It was not an extensive library, but I would not have cared to attempt examining the pages of every book in it. However, that thought was not one which Holmes found troublesome. 'Let us begin with those volumes which appear to have some relevance.'

'We may leave the *Flora and Fauna of Oxfordshire* to last?'

'I think so. I can see that the spines and tops of the books do receive some dusting, but at intervals that will assist me in identifying anything that might have been examined recently.' Holmes inspected the shelves and removed some histories, and Luckhurst and I did the same.

'And here is a rather fuller account of the tragedy at the inn,' said Holmes. 'William Gilmartin was of good though not noble stock. He was aged forty and married to Alice Fernley. They had a daughter, Annabel, and a son, Robert Fernley Gilmartin, who was seventeen. Father and son were both in the king's light cavalry. During the routing of the troupe, William was injured, and his horse killed. The son refused to leave his father to save himself, and he determined to conduct his parent to safety. He took him to the inn, where he believed he would be cared for. The forces of Colonel Keogh, realising that the fleeing Royalists were sheltering at the inn, dispersed their horses and set fire to the inn. Both father and son were able to escape on foot, but were refused sanctuary at Charlbury Park, then in the ownership of Stephen Maxstead. William was killed at the gate by Colonel Keogh, and Robert plunged into the river. The waters being high, he drowned. His body, weighed down by his cuirass and leather buff coat, was never found.'

'I read that Keogh was betrothed to Maxstead's daughter,' I said.

'Which is confirmed by this work, but it appears they were never married,' said Holmes.

'And did Keogh change his name to Kingsley?'

'Apparently not. He was extremely ill-thought of and decided to avoid possible retribution by taking up residence at Charlbury Park. It is asserted here that his actions preyed upon his mind, and he was haunted by the ghosts of the innocents he had slain. He thought they whispered to him at night. Some while later, he was found hanged in the stables.'

'Then he has no descendants, called either Keogh or Kingsley?'

'I would think not. But that idea has been given weight probably by the efforts of the Maxsteads to deal with the death as quietly as possible. It is hard to be sure nowadays, but a nearby crossroads may one day give up its secrets.'

CHAPTER FIFTEEN

The library appeared to have told us all we were likely to discover. However, Holmes asked Lord Redcar if there were any other papers or books relating to the history of the area. 'There is a box of papers regarding the history of this house and our family,' said his lordship. 'Letters and monographs and suchlike.'

'I did not find such a box in the library.'

'No, it is still in my study, I think. Would you like to see it?'

'If you wouldn't mind.'

Redcar went to rummage in his study, which was rather tidier than Holmes's rooms, but less well organised, and eventually he emerged with a deed box. 'Mainly old legal papers,' he said. 'I am sure they have been well thumbed already and my solicitor has copies, but you are welcome to see them.' He looked suddenly weary and aged. 'And now I must leave you for a while. Inspector Marsh and I must go to Charlbury for the inquest. I only hope that something may emerge which will cast some light on this mystery.'

We took the box to the library and spread out the contents on the table. We were not very surprised to see a small slip of notepaper fall from the box, but if it had marked anything, it had been dislodged. Holmes took up the paper and went to a window, where he held it to the light.

'Is there a watermark?' I asked.

'No, not on this piece, but I think there is a very slight violet dye.'

There were, as we had been told, a number of legal documents as well as papers relating to family events. When the Redcars had acquired Charlbury Park about a century before, they had purchased a burial plot in the ancient church of St Cuthbert in Charlbury. We found a printed paper relating the history of the church, which had been compiled by the church council in 1857. This church was the burial place of the victims of the tragedy at the inn, and it included the name of William Gilmartin. Additional study by the diligent historians, which required the clearing of moss from old gravestones and the reading of faded documents, had uncovered further details. Alice Gilmartin had followed her husband to the grave in 1650, at the age of forty-four, and there was a further Gilmartin burial, the couple's only daughter Annabel, who had died in 1649 aged thirteen.

'That means Annabel Gilmartin cannot have been presented at the court of Charles II,' I said. 'And she was the only daughter.'

'Neither Annabel nor her mother could have been the mother of Robert Fitzroy Gilmartin,' said Holmes. 'Who was the man who was made a viscount? His elevation is on record, but not the rest of the story, which must have been family legend and assumed to be true.'

'And is Northam really of royal blood?'

'Only if we can be sure of the first viscount. I have established that the family tree does not include intermarriage with any of the other families claiming royal descent.'

Those of my readers who are familiar with John Watson's memoirs composed during his later association with Holmes will know his habit of solving problems alone, with only his pipe for company. Lady Redcar's aversion to the smell of tobacco, a sentiment I shared, meant that the opportunities for smoking indoors at Charlbury Park were limited. Lord Redcar undoubtedly took to the pipe in his study, where there was a rack with a selection of well chewed specimens. There was a smoking lounge for visitors near the rear of the manor, a fine place for any man who liked to sit in a room where his vision was wholly occluded by acrid fumes. It was not, in my opinion, a place for serious thought. Naturally I had remonstrated with Holmes over his addiction to tobacco. We both had seen the blackened lungs of smoking men on the dissection table, and we both knew that a healthy lung was not meant to be that colour. But Holmes said that pipe-smoking assisted his thoughts, and that was more important to him than breath. There are, of course, some individuals who manage to keep smoking into old age with no apparent harm, and it would seem that Holmes is of that fortunate few.

At Charlbury Park, his preferred places for long rumination in the company of his briar were the open grassland, where he would stroll, puffing out clouds of smoke like a steam engine. Sometimes he would sit on the log seat for up to an hour, wreathed in fumes that wafted up in the breeze.

Having given the matter of Viscount Northam's descent a generous amount of thought, mainly over a number of pipes smoked while walking around the aged trees that surrounded the denser woodland, Holmes returned indoors all smiles.

Lord Redcar had just alighted from his carriage with the inspector, and we learned that the inquest had been brief, concluding only that Sir Walter Kingsley had been murdered by a person or persons unknown. His lordship disappeared into his study, and Holmes and I retreated to the library.

'Let us consider the events of February 1646,' said Holmes. 'Robert Fernley Gilmartin, aged seventeen, alone and on foot, has seen Colonel Keogh slaughter his wounded father before his eyes. He cannot hope to escape on foot along the open road, so he takes a desperate measure. He plunges into the river Charle, hoping to be borne along into the grounds of Charlbury Park, where he might find a place to lie low. But he encounters an unexpected obstacle. The iron bars, which protect the culvert from being choked with debris, prevent him from entering the park. He is a strong, courageous, quick-thinking young fellow — we know that from his efforts to save his father. He is in danger of being weighed down by his battle clothes, which are far from ideal for swimming. Light cavalrymen of that time did not wear full armour. There was a helmet and a cuirass, consisting of a breastplate attached at the shoulders to a backplate, worn over a leather buff coat or jerkin. A slender boy might well have been able to slip though the bars, if he could doff that thick clothing. If he had presence of mind, he might even have pushed those items through the bars ahead of him. We know that they were never found. Let us suppose he did so and made his escape.

'There he is, in Charlbury Park, hoping that no-one will follow him. Maybe the Parliamentary troops were unwilling to plunge into the river, or if they did, they saw the obstacle of the bars and turned back, and he was given up as drowned. But if he survived, he should have been able to hide his battle clothes and anything else that might have revealed who he was and emerge with nothing about him to show his true identity. Many Royalists went into hiding as humble folk, and did not emerge until the Restoration, and he might have done the same. He could have represented himself as a servant from the inn.'

'He stayed in Charlbury Park?'

'It was as good a place as any. And he had a skill with which to support himself. He knew how to care for horses. Perhaps he found a place as a stableboy. It must have been quite a shock when the infamous Colonel Keogh, his father's killer, later went to live there. Did young Robert frighten the colonel with whispers, pretending to be the ghost of his father? Or even his own ghost? And then one day, when at work in the stables, Keogh himself appeared. Robert Gilmartin saw the chance to exact his full revenge, and he took it.'

'You can't know all this, Holmes.'

'No, but it is what I would like to believe. I am not at present in a position to do a great deal more research, but when I do, the truth might well emerge.'

'Then who was made a viscount?'

'If I am correct, then after the Restoration, Robert Fernley Gilmartin presented himself at court with sufficient means to prove his identity and was granted the title in honour of his and his father's services to King Charles I. Family legend translated Fernley to Fitzroy.'

'And Northam is descended from him?'

'Quite probably.'

'I wonder who he married?'

'That would be interesting to discover. A stableboy might not aspire to the hand of a lady, but I am sure he found a worthy wife.'

'Was this the great secret Kingsley was going to expose?'

'I think so.'

'I know I only saw Kingsley a few times, but he didn't appear to be a patient or indeed an intelligent researcher.'

'He was neither, but I can deduce how he discovered what we now know. Those little slips of violet notepaper are suggestive. Whether he actually told Northam what he knew, thus giving him ample motive to murder him before he could reveal all, is another matter.'

'This story all hinges on Robert Gilmartin being able to survive his plunge into the river.'

'It does, and we may be able to find confirmation one way or the other.'

'Where?'

Holmes smiled, and I realised where we would soon be bound. Sadly, I did not have waterproof boots amongst my luggage.

CHAPTER SIXTEEN

When Holmes told Inspector Marsh that we were making an examination of the culvert, the inspector said his men had already searched it for the missing murder weapon and found nothing, but he was content for us to proceed. None of the policemen who had already explored the culvert showed any anxiety to do so again. Holmes also had a brief word with Mr Gorringe to explain what we were intending to do. Gorringe, unsurprised by the eccentricities of gentlemen, did not attempt to dissuade us, but handed us an old garden rake with which to explore the waters.

'Of course,' said Holmes, as we made our way towards the mouth of the culvert, armed with an oil lamp and the rake, 'we may find some rusted armour and a set of bones which will quite explode my theory, but I rather think we will not.'

The culvert appeared to date from the construction of the estate. The entrance, which we reached by negotiating a steep, grassy slope, presented itself as an arch of coarse red brick, and what we could see of the upper part of the interior appeared to be a low, curved, stony vault. The river was thankfully low enough at this point to reveal a narrow path of rough cobbles on either side. We were able therefore to make our way inside, but with great care, as it was necessary for both of us to bend our knees and backs as we went. It was best, as we soon discovered, not to touch the walls for support, since they were coated with an especially nasty slime. The stench, of course, was rather unpleasant, the gases of decaying matter rendered violently pungent by the warm weather.

We crept along as best we could, Holmes leading the way, holding up the lantern while I carried the rake. I had no idea how long the culvert would be. Due to its age, it was quite possible that there would be fallen stones impeding our progress, or even — and this was a ghastly thought — slabs in the curved roof above which were in danger of falling, and which might be dislodged by the vibration of our footsteps.

At length, Holmes, holding the lantern high, exclaimed, 'Now, this is very interesting!'

'What have you seen, Holmes?' I asked, my voice sounding even more apprehensive than usual as it echoed in the grim tunnel.

'Something I mean to explore further. Hand me the rake, and stay there, Stamford.'

'But —'

'I will return very shortly.'

I stood still, wondering what Holmes was doing and why he wanted me to stay back. Was he entering a dangerous area and required me to remain in case it was necessary to send for help? I listened to the sound of his footsteps, his figure obscuring my view of what lay up ahead. He was holding the lantern before him, and it cast a yellow glow over the glistening walls. The sounds grew gradually fainter as he moved on, as did the light, and eventually, and rather worryingly, both ceased altogether. All I could hear was the trickling water and my own nervous heartbeat fluttering in my ears. I thought of calling out, but I didn't want to startle Holmes and place him in even more danger. Time passed, and I was becoming afraid that Holmes was trapped somewhere and unable to call out, or had fallen and drowned, or suffocated in poisonous gases. I had no idea what to do for the best.

Then I heard a sound behind me, and I turned around and saw a figure approaching, holding a lantern. I thought at first it might be Gorringe, but to my astonishment, as he drew closer, I saw it was Holmes. He chuckled at my obvious surprise. It was not often that Holmes felt any guilt at giving me a terrible fright. This was not one of those occasions.

'How did you come to be there?' I demanded. 'I know you didn't creep past me.'

'Not at all,' he said. 'Let us move on and I will show you. The iron bars are still there, but in places they are almost rusted away, leaving a gap that I was able to step through quite easily. I went round to the gate and Gorringe let me in. However, enough remains of the original bars to give us an impression of whether a boy of seventeen could have escaped through them if he removed his armour and buff coat.'

We moved forward, and at last I saw a set of bars, six in all, of which two were so rusted away that they appeared like rotten teeth, with enough space in the jagged jaws for Holmes to have made his escape.

'Can you get through the undamaged bars, Stamford?' asked Holmes.

'Possibly. Did you find any remains of Robert Gilmartin?'

'No. I explored the stream most thoroughly on both sides of the bars and found neither armour nor bones. That is not conclusive, of course.'

I examined the four whole bars, which were slimy to the touch. Then I decided to remove my jacket and handed it to Holmes to hold, which I thought was the least he could do under the circumstances. I had a pocket handkerchief, which was required to give up its useful life to the cause of investigation, and managed to clean off as much filth from the bars as possible before I made the attempt. I had to hold my breath, but I was able to pass between two of them without any difficulty and emerge on the other side.

'Did Gorringe know about the state of the bars?' I asked.

'Yes, he told me they were broken in places, eroded by time, but that this would only be apparent when the waters were low. He conducts regular inspections of the culvert in case anything should fall in and require removal. He is not aware that anyone else goes down here. Gorringe was proud to tell me he has served this estate for forty years, and I doubt there is anything he does not know about it. But his loyalty to Lord Redcar is strong and resolute, and he may choose not to tell all he knows to a stranger.'

Once we had returned to the manor, I hurried to perform some ablutions to make myself presentable again, thankful that I had brought a spare shirt. Mrs Pescott was able to take charge of my dirtied clothing, without exhibiting any curiosity as to how the stains had arisen. Holmes, who had not attempted to squeeze between the undamaged bars, had managed to deal with his garments by using a stout brush.

We returned to the library, where Holmes, fired by his recent conclusions, hoped to see if it was possible to discover the year in which the first Viscount Northam was born. We both made diligent searches to see if any of the standard directories might provide this, but without result. The next possible source were volumes recording notable persons in the county of Oxfordshire. These provided only fragments, none of which were of any assistance. Although we were not able to examine church or burial records, there was a large book describing the major churches of the county, usually referring to their history, architecture, and important monuments and mausoleums. Holmes proceeded to examine it, and I occupied the time with other volumes, including one on the rivers of Oxfordshire, which included a brief mention of the Charle. But I paused occasionally to look on in admiration at the painstaking dedication of my friend, who, it should be remembered was at the time a mere student, just twenty-three years of age. I knew of course that he was a very great man, but I had no inkling that one day he would be the most famous and sought after detective the world has ever known.

It was slow work. There was no means of Holmes knowing precisely what he was searching for, or even if the crucial piece of information was there to be found. Eventually, however, I saw him smile and make an exclamation. I rushed to his side. A long, pale finger tapped a page. He had discovered a description of a church in the city of Oxford, which included a commemorative plaque to the Viscounts Northam. It had been erected in 1715 by the first viscount's grandson, William Robert Gilmartin. The description referred to Robert Fernley Gilmartin, the first Viscount Northam, 1629–1699.

'So now we can be sure,' said Holmes. 'The first viscount would have been seventeen at the time of the tragedy at the inn.'

'It seems that Northam has not taken the trouble to study his ancestors,' I said. 'He has taken the entry in Burke's *Peerage* as fact, but now it seems it was flawed.'

'Maybe he feared what he would find if he looked further,' said Holmes.

'Was this the secret Kingsley wanted to reveal?' I asked. 'Northam's humble origins? He would have taken pleasure in doing so, I am sure.'

'And if Northam discovered that Kingsley intended to tell the world, that might well have been a motive for murder.'

CHAPTER SEVENTEEN

Two days after the death of Sir Walter Kingsley, Lord Redcar was able to welcome his widowed daughter to the estate of her birth. The essential arrangements were in progress: letters had been written, serious gentlemen consulted, and mourning clothes ordered. We did not see Lady Kingsley arrive, but I was told that a curtained carriage had been seen passing up the driveway. It did not stop at the front door, but circled around the manor, so the passenger, who was accompanied by Inspector Marsh, could alight unseen, and be greeted by Lady Redcar and her mother, Mrs Fenton. Lady Kingsley was then quickly conducted to Garden Cottage, where she would remain for as long as she wished, certainly until the gentleman visitors had departed.

The sporting guests were still hoping to be allowed to leave the estate. We were told by Inspector Marsh that once the police searches were drawn to a close, which he hoped would not take more than a day or two longer, he would permit us to do so.

Although there were no visitors to the estate who had not been thoroughly approved by the police, there were deliveries of letters, which were brought to the front gate by post boys and handed to Gorringe. Then, by a process we were not privileged to observe, they arrived on the dining table. On the morning after our adventure in the culvert, both Brambilla and L'Épine received letters they had not been expecting. The letters were duly opened as we breakfasted, and once read the contents were not greeted with pleasure.

Brambilla made a great many pronouncements in Italian. Many of the words he used were somewhat forceful, and I was pleased not to understand them. He folded his letter roughly and thrust it into his pocket. The other gentlemen, assuming he had received bad news of a personal nature, decided out of politeness not to ask the reason for his discomfiture. Moments later, L'Épine barked out annoyance at the contents of his missive. The paper, crumpled in an angry fist, was hastily put away. The two sword masters stared at each other across the table but said nothing. The rest of us attended closely to our breakfast plates.

When coffee was served, Brambilla and L'Épine left the room separately, presumably to deal with the unwanted correspondence.

'I suppose you can tell us what has just occurred?' I asked Luckhurst when Holmes and I were able to speak with him in private.

'Yes, and it is nothing to do with the situation here. Brambilla's letter was from his wife; it seems there are family matters which require his presence in the near future. L'Épine's letter was from his lawyer, who wants to see him in order to sign some papers. I didn't get the impression that there was anything distressing involved, but they were clearly annoyed by the inconvenience.'

'Both of them,' said Holmes.

'Yes. I think it upset some other arrangements they had.'

Holmes nodded, knowingly. 'I think I observe a subtle plan they might not have detected.'

A little later we found Brambilla on the terrace in a contemplative mood, studying his letter, and Holmes decided to join him. 'It is very frustrating, is it not,' he said casually, 'to be confined here and not be able to attend to our own business?'

'It is a great nuisance,' said Brambilla. 'I was hoping to be permitted to leave tomorrow, as I have an important engagement, but this letter from my wife tells me of urgent family matters which I must attend to, and which entirely defeat my plans. She is most insistent, and I cannot disappoint her.'

'The Chevalier L'Épine appeared to be similarly inconvenienced,' observed Holmes.

'You speak French?'

'Just a little. Might I be so bold as to ask if your engagement and his were the same? A meeting of the two of you in Paris, to decide who is the superior man with the sword? There have been rumours in the fencing clubs.'

Brambilla hesitated but was obliged to agree that this was the case.

'Was the baroness informed of the date of that engagement?'

'She knew I was to be in Paris that day.'

'And I would not be at all surprised to learn that L'Épine's lawyer also knew he was to be there.'

'I am not sure I understand you, Mr Holmes.'

'Have you ever considered why it is that the arrangements you make to meet have always failed to take place?'

'We are busy men,' said Brambilla with a shrug. 'It is not always convenient. But of course, here we both are.'

'But I understand that you have agreed to a truce while on English soil,' said Holmes.

'We have, yes, on the advice of Lord Redcar. We intend to test our claims to pre-eminence in the only meaningful way, open combat, which we are told would not meet with the approval of English law.'

'Could you not test each other with the foil?' I asked. 'You might do that here, once the fencing hall has been opened for competition.'

'The test which was to have taken place in Paris would have been with rapiers. It would only have ended when one man marked the other and drew blood,' said Brambilla. 'We will have to arrange another day, another place. And next time, nothing will be allowed to stand in our way.'

'Has it not occurred to you, as it does to me,' said Holmes, 'that your families and advisors may have been quite deliberately, and with the best of intentions, preventing the two of you from conducting a duel?'

Brambilla stared at Holmes in astonishment.

'Since you were not intending to do anything other than meet in sport while here, there was no need on this occasion for them to interfere with your plans. They may even have entertained hopes that the discipline of the fencing hall would prove to be sufficient to end the dispute, and the two of you would part in peace. Might I suggest that this is the best option to pursue?'

Brambilla was plunged into a thoughtful silence. We could see that the fencing master had been affected by Holmes's words and left him alone with his deliberations.

It was a quiet morning. The police had temporarily retired from the scene but instructed us all not to leave the estate until we received official permission. There was some desultory talk of a game of cards, and it was agreed that we would gather for this after lunch. Northam had brought some sporting journals to read and retired with them to the drawing room. Prince Rampal went to enjoy the peace of the gardens, Grey had gone out for a run around the parkland, and Winchip had shuffled off to take a nap. There was no sign of the ladies.

Lord Redcar had grown impatient with our exclusion from the fencing hall. 'I don't see any reason why we should not at least recommence practice,' he told Holmes. 'I am satisfied that Grey was the man who murdered Kingsley, but I can hardly imagine he means to cut us all down. It was clearly a private quarrel. He will be proven guilty in due course, the law will take its revenge, and good riddance. I doubt that the rest of us are in any danger.'

Holmes, as ever, advised caution, but Redcar was certain he was right. There was an expression his lordship adopted in those circumstances, a determined frown with an intense furrowing of the brow, and his lower lip thrust out, which was a sure sign that nothing, even common sense, would shake his opinion. He strode away to give orders that the fencing hall should be re-opened and thoroughly cleaned, so practice could resume forthwith.

Holmes and I had decided to return to the library in case it had further enlightenment to offer, and were examining the available volumes when Mr Xavier peered in. 'Gentlemen,' he said, 'I do not wish to alarm you, but might I ask if either of you know where his lordship's sabres might be?'

'If they are not in their glass case, that is a matter of concern,' said Holmes. 'When did you notice they were missing?'

'I unlocked the fencing hall this morning as his lordship required and made my usual inspection. Everything was in its proper place. I then consulted with Mrs Pescott about what needed to be done to prepare the room for the competition, and when I returned, I noticed that the sabres had been taken from their case. I have searched the room most thoroughly, as it was possible that they had simply been moved, but they are not there. Mrs Pescott has assured me that they have not been taken from the hall by the servants for cleaning or storage. Those gentlemen I have spoken to thus far say they know nothing about them. His lordship would certainly have informed me had he wanted them moved to another location.'

'Where is Lord Redcar?' I asked.

'I believe he may be in Garden Cottage, where he would prefer not to be disturbed.'

We accompanied Xavier to the fencing hall, where the sabres were still absent.

'This case is always kept locked?' asked Holmes.

'It is, but I fear that the lock is an old one, and a determined person might easily open it without a key.'

Holmes examined the lock with his glass. 'It has been forced. There are some scratches here. The tool used slipped and marked the wood.'

'Was it done with a knife?' I asked, worried that the estate still held carefully concealed weapons that had eluded the police searches.

'Nothing so sharp,' said Holmes. 'A pair of scissors, I believe.' He leaned close. 'With an interesting scent. The sabres were taken by a man with a carefully groomed moustache. Where are Brambilla and L'Épine?'

'I have not seen them recently,' said Xavier. The implications were obvious to us all.

We were making for the door to commence urgent searches when it opened and Brambilla entered, sabre in hand. He had the decency to look embarrassed.

Holmes stared at him. 'Baron Brambilla, please explain yourself. Why have you abstracted a duelling sabre, and where is the other one?'

Xavier with a gentle cough, approached Brambilla, carefully took the sabre from his hand and inspected it, then nodded with satisfaction. 'It is unused,' he said.

Brambilla was perspiring and sighed heavily. 'Mr Holmes, after our conversation this morning, I decided to speak to L'Épine. It was now apparent to us that the failure of our arrangements for meetings was not due to chance or the cowardice of either of us, as has sometimes been alleged. It was, unknown to us both, a design by our families and friends to keep us apart, lest one of us slays the other. You were quite correct. The only reason no-one interfered with our meeting here was that we had announced a truce on English soil. L'Épine and I therefore agreed to end our truce, and settle our differences here and now, in the time-honoured way, as we might not have another chance. We did not come prepared with our duelling swords but thought that the sabres would do very well for the purpose.' He stroked his moustache. 'It was not hard to open the cabinet. Naturally we were obliged to meet in secret. We thought it would appear suspicious if we were both seen proceeding outside together. L'Épine said he would walk out to a place where, if one goes just past the log seat, there is a clear area sufficient for our purpose, hidden from the house by trees, and he would wait for me there. Then after some minutes had passed, I was to follow. It was a risk, of course, but we thought that if we held our swords in front of our bodies, it would not be apparent if seen from behind that we had them. If either of us happened to be questioned on the way, then we could always claim we were practising the apple trick alone. For this reason, we both took an apple with us.'

'You appointed no second?' demanded Holmes. I could see that he was appalled by the fact that his suggestion for a peaceful resolution between the two men had been turned in this dangerous way.

'No, we told no-one of our intentions, since we did not wish to be prevented. And we are gentlemen of honour. We both agreed to yield to the superior man. With a true sword, it hardly needs a director to call out a hit. I said to L'Épine, "Today we battle as sworn enemies; tomorrow we may meet as friends." A little blood will settle the matter.'

Holmes was not placated by this. He folded his arms and fixed Brambilla with a piercing stare. 'And what was the outcome? Where is L'Épine?'

'He was not there to meet me. We never fought. I waited for him. I thought I heard someone in the woodland. It might have been he. I assumed he was attending to his comfort before our contest. I decided not to call out but waited in the appointed spot, expecting him to come and join me, but he did not. Then I thought he must have changed his mind and returned here.'

'The other sabre is still missing,' said Holmes. 'If he had returned, I assume he would have brought it with him.'

'Perhaps he has fallen and injured himself,' I said. 'Or you mistook the place, and he is still there waiting.'

'We must find him!' said Brambilla.

Holmes gave a curt nod. 'Let us go.' He turned to the butler. 'Mr Xavier, see what extra resources you can muster and bring them at once to make a thorough search.'

Xavier hurried away and the rest of us proceeded outside, where we found Luckhurst sitting in a shady spot on the terrace reading a book, while Sir Jasper Grey, having completed his run, was nearby, doing his daily exercises.

'The Chevalier L'Épine cannot be found, and he has a sabre with him,' said Holmes, tersely.

'Oh my word!' said Luckhurst. He put down his book and stood up. 'I'll help you look.'

Grey said nothing, but wiped his neck with a towel, threw it down, and joined us.

'He may be in the woodland, but we cannot be sure,' I said.

'What was he doing in the woods with a sabre?' asked Luckhurst.

'He was going to practise the apple trick,' said Brambilla, quickly. 'I went to see how he was progressing, and I thought I heard him moving about, but I didn't see him. I will show you the place, just past the log seat.'

'A very private location,' observed Grey. 'If you had been intending to fight a duel, you could not have chosen better.'

'As far as we know, he was alone,' said Holmes. 'If we are fortunate, we may have to deal with no more than a man who is lost or has stumbled.'

L'Épine was not to be seen anywhere on open ground, and we plunged into the woods and gradually spread out. We called out for the missing man but received no response. There was no movement of any note, a welcome breeze did no more than stir the upper branches, and leaves high above our heads were rustled by passing squirrels. As we lost sight of each other, it was easy to imagine that the sound of our fellow searchers was an indication of the man we sought.

Briefly I stood still, looking about me, judging where my companions were, hoping to sense something that would offer a clue. Somewhere distant, there was the crunch of dry twigs underfoot. A man was moving. I called out for L'Épine again, but something flew past me, almost brushing my ear, giving the momentary impression of a large insect or a bird. Then an arrow buried itself in a nearby tree, making a loud thumping noise as it did so. For a moment I was unable to move, frozen to the spot by the realisation that I was being shot at. I realised I should run and hide myself in the woods, but without any idea of where I would be safe, I could not choose a direction. In the event, I never had the chance, for I was suddenly struck with great force and borne to the ground.

CHAPTER EIGHTEEN

I have never been hit by a moving carriage or a galloping horse, but in that moment, I had some impression of what such a fate might be like. The impact knocked the breath from my body, and I crashed onto the forest floor. I lay on my back, helpless and pinned down by a huge weight, while a powerful hand the size of a great ape's clamped over my mouth. A low voice hissed in my ear, 'Quiet.' At almost the same moment there was another thumping sound, and to my horror I saw a second arrow sunk deep into the trunk of a tree. Had I been standing, I would almost certainly have been struck.

My attacker — or saviour, as I now realised — was Sir Jasper Grey, with locks of his raven hair stuck to his face with perspiration, and fresh blood soaking into one shirtsleeve. I made no attempt to move or speak; I merely watched him as his darting eyes took in the surrounding scene. Someone was lurking nearby, but as we lay there, hardly daring to breathe, the sound of footsteps slowly faded away into the distance.

Then, to my relief, we heard the arrival of Xavier's band of reinforcements, men plunging pell-mell into the woods and calling out loudly for L'Épine. Grey slowly sat up, took his hand from my face, and leaned against a tree. 'That will frighten the fellow off,' he said.

I dared to raise my head. 'Did you see who it was?'

'No, there was just a shadow moving in the trees.'

I sat up rather cautiously. 'I — thank you. I don't know what to say. But you are injured.'

'Yes, an arrow seems to have grazed me,' he said carelessly.

'Let me take a look.'

'It's nothing, I'm sure.'

'The least I can do is tend to it. Please allow me. I am something of an expert in dressing wounds.'

He smiled and removed his shirt, revealing a torso that would have looked well on a Greek athlete. There was a long, shallow cut on one shoulder. Fortunately, I had my medical supplies in my pocket, and was able to staunch the bleeding with a pad of surgical lint and apply the antiseptic lotion I had prepared. I warned him that it would sting, but he took it without flinching. 'Should you require a bandage, Mrs Pescott has ample supplies in the kitchen. If you were anyone else, I would be asking which was your sword arm, but I understand you have two.'

'I do. The right is stronger, but the left —' he made a wicked tilt of the eyebrow and flexed his fingers — 'delivers more surprises. I shall need both if Redcar decides to call me out.'

I blinked in amazement. 'You — think he might?'

'His lordship is somewhat transparent.'

'Would you accept a challenge from him?'

'Why not? It's better to meet these things than avoid them. I need to put him straight. He thinks I insulted his daughter.'

'And did you?' I dared to ask.

'The only man who insulted Redcar's daughter was her husband, and she is well rid of him.'

Further emboldened by this statement, I continued. 'So — I hope you won't mind my asking — what did happen that night at the Countess of Eastleigh's ball?'

Grey examined his torn shirt, which probably cost more than every garment I was wearing. 'I won't ask you to believe me, but now that the fellow is dead, I can tell you. Kingsley was well in his cups that night, and I heard him criticise his wife for her appearance. He said he was ashamed to acknowledge her as his, but there was no recourse for him but to accept the situation. He said she was from "common stock" and had been foisted on him, and she must never forget it.'

'Common stock?' I exclaimed. 'Whatever did he mean by that?'

'I don't know. But that was when she ran onto the terrace. I could see she was distressed, so I went to speak to her. I can never resist a lady in distress. I tried to reassure her that her husband's words were worthless. I praised her appearance. I usually do, and it is always appreciated. She could barely speak for emotion and left me.'

'Then there was no insult?'

'No, but it is pointless for me to say so, as I am a renowned scoundrel and dissembler, especially where women are concerned. I am obviously lying.'

'She said that she was repulsed and frightened by your behaviour.'

'Did she now?' he drawled.

Encouraged by his calm manner, I added, 'I have heard you called the worst man in England.'

He grinned. 'I may be. Any rivals I had for that title have already been hanged or murdered.'

I was beginning to think that Grey was a far better man than he was made out to be, when we heard footsteps approach. To my relief, it was Luckhurst. He stared at us speechlessly for a moment or two, and I realised that with Grey's state of undress and the leaves and twigs clinging to my garments, we must look like a pair of ragamuffins who had been wrestling in the dirt. I brushed down my clothes.

'We've found L'Épine,' said Luckhurst. 'He's dead.'

Grey pulled on his shirt and we followed Luckhurst, who led us to where the Frenchman lay face-down in the undergrowth.

The sabre, still in its sheath, was clasped in his hand. The searchers, who included Mr Xavier, Holmes, gentlemen guests and male servants, were grouped around him. An arrow protruded from his neck, and a substantial pool of blood had flowed from the wound.

'Poor fellow,' I said as I knelt beside the body.

'I suppose there is no hope?' asked Brambilla.

I shook my head. 'The arrow has pierced an artery. He has bled quite copiously and must have been dead in minutes.'

'How long has he been dead?' asked Northam.

'Not long. I think he was last seen alive less than an hour ago. The blood has not yet dried.'

'Why did he have the sabre with him?' asked Rampal. 'I hope he was not intending any harm.'

'I have been told that he was planning to practise the apple trick in private,' I said, which was very nearly true. This explanation was greeted with all the credence it deserved.

'But who would want to kill L'Épine?' demanded Brambilla. 'For all his faults, he was not a bad man. I don't believe he had an enemy in the world!' A number of incredulous faces turned to him, but he seemed oblivious to their stares.

'He was not the only target,' I said. 'I believe that the same person who killed L'Épine tried to kill again soon afterwards.'

Several persons spoke at once, demanding an explanation. I rose to my feet and waited for silence. For once, I found myself in the position of Sherlock Holmes, as the man who had the evidence and was about to make a pronouncement.

As carefully as I could, I recounted the details of the near-misses I had experienced only moments before greeted by horrified gasps and shocked expressions. Grey added corroboration, and for once he was believed. His spilt blood spoke for him.

'You are unhurt?' Luckhurst asked me, with a little tremor in his voice.

'Yes,' I reassured him, probably sounding braver than I felt.

'We have a murderer in our midst!' exclaimed Northam, on the edge of panic, looking wildly about him. 'An arrow in the forest might well have been meant for me!'

'Perhaps,' said Holmes, calmly, 'the killer is standing amongst us now.'

We all stood still at the implication of his words and looked about the little circle of men. Assuming that there were not two murderous archers in the woods, and Grey and I had been shot at by the same man who had killed L'Épine, we at least had been exonerated from blame, but what of the others?

'We cannot say precisely when L'Épine was killed, but the second attack was only a few minutes ago,' said Holmes. 'That does, however, leave enough time for the killer, on hearing the second band of searchers arrive, to cast aside his weapons. If he had circled about, he could have joined us and be standing here, now. Or he might have left the area and returned to the manor, hoping he would not be seen to do so. He might then claim that he had been there all the time. The rest of us were dealing with this tragedy and might not have noticed someone slipping away. If we wait here, he might even arrive, all innocence, as if attracted to the spot by the sudden activity.'

'What's all the commotion?' came a voice, and Lord Redcar appeared with Winchip trailing in his wake, yawning. His lordship's face as he was informed of what had occurred was a picture of despair.

'My lord,' said Xavier, quietly, 'I think I should send a man to Charlbury to advise Constable Bennet.'

'Yes, yes, do whatever is necessary,' said Redcar, wearily.

'I suggest,' said Holmes, 'that the place be marked, but no-one should disturb the body. The woods should be out of bounds until the police have searched the area. I shall offer my services to the inspector as before.' There were some surprised faces as he said this. 'In my capacity as a student of anatomy and chemistry at Barts, I have been called upon by Scotland Yard more than once to make detailed studies of scenes of crime,' Holmes explained, 'many of which include murder.'

'You claim to have caught murderers?' said Northam, incredulously.

'I have either laid hands upon them myself, or directed the police to where the killer can be found.'

'That is true,' said Lord Redcar. 'Inspector Marsh has confirmed it. And Mr Stamford here has acted as Holmes's assistant.'

'Then I wish you success,' said Grey, who, with his torn and bloodied shirt looked more like a murderer than anyone else present.

'And pray for no more deaths!' exclaimed Redcar.

It was a miserable party which wended its way back to the manor. All of us were affected by this second death, Brambilla most of all. When we were next gathered together, he delivered an emotional eulogy to his rival, for whom he expressed the greatest respect. He then said that he was intending to go for a walk in the grounds so as to be alone with his thoughts but was gently dissuaded from doing so. Holmes suggested that no-one should go outside without a companion, and on his advice the door of the room where the archery supplies were kept and the fencing hall were sealed. The next time those rooms opened would be for the inspection of the police.

At the first opportunity I revealed to Holmes what Grey had told me concerning the evening of the Countess of Eastleigh's ball, and the behaviour of Sir Walter and Henrietta Kingsley.

'Do you believe this account?' asked Holmes. 'It does tend to show Grey in the best possible light, and he is not noted for his truthfulness.'

'That's the thing,' I said, 'practically everything he says is designed to show him in a bad light. I think he rather revels in it. He likes the notoriety.'

'Take care he does not lead you into iniquity,' warned Holmes. I could see his point. My friendship with Holmes had endangered my life and shaken my nerves, but at least my good name was intact.

'But whether or not Grey is speaking the truth, I don't think Redcar would be inclined to believe him innocent in the matter, unless his daughter confirmed the story,' I said. 'And perhaps not even then. Would she really disclose her husband's accusations to her father? She might have thought it better simply to allow Sir Jasper Grey's reputation to apportion blame.'

'You may be correct,' said Holmes. 'Still, the attempt must be made to convince Lord Redcar that there was no insult for him to revenge. Any opportunity of dissuading him from foolishness must be taken. We have promised Lady Redcar as much. But we must move slowly in a question of such delicacy.'

'You think his lordship is still determined to punish Grey?'

'I have no doubt of it. If Grey is not arrested for the murder of Kingsley, then Redcar will seek to obtain justice for his daughter by the sword.'

'And the accusation Kingsley levelled against his wife? That she was of "common stock"? Is there any truth in it, or is it just his fancy? Some men would happily ignore a wife's humble origins for love or beauty or character, but I fear that he was not a man who would do so. I have seen the portrait of Lady Kingsley and if that is a good likeness, it is true that she does not resemble her father. Brambilla described her as a pearl emerging from an oyster. Might that be the reason for her husband's suspicions?'

'It is impossible to prove the truth with any certainty,' said Holmes. 'The world is told that Lady Kingsley is the daughter of Lord Redcar. Any accusation to the contrary is a grave insult to his lordship, his late wife, and their daughter.'

'Kingsley might have been killed to silence him on the subject,' I said. 'Lord Redcar knew where he was to be found, and we only have his account of the conversation between them. And I think Winchip would support any story told by his cousin.'

'We would know a great deal more if we could discover the weapon used,' said Holmes. 'But I do not think I can progress my enquiries much further without interviewing Lady Kingsley.'

CHAPTER NINETEEN

While we were waiting for the police to arrive, Holmes and I went to see Lord Redcar, who was in his study. He had some letters on his desk, but if he had been reading them, he had stopped and seemed to be staring at nothing.

He looked up at us with a haunted expression. 'Please don't tell me there is more bad news! I couldn't bear it!' he exclaimed.

'Not at all,' said Holmes. 'I have come to ask you if Lady Kingsley has revealed any facts to you which might cast some light on the unfortunate death of her husband.'

Redcar pushed away the pile of papers, which teetered precariously on the edge of his desk. 'She has not. The shock to her has been very great. My poor girl. Sir Walter told us he had locked her up, and I could hardly believe it, but it is true! When the police went to inform her of the tragedy, they found her a prisoner in her suite. She was comfortable enough, and provided with all necessities by the housekeeper, but all the same, it was a shameful way to treat a blameless wife. And to dismiss her personal maid, a devoted and loyal servant, on a mere whim!'

'Might I have your permission to speak to Lady Kingsley?' asked Holmes.

Redcar frowned. 'What would she tell you that she cannot tell her own father?'

'Sometimes,' said Holmes gently, 'sensitive persons find it easier to reveal their deepest feelings to strangers than to their closest family.'

Redcar reflected on this for a moment, then nodded. 'You may be right. Very well. I will see what I can do.' He rose and left the room. As he did so, he was so preoccupied that when he brushed past the papers and caused them to tumble to the carpet, he did not appear to notice.

Holmes picked up the papers and restored them to the desk, but he could not resist glancing at them before he did so. One does not usually pry into a gentleman's private correspondence without his permission, but in the circumstances, I could understand Holmes's action. 'Lord Redcar has been making enquiries as to the value of the Charlbury Park estate, should he wish to sell it,' said Holmes.

'I wonder if that has any bearing on what has happened here,' I said.

'It may mean something or nothing,' said Holmes. 'Sometimes it is not one fact that creates a situation of danger but an accumulation of small, individually trivial facts which taken together can be deadly.'

When Redcar returned, he beckoned us to go with him. 'She has agreed to speak to you, but only for a few minutes,' he said. 'Please, I beg you, be very careful with her. I have not yet informed her of the recent tragedy, and you must not. She will learn of it soon enough, but not before I permit it.'

The door of Garden Cottage, peeping from under a bower of trellised blooms, was opened by Lady Redcar's maid, Molly, who was expecting us and ushered us in. Everywhere I sensed the hand and tastes of Lady Redcar. The entrance hall was bright and airy, with patterned wallpaper and little tables for the display of decorative trinkets. The room we entered, rather cautiously, as we knew we were there under strict approval, was arranged as a lady's parlour. A circular table laid with a lace-edged cloth was enhanced by a bowl filled with fresh flowers, and there was a silver tray of chinaware painted with roses. The air was fragranced by some exotic tisane. The only persons before us were Mrs Fenton, Lady Redcar, and the widow of Sir Walter Kingsley.

When a lady finds herself suddenly and unexpectedly widowed, one of her first actions is to be fitted out with suitable mourning attire. It is a purchase of great significance, since she is to live in weeds of utter black for many months, the deep colour of her garments fading as the mourning period progresses. Lady Kingsley, having been transported from her home to that of her father without the opportunity of having her new wardrobe completed, had had to make do with her most sombre day gown. She had chosen mauve silk, the colour widows wear when they still have to appear to be in mourning, but the grief of their loss has largely worn away. A black lace wrap was around her shoulders, and she also wore a black trimmed cap and lace mittens. I guessed that these might have been loaned to her by Lady Redcar. I saw at once that any gown Lady Redcar had worn when she mourned her late father would not have fitted Lady Kingsley, who was of larger form and comely in a different way. From what I could see of her features, partially hidden as they were by the lace frill of the cap, her portrait had not been excessively flattering. I could certainly see why Baron Brambilla admired her.

We bowed respectfully and offered our formal condolences as Lord Redcar introduced us. He gave us a sad look as he withdrew from the room. Molly remained in attendance.

'Please be seated,' said Lady Redcar. 'Would you like some tea?'

We sat and accepted a clear, fragrant liquid with a thin slice of lemon in tiny cups.

While this was being provided, I could not help but study, as unobtrusively as I could, the face of Lady Kingsley to see if I could detect any hint of similarity to that of Lord Redcar. I tried to imagine his lordship much younger, beardless, with unlined, rounder features. Did I see anything? I could not be sure. And then there was the portrait of her mother, the first Lady Redcar, whose poor health was apparent even through the paint of what might well have been an image fashioned to please the subject. There was nothing to learn there.

'I would like Lady Redcar and Mrs Fenton to stay,' said Lady Kingsley. Her voice was quiet but firm.

'As you wish,' said Holmes, deferentially. He sipped the drink and set it aside. 'I have been asked to provide the police with advice of a medical nature; however, it would assist me if I could learn more about your late husband, whom I had not met before the day of his sad demise.'

Lady Kingsley inclined her head in assent. 'What would you like to know?'

'He struck me on a first impression as a man who was quick to anger. Is that correct?'

Her expression did not change. 'It is.'

'Men who are quick to anger often regret their passion almost as soon as it seizes them. But when in the throes of the storm, they are likely to say things they afterwards wish they might take back. Does that describe your husband?'

She toyed with her cup for a while, as if seeking an answer in the few floating fragments of green leaves. 'He may in his heart of hearts have secretly regretted certain things he said, but I have never known him to apologise either in spoken words or by letter to anyone he insulted. Neither have I ever heard him admit he was in the wrong on any subject.'

'He may, without realising it, have made many enemies,' said Holmes.

'He did, but I cannot imagine that would have concerned him.' She gave a faint smile. 'I can see where you are tending with these questions. You want to know if there were men who wished him harm. There could have been several. But for every hundred men who utter threats or speak of the bold and desperate things they might do, you would be hard pressed to find one or two who would actually act upon their words.'

'And do you think your husband might be one of that rare kind?'

'I have never seen him come to blows over a dispute, but that does not mean he would not. Are you saying he might have provoked an attack upon his person?' She considered this. 'Yes, he might well have done. A man who would not strike him in cold blood could easily do so in retaliation.'

'When your husband came here, he uttered threats against Sir Jasper Grey regarding an incident at the Countess of Eastleigh's ball. In fact, he challenged Sir Jasper to settle the question by combat.'

'That was unwise. Did they fight?'

'You father made them both promise not to. He urged your husband to return home in a calmer state of mind and restore peace to his household. It took some persuading, but eventually your husband said he would go home. But do you think that despite his promise, he might have determined to fight Sir Jasper Grey if the opportunity arose?'

'He was never a man one could trust to keep his promises,' she said.

'Would you be prepared to enlighten me as to what passed at the Countess of Eastleigh's ball? The circumstances which so enraged your husband?'

She shook her head. 'It is gone; it is past. I do not wish to speak of it. Things were said which were untrue and therefore unfit to repeat. How can it have anything to do with Walter's death?'

'All I know at present is that your husband met his demise at the hand of another. It is a mystery that demands to be solved. Every fact must be examined with great care, and if not relevant, dismissed, until finally only the truth remains. Lord Redcar has asked for my help, and I mean to do all in my power to find the answer.'

'So,' said Lady Kingsley, with a look that denied any possibility of contradiction, 'I must either confirm the shame that has been unjustly heaped upon me, in which case my poor father will be deeply affected, or, if I reject that account, I will be exonerating a scoundrel from blame and might appear to be in league with him. It is better to remain silent.'

'Dear Henrietta,' said Lady Redcar, gently, 'you should tell your father that he is not to distress himself over the past. His only concern now must be for your future happiness.'

'That is good advice, my dear,' said Mrs Fenton.

'I agree,' said Holmes. 'I am anxious to save Lord Redcar from any further pain and distress, lest he attempt any action that might prove detrimental to his safety or his honour.'

At that moment there was a soft knock at the door. Lady Kingsley gave a slight frown at the intrusion, but when the door opened to reveal Mrs Pescott, her face softened into a happier expression.

Mrs Pescott addressed us. 'Gentlemen, Lord Redcar wishes to speak with you,' she said. 'He is in the library.'

We rose and took our leave. Lady Kingsley made no effort to conceal that she was pleased to see us go. At the door, Holmes turned and made a slight bow. 'I thank you, Lady Kingsley, for agreeing to speak with us at this sad time. If there is anything further you wish to say, even if it should seem to you to have no importance whatsoever, you have only to request our presence and we will oblige.'

Holmes's exquisitely polite and controlled manner only revealed his frustration that Lady Kingsley would not tell him all. A truth was being hidden, and he was not yet in a position to extract it.

As we proceeded to the library, Mrs Pescott said, 'Lord Redcar expressly asked me not to mention in Lady Kingsley's hearing that the police are here.'

'I understand,' said Holmes. 'She is a remarkable young lady. Very firm of character. I am sure that she will be able to endure the news when she is told.'

Mrs Pescott smiled. 'Oh, yes. Even as a child she was strong-willed, yet never fretful. Lord Redcar is extremely proud of her.'

'How old was she when she lost her mother?'

'Almost three. The first Lady Redcar was never very strong, and she was an invalid after the child was born.'

Holmes paused. 'I must apologise in advance for raising a subject which might be considered indelicate, but I am engaged in examining all the facts which might be relevant to the death of Sir Walter Kingsley, and I am endeavouring to know more of his character.'

Mrs Pescott was firm in her position. 'Lord Redcar has issued instructions to the servants that we are to answer all your questions. I will do whatever I can to assist you.'

'I have been told that Sir Walter Kingsley had been heard to cast doubts on Lady Kingsley's parentage. He accused her of coming from "common stock".'

This came as no surprise to Mrs Pescott, who nodded, sadly. 'She has mentioned something of the sort. He was generous with his insults but little else. But I can assure you, Lady Kingsley is a Redcar, and had she been born a son, that boy would rightfully be the next duke.'

'Were you present at the birth?'

'I was. She was born in this house, and there was a doctor in attendance.'

Holmes said nothing in response, but the conversation had given him something to think about. He remained silent until we reached the library, where we found Lord Redcar with Inspector Marsh, who was studying the estate map.

CHAPTER TWENTY

'How was my poor girl?' asked Lord Redcar.

'You need not fear for her,' said Holmes. 'She has great strength of character. But she is not yet ready to talk of those things which most concern her husband's death.'

We gathered around the library table. There was a carafe of water and some glasses on a tray and as the day was hot, we refreshed ourselves.

'We have found out little that is new from her regarding her husband,' said Marsh. 'I have yet to discover anyone who had a good word for him. I have also spoken to Lady Kingsley's maid Agnes, who as we know was turned out of the house simply on the suspicion that she was passing love notes between Lady Kingsley and an admirer, something she strongly denies. We found no such notes at the property, and I am inclined to believe her.'

'I hope the maid was able to find shelter,' I said.

'As it happens, she has an aunt in the village of Lowhampton and is there with her now, but it was a long way for her to go. She had to spend a night in a field. Then she was able to beg a ride on an ironmonger's cart. Her aunt was furious at seeing her arrive with her garments so dirtied and had a lot to say on the subject. When I told her Sir Walter Kingsley was dead, she was not sorry to hear it, and said had he been alive she would not have allowed her niece to return to that house, however much she was wanted. Now, of course, Miss Agnes says she would dearly like to attend Lady Kingsley if she could have her place again.'

'The maid could not suggest who might have killed her master? Had he received any threats?'

'I had the impression that quarrels were meat and drink to him. The maid did tell me, and I am sorry to say it, Lord Redcar, that Kingsley neglected your daughter, and was often absent from home. His manservant revealed that there was an apartment in Oxford where a single lady resided, for which Kingsley paid the rent, and he was more often there than he was with his wife.'

'The key on his watch chain?' asked Holmes.

'Yes, we had imagined that that would open the door of the suite where Lady Kingsley was confined, but it was not the case. That key is in the possession of the housekeeper, Mrs Crane. No, we think the key on Sir Walter's watch chain was for the apartment in Oxford.'

Redcar shook his head in wordless misery.

'Did Lady Kingsley know of this?' asked Holmes.

'She had her suspicions, but she would never have confronted him with them. However,' continued Marsh, 'I remain sure that Kingsley was killed by a personal enemy, and I cannot see that it was a chance encounter. Whoever killed him must have known he was here, and whereabouts he was to be found alone where the murder could be carried out unobserved.'

'That leaves us with a very small number of suspects,' observed Holmes. 'Has Mr Armitage completed his examination?'

'He has. The deceased was in good health and not under the influence of alcohol or any drug that might have impaired his actions. The weapon was thrust right through the body with some force. It passed through the back and front of his shirt, but not the coat and waistcoat. These were unbuttoned, probably due to the hot weather. In view of the strength required, the murderer is more likely to be male than female. The exit wound was the same width as where the weapon entered. It was a clean, smooth cut with no debris, and it is estimated that the blade must have been at least twelve inches long. So most probably a sword.'

'You have not located the weapon?'

'Not yet. It might be hidden in the woods or at the bottom of the river. But we will continue to look.' He uttered a deep, weary sigh and opened his notebook. 'And that brings me to the sad demise of the Chevalier L'Épine, a man who appears to have had no enemies at all, apart, possibly, from Baron Brambilla. But I detect friendly rivalry there rather than hatred, and something more likely to be settled by the sword than an arrow in the neck.

'I have now examined the room where the archery materials are kept, and Lord Redcar tells me he believes that some items are missing. Are they always kept in that room?'

'Yes. All the gentlemen invited here were shown where they were. We were due to have archery practice after the cricket, but...' Lord Redcar sighed.

'The room was not kept locked?'

'No, I think the key was lost long ago. The cricketing equipment is there as well. I mean, I could never have expected what happened. All sports have some risk attached.'

'Did anyone state their intention of practising archery?'

'No. None of the targets have been put in place. I expect Gorringe would have helped with that, had it been required.'

'I have shown you the arrows we took from the tree near where Mr Stamford was standing. We have found others, one of which dispatched a squirrel. The fatal arrow remains in the body and will be removed and examined in due course, but it looks very like the others. Can you confirm that the arrows I have shown you belong to the estate?'

'I am not sure. Mr Gorringe would be able to advise you.'

'Was anyone seen with a bow and arrows prior to Chevalier L'Épine's death?'

'No.'

'Do you know why L'Épine had a sabre with him?'

'Sword practice,' said Redcar, firmly.

'Alone?' queried Marsh.

'Yes, there are exercises which may be performed alone. With an apple.'

Marsh raised his eyebrows, then flicked through the pages of his notebook. 'An apple was found in his pocket,' he admitted, and did not pursue the point. 'I am told that it was you, Mr Holmes, who gave the alarm. What brought you to the woods?'

'I was told that a sabre had been taken from the fencing hall and L'Épine was not to be found. He had mentioned exercising somewhere near the woodlands. We were concerned for his safety and decided to look for him. He was not used to the sabre, and we all feared he had perhaps fallen and done himself an injury.'

'And you, Mr Stamford, I am informed that you had a narrow escape.'

I was obliged to describe my near encounter with the arrows and the injury to Sir Jasper Grey. I could see Redcar was unimpressed by Grey's heroic action. 'Are you sure he was struck by an arrow?' he asked. 'I mean, he might have marked himself to avoid suspicion. I wouldn't put anything past that man.'

'I saw the injury and given its position, I cannot imagine that anyone could convincingly inflict it on himself,' I said. I almost added that it would be futile for Grey to try and avoid suspicion, as he seemed to be surrounded by it. Redcar merely snorted in disbelief.

Constable Bennet arrived, bringing with him some items wrapped in oilcloth, which proved to be an archery bow, a leather quiver and gloves. All had obviously suffered some soaking in the river. On being asked where they had been found, Bennet pointed out the place on the estate map, which suggested it was not far distant from where L'Épine's body had lain.

'They are similar to the others I have seen which are held here,' said Marsh. 'Can you comment, Lord Redcar?'

Redcar looked at the sodden items. One arrow is very like another, but from the design and signs of wear on the quiver and gloves, he was able to confirm that they were his property. He had no doubt that they were the very items he had told the police were missing from the storeroom.

'I am going to have to insist that the remaining archery supplies are placed under lock and key until such time as I say they may be released,' said Marsh. Lord Redcar had long abandoned any thought of sporting competitions and made no protest.

We appeared to be no further forward in finding either murderer, assuming there were two of them, and once our interview was over, I commented to Holmes that it was a shame that Lady Kingsley had not been able to tell us more.

'Sometimes,' said Holmes, with that enigmatic smile that could be quite frustrating at times, 'it is not what someone says but what they do not say that is the most informative part of the conversation. But now I wish to have a further word with the man who is probably better acquainted with the parkland than any other. The man who knows all the secret places where the weapon that killed Kingsley might be.'

'Mr Gorringe?'

'Indeed. He may have information he does not realise is important, or if he does so realise, he prefers not to reveal it, to protect his master.'

As we made our way outside, it occurred to me that our pledge to Lady Redcar to protect her husband from his own impulses might be waylaid by the discovery of his involvement in murder.

Holmes has always taken his promises very seriously, and his promise to Lady Redcar was no exception. I am sure that he was not moved by her beauty. He did not judge a person's character by outward appearances. He appreciated beauty of every kind, but it did not drive him, and he never allowed it to control him. He liked a mystery, a challenge to his intellect, a mission where quick, bold, and determined action was required. He would do all in his power to protect a woman under threat or in distress, but he was also aware that there are those who can be as wicked as men, or even worse. He once said that a woman's wickedness can either be violent and ruthless, or so subtle that one does not see it until it is too late.

Luckhurst had naturally made a comment to me earlier on the subject of the curious and seemingly ill-matched marriage of the bluff and hearty fifty-five-year-old Lord Redcar and his gracefully lovely wife, who was less than half his age. 'It can hardly be thought of as a love match,' he said, 'more like a financial arrangement that suits both parties.'

'I do feel that they are very fond of each other,' I replied, recalling that Lady Redcar's anxiety for her husband had been expressed entirely in terms of her affection for him. Had she not cared for her husband, and married solely for advancement, then any harm that came to his lordship would not have concerned her. Widowhood would, however, confer on her a tremendous benefit, both financially and in the personal freedom that only a woman who was both single and wealthy could enjoy.

As Holmes and I went to interview Gorringe, I thought once more of his lordship's plan, which we had only known about because Lady Redcar had revealed it to us. He meant to punish Sir Jasper Grey for his misdeeds but in such a way that he would escape all suspicion. Not out of cowardice, I was sure, but consideration for his wife.

It was as I reflected upon this that I suddenly perceived a flaw in what Lady Redcar had told us. Any harm that befell Sir Jasper Grey which appeared to be purely accidental could not escape suspicion as Lord Redcar hoped, because Holmes and I had been warned of his lordship's secret plans. Was the confidence she had shared with us intended to work against her husband rather than for him? And if that was the case, how would we ever prove it?

I also wondered how Redcar's plans to sell the estate affected the situation. If he did sell it, might he have to make changes to his will? Did Lady Redcar know about his intentions? Would she lose her sanctuary of the Garden Cottage? Would she do anything in her power to prevent the sale? Did she, so far from trying to protect her husband, actually hope for his death, and for it to take place sooner rather than later?

Despite the fact that Holmes usually attributed little value to my musings, I felt obliged to mention these thoughts to him. He listened without comment or change of expression. Of course, nothing I had said could have escaped him, but he kept his conclusions to himself.

CHAPTER TWENTY-ONE

We found Gorringe in the cottage garden, where he was wielding a hoe, skilfully applying it either firmly or with tender care as appropriate. I could imagine one of his ancestors, wirily strong with his face set in a determined scowl, bearing a pikestaff into battle.

Holmes engaged him in conversation regarding how well the garden was growing, and Gorringe told us that Lady Redcar and Lady Kingsley both liked to walk there, arm in arm, to admire the flowers. 'Like sisters, they are. And Mrs Fenton, she is always there with them to see they don't get troubled by the gentlemen.'

'Mrs Fenton does not fear the gentlemen,' said Holmes with a smile.

'Not at all. In fact, she —' Gorringe stopped.

'Yes?' said Holmes.

'I won't say no more,' said Gorringe, shaking his head. 'She is a widow lady of mature years and can do as she pleases.'

The subject of conversation underwent an abrupt change, and there followed some general talk of the weather and how prolonged lack of rain made life hard for the gardener. This matter having been disposed of, Holmes said he hoped Gorringe had not been troubled too much by the police being everywhere asking questions.

Gorringe merely shrugged. 'They have their work to do, just like me,' he said.

'I don't suppose you saw anything which might assist them in discovering the murderer of Chevalier L'Épine?' asked Holmes.

'All I know is, none of the gentlemen said they wanted to practise archery, or I would have taken the targets out,' he said. 'I went along to the kitchen, where Mrs Pescott said they were making a nice pie for my dinner. Then we heard all the commotion, and I was told the police had been called again.' He shook his head. 'Never known anything like it.'

'Since you know the estate so well, you must have been able to offer the police considerable help in their searches for the weapon used to murder Sir Walter Kingsley,' said Holmes.

'I did all I could. Some sort of sword, they told me. And his lordship said it can't have been one from the house. I keep my eyes open all the time, of course, but it's not easy searching the woodland. It might be at the bottom of the river.'

'But where did it come from?' asked Holmes. 'That is the question. None of the visitors admits to having brought a sword to the estate. None of those living here seems to have owned one.'

'Oh, there's plenty of old iron around here,' said Gorringe. 'All those battles in the old days. People still sometimes find things in the soil. I have some bits of it myself.'

'Really?' said Holmes. 'I would like to take a look, if I may.'

'Now, there's nothing that might be suspected,' said Gorringe. 'Rusty old pieces, some of them quite broken up. I showed them to the police.'

'All the same, I would be most interested to view them,' said Holmes. 'The history of the county is quite fascinating, and surely even such humble items might have a story to tell.'

Gorringe pulled a kerchief from his pocket and mopped his brow. 'They're in my cottage, if you want to come along now.'

'Thank you,' said Holmes.

We trudged up the drive. Gorringe's home was a venerable stone-built edifice, a lower floor with a tiny attic room, and a small outhouse attached. Generously growing creepers clothed it so abundantly in green that it might at first glance have been thought part of a hedge or a topiary sculpted into the shape of a cottage.

An oak door opened into a small parlour with a large fireplace and a blackened pan hanging above it. On another wall were two iron hooks on which rested a very old blunderbuss. A powder horn hung from another hook nearby, and a small shelf carried a lidded box and some torn scraps of paper. The furniture was strongly made and serviceable, and there was a platter on the table, draped in a cloth, as well as a covered jug suggesting the hearty repast awaiting Gorringe after his labours. There was a small door to another room, and a set of stairs just wide enough for the passage of one person.

'How often do you use this weapon?' asked Holmes, examining the blunderbuss.

Gorringe chuckled. 'Not often. I sometimes bring down a squirrel or two. If the local boys try to climb the gates, I find waving it at them soon sends them back down again.'

Gorringe climbed the stairs and returned with a small hessian sack. Pushing the platter aside, he opened the sack and there tumbled onto the table some pieces of ancient weaponry, all very worn and eaten by rust. We identified two broken pike heads, a small dagger with the tip missing and a short sword, its blade slightly bent and the edges notched from violent combat. It was obvious at a glance that none of these items could have recently been used to commit a murder.

'And these are all from the Civil War battle fields?' asked Holmes.

'Oh, yes. Always finding pieces of old ironmongery hereabouts, even now.'

I examined the sword. 'This doesn't look like a foot soldier's weapon,' I said.

'Ah, well, that is what they used to call a tuck sword,' said Gorringe. 'It was carried by the pike men in case they broke the pikestaff and needed to fight close up.'

Holmes studied it with some care. 'Light to carry, but just as deadly,' he mused. 'A wide double-edged blade, and a scrolled cross bar.'

'Surely this can't be —' I exclaimed.

'No. This is not the weapon used to kill Sir Walter Kingsley. The rust has not been disturbed. If there had been traces of rust in the wound, the police surgeon would have detected it. And it could not have left such a clean, straight cut. But I would say that he might well have been killed by a weapon of this type, one that is smooth and clean. Mr Gorringe, do you know of anyone who might have such a thing?'

'I wouldn't be surprised if a few other people in the county had one.'

Holmes took a notebook from his pocket, and I saw him mark down some estimates of the measurements of the tuck sword, then make a sketch of the curled iron of the pommel. 'I don't believe Lord Redcar has a similar example in his collection,' he observed.

'But it had to be something already here on the estate, or recently brought here and then carefully hidden,' I said. 'The police have searched everywhere, including people's rooms.'

'I don't know what any of the guests might have brought with them, but I can say for sure that Lord Redcar does not have a tuck sword,' said Gorringe. 'He has seen this one and said how much he would have liked to find one in good condition so he could have it for his collection.'

'I believe that the police are considering him as one of their suspects,' said Holmes. 'But he does not strike me as someone who would kill an unarmed man in cold blood. In fact, I am quite certain that he is innocent of all wrongdoing, and I hope to be able to prove it.'

'I hope you do,' said Gorringe, warmly. 'And — well, there was something I didn't say to the police, because I didn't want them to take it the wrong way and think that his lordship might have had something to do with it. But since you are of my mind I can tell you about it now, as it proves to me and will prove to you that Lord Redcar never had any thought of murder.'

'I admire his lordship. He is a noble and honest gentleman, and I would be most relieved to hear your proof,' said Holmes.

'Well, this was the thing,' said Gorringe. 'I was working in the garden not so long ago, and I saw Lord Redcar and Sir Walter Kingsley walking along, deep in conversation. And I could see that it was getting rather heated. I thought they wouldn't want my company, so I picked up my tools and left.' He paused. 'But then, I admit it, I crept back to listen. I mean, I thought if there was to be any difficulty for his lordship he might want to call out for assistance, and if he did, then I would be to hand.'

'Of course,' said Holmes, smoothly, 'that is most commendable.'

Gorringe looked relieved at this reaction. 'The subject of the altercation was Lady Kingsley. Now, I just want to say that she is a fine lady I have known since she was a tiny mite. No father could be prouder of a daughter than his lordship. He used to teach her all the sports just as if she was a boy; it made no difference to him. And she took to it as well as any boy. Kingsley, I never liked him, but it wasn't my place to say.

There were rumours about how he loved money and only courted ladies with a good settlement. I don't know how true that was. He came here and was as charming and mild as a man could be, but it was all a sham. After they were married, I could tell, every time she visited, she was not happy. She didn't have the spirit I had seen in her before.

'On that day, I heard Kingsley say such dreadful things. Shocking, they were. I never heard anything like it from the mouth of a gentleman. He refused to believe his wife was Lord Redcar's daughter. He said he had learned that the first Lady Redcar had been in poor health for years, and accused Lord Redcar of adopting a child of humble parents and pretending that she was of noble blood. He said he did not want the public scandal of casting her aside, but — you must excuse me, sirs — I only repeat what I heard — he said Lord Redcar should not expect to welcome any grandchildren.'

'How shocking!' I exclaimed. 'Did Lord Redcar deny this accusation?'

'He did. Most strongly.'

'Do you know what provoked Kingsley to this belief?' asked Holmes.

'It seems he had chanced to see a young woman of humble birth whom he thought resembled Lady Kingsley and imagined that they might be related. Then he made further enquiries, which seemed to support his notion. But that is all I know.'

'But this dispute between the two men — it did not come to violence?'

'Only in words.'

'Was there any resolution reached?'

'Lord Redcar was very angry. He said he did not want his daughter to remain in a household where she was not properly regarded. He said he would seek advice in law on arranging a separation of husband and wife. But he made it clear that should that separation take place, Kingsley would be expected to make a generous settlement.'

'How did he respond?' I asked, although I strongly suspected what the answer might be.

'With oaths and threats. He said he would not part with a penny. And worse than that, he said if Lord Redcar attempted to arrange this separation, he would make his allegations against his wife public and put her to shame. Then he walked away, and his lordship just stood there for a while, looking very unhappy. But you see, sirs, that what I overheard shows that Lord Redcar wanted to settle his differences by lawful means.'

Holmes thanked Gorringe and we left him to his work, returning to the house.

'Lord Redcar was in a very difficult position,' Holmes observed. 'He would not have wanted his daughter's name dragged through the mud. I am sorry to say that despite what Mr Gorringe might think, this does give him a powerful motive to murder Sir Walter Kingsley.'

CHAPTER TWENTY-TWO

Inspector Marsh had gone about some police business, and we were able to obtain a private interview with his lordship in his study. The air was thick with pipe smoke, but unlike Holmes, I thought the activity brought our host little comfort. He looked haggard, and the dark blotches under his eyes showed that restful sleep was merely a memory.

'What is it you have to say to me, Holmes?' asked Redcar miserably. 'Do not be afraid to speak. I need to know everything, anything that might resolve this catastrophe.'

Holmes paused, choosing his words carefully. 'It is apparent to me that Lady Kingsley is bearing up very well, following the loss of her husband,' he said.

'My poor daughter,' said Redcar. 'Yes, you may well think she has little reason to mourn him.'

'Was there ever any prospect of freeing her from the marriage by some means acceptable to them both?'

'None. I explored that, but Kingsley always had some obstacle to put in my way. Henrietta would have endured much to be free, but he wanted to keep her if only to punish her. And now, I fear she has further ordeals to endure. Not only did her husband suspect her of betraying him, as you saw from his frightful behaviour when he came here, but he levelled other accusations against her which were as disgraceful as they were untrue.' He paused with a sigh, and we waited for him to go on. 'I must tell you something now which for the moment must not be discussed with anyone else. The world will know soon enough if it becomes public.' We continued to wait. 'Kingsley's death will not put an end to my daughter's sorrows. He will have his revenge from the grave.'

'What do you mean?' asked Holmes.

'You are aware, of course, that in the usual way of things, a childless widow is the deceased husband's next of kin. Henrietta is of full age, and would have expected to inherit his estate, since he had no other close relatives — at least none with whom he was on speaking terms. At the very least he might have put his property in trust for her and appointed a manager, but no. When I spoke to him last, Kingsley revealed to me that he had made a will in which he left the bulk of his fortune to the university. Henrietta was to receive a nominal sum more in keeping with a bequest to a servant. And I think that that paltry amount was only included in the terms of the will so it could not be maintained that she had been omitted by mistake. Worse still, much worse, the will described in full his reasons for this cruel and insulting arrangement. So not only will she now be almost penniless, but her reputation will be ruined. I will contest the will, of course, on the grounds that not only are the accusations untrue but the document itself cannot be valid, as Kingsley cannot have been in his right mind. I don't know how successful I might be. It could take months, years —'

'I assume you have not seen the will?'

'Not yet. My solicitor has been informed.'

'You must be able to prove that Kingsley's disgraceful accusations are untrue?'

'I am sure I can. I hope I might do so without taking action in a court of law, but if it goes that far, I will do everything possible to ensure a closed hearing. To have my daughter's name exposed to common tattle in the newspapers would be insupportable. The matter must be settled without it becoming public.'

'Does Lady Kingsley know the terms of her husband's will?'

'He had taunted her with it, yes, although she has not seen it. But the dear girl sets no store by money. I think if she is able to return to her family who love her, not only to me, but also my dear wife who is almost a sister to her, she would be content. But a public scandal, even based on lies, might mean she would not be able to move in society. Memories of that sort do not fade. There will always be some who like to believe the worst, and there would be houses which would not receive her.'

'Lord Redcar,' said Holmes, in his most gently persuasive tone, 'I know this is a delicate matter, but any information you can provide which could guide me to a solution of Sir Walter Kingsley's murder would be appreciated. Would you be prepared to elaborate on the nature of his accusations?'

'Yes, yes, of course.' Redcar sighed. 'But this must be in strict confidence. For now, at least, before anyone else learns of the will. I don't yet know the precise wording, of course. Kingsley implied that Henrietta is not my daughter but was adopted from a family of humble status. This is quite untrue. I have her birth certificate. It shows that she was born in this very house, and my dear late wife and I are her parents. I told Kingsley of this, and his retort was that papers can be forged, and persons may be bribed to tell lies. He had not one shred of evidence for his accusations. But let me show you the proof. I have it here.'

Lord Redcar took a document box from a shelf and brought out the certificate of his daughter's birth. Henrietta Sophia Redcar was born on 11 February 1855, at the manor house, Charlbury Park, Oxfordshire. Her father was Montague Charles Redcar, and his rank or profession was Baron Redcar,

Duke of Charlbury. The name and maiden surname of her mother was Maria Henrietta, Baroness Redcar, Duchess of Charlbury, formerly Broughton. The signature description and residence of the informant was that of Catherine Pescott, the housekeeper, who had been present at the birth. The date of the registration was 25 February 1855.

Once we had left Lord Redcar, I asked Holmes, 'I suppose documents can lie?'

'They can and they do,' said Holmes. 'The introduction of certificates of birth, marriage and death opened up a world of opportunities for falsehood; but in any court of law, they are powerful evidence. All the same, what father would be happy about having doubts about his daughter's parentage exposed to open debate? What steps might he take to avoid it? But now, I must speak to Mrs Pescott once more.'

The housekeeper was in her tidy little office room, made cosy by the account books of the estate, which were shelved around her. She was at a desk with pen and ink and invoices but rose at once as we entered.

'What can I do for you gentlemen?' she asked. 'Please make yourselves comfortable. Would you like me to order some refreshments?'

'Thank you, Mrs Pescott. That will not be necessary. I have been speaking to Lord Redcar about the late Sir Walter Kingsley and I would value your observations.'

'Of course, I will tell you whatever I can,' she replied. We were seated, and while the housekeeper was undoubtedly wearied by work and worry, she appeared more than willing to assist us.

'It cannot have escaped anyone's attention that Sir Walter Kingsley was a strange man who sometimes adopted strange ideas for no apparent reason,' said Holmes. 'The question of his wife's birth, which we have already spoken of, is a case in point.'

'That is one way to put it, sir,' she said. 'He was a strange man indeed. He was much given to curious fancies, and some of them he used as sticks with which he would beat others.'

'It appears that Kingsley openly accused Lord Redcar of adopting the child of another family entirely, no doubt worthy but not of noble blood. Yet all the evidence shows that he was mistaken. Can you suggest to me how this idea might have come about? Was there some gossip amongst the servants, or a story being told? Even an old legend? Lord Redcar has just shown me the birth certificate, and there really cannot be any doubt in the matter.'

She smiled. 'Well, sir, I think I know how the misunderstanding might have arisen.'

'I would be very grateful if you would enlighten me.'

'You might know the Traveller's Rest, the inn not far from here?'

'I passed it by on the way here. It was the scene of the terrible fire in 1646 which we have read about in the history books.'

'Well, the landlady of the inn, Mrs Stevens, is a widow with two fine grown daughters and a son. Some months before Miss Henrietta was born, Mrs Stevens and her husband were hoping to welcome another child to the family. But then a terrible thing happened. Mr Stevens died in an accident when the cart he was driving overturned. The shock to his poor wife cannot be imagined. Her position was one of great grief and distress. I went to see if there was anything I could do, as the three children were very young and needed a mother's care. But the ending was a sad one. The child she was expecting came early, far too early, and it did not live.'

'I think I understand,' said Holmes. 'But please continue.'

'I heard that Sir Walter Kingsley had been making enquiries about children that might have been given away by poor families. He knew that the first Lady Redcar had always been of a delicate constitution, and that led him to suspect that she might not be Miss Henrietta's mother. He was told of the death of Mr Stevens and the child that was due, a child which no-one ever saw. He concluded, with no evidence at all, that Lord Redcar, not having an heir and despairing of one, had agreed to help Mrs Stevens by adopting her child when it was born, and that child was a daughter, named Henrietta.'

'But that is not true?' said Holmes.

'No, sir. It is as I told you: Mrs Stevens's child did not live. This was explained to Sir Walter Kingsley, but given the importance of the situation, and his reluctance to admit he was mistaken, he was not convinced and thought everyone was telling lies to cover up what he believed had occurred. The doctor who attended Mrs Stevens, a Dr Price of Charlbury, was the same man who was present at Miss Henrietta's birth several months later. The payment to him and its purpose are recorded in our books of account. I suppose a professional man might have been believed, but unfortunately Dr Price passed away some years ago.'

'I think that everything we have been told would make good sense to anyone other than Sir Walter Kingsley,' I said to Holmes after we had thanked Mrs Pescott and left her to her work.

'I agree,' said Holmes. 'It makes perfect sense to me.'

CHAPTER TWENTY-THREE

The next morning was a Sunday, and after breakfast we were all asked to gather for solemn prayers for the souls of the deceased. Holmes rarely referred to his religious beliefs, which I think he saw as something which ought to be highly personal. He sometimes expressed his conviction that life must have a meaning, a purpose. It was the ultimate question to which he might never know the answer. But he understood the value of prayer as a comfort to the living. In deference to individual preferences, Lord Redcar, after initiating the prayers, allowed us all to engage in silent contemplation. He might have hoped that something might arise from the conscience of the guilty, made aware of the divine judgement that awaited, prompting him to a confession; but I could only conclude that the killer must have felt no remorse, and kept his thoughts to himself.

It will not have escaped my readers' notice that whenever Holmes and I wanted to have a conversation at Charlbury Park with the least possible chance of interruption, one of the best places to do so, apart from outdoors was his lordship's library, where so much of the material we wished to explore and discuss was to be found. None of the less academic gentlemen appeared to be devotees of the kind of volumes that were on its shelves. Prince Rampal had, soon after his arrival at Charlbury Park, donned a little pair of spectacles and after examining the material, regretfully declared it too antiquated to be of interest to his studies. It was therefore a room the sporting guests never entered, and it also had the advantage that if we were wanted urgently by Lord Redcar, Xavier,

Inspector Marsh, or Mrs Pescott, they usually knew where to find us.

When Holmes wanted to study alone, he settled himself at one of the tables, and I knew better than to interrupt him. I could see that he was still reflecting on our conversation with Mrs Pescott and suspected that the period of silent prayer had enabled him to arrange his thoughts. This may appear to be irreligious, but there must be more than one kind of spiritual comfort. The solution of a tragic mystery is undoubtedly a worthwhile object. Holmes told me he would pursue his deliberations in the library, and I might join him in an hour.

Not wanting to spend my time alone, I enjoyed a conversation with Prince Rampal, who told me of the forthcoming marriage of his sister. This event was of great importance to the family, securing a prestigious connection, but I was pleased to learn that respect, love, and harmony between the couple were also a prominent consideration. This led to a discussion of the cruel marriage of Lady Kingsley. Neither of us doubted that her release from that arrangement, however distressing the circumstances, had been a relief.

When I went to the library for my meeting with Holmes, I found him seated at the long table, with pen, ink and paper, and a great many books spread out before him. I drew up a chair, expectantly.

'Let us begin with the death of Sir Walter Kingsley and start from first principles,' he said.

I understood that Holmes was about to think aloud, and I would be the recipient of his words. I stayed silent but attentive.

'Sir Walter Kingsley was undoubtedly murdered, and it was not a situation in which he could have been mistaken for another individual. But no-one who was in a position to commit the crime, and had a motive to do so, would have come to the sporting event prepared to commit the murder, since none of us knew that he would be here until he arrived. However, most if not all of those in the manor, even if they were not actually present when he burst in, would soon have known of his unexpected appearance. The schedules of events had already been widely distributed. Kingsley's decision to take part in the steeplechase through the woods was very much a last-minute one, but any changes made to accommodate the new participant would have been carried out promptly with Mr Xavier's customary efficiency. Someone who had a motive to kill Kingsley saw his chance and took it.'

I merely nodded agreement.

'The deceased was not seen with a weapon of any kind, although initially I did wonder if he might have had something concealed about his person. Men have been known to have pockets made in their clothing for that purpose, and I thought that might have been why he declined a change of costume. He could have brought a knife with a crossguard similar in form to that of the old tuck swords, which would explain the shape of the bruising. If he drew the knife in a quarrel, it might have ended up in the hands of his enemy.' Holmes paused. 'But on hearing the report of the police surgeon, I was obliged to discard that theory. The blade of such a knife would have tapered toward the end and could not have left the exit wound Mr Armitage has described. He is of the opinion that Kingsley was killed with a sword, and I must reluctantly agree. And it seems there was nothing unusual about the clothing, nowhere Kingsley might have hidden such a weapon. Which still leaves us with the question of where the sword came from and where is it now?'

He seemed rather despondent at this. I waited for more on the subject, but he had nothing more to add.

'I leave motive to last,' he continued, 'although I fear that five minutes in Sir Walter Kingsley's company might have roused many a man to consider the pleasures of running him through with a sword.' Holmes showed me a paper. 'Here I have written the names of everyone who was on the estate at the time of death. Can any of them be ruled out of consideration? I believe so. Mr Xavier was standing in full sight of several people during the run. The large number of guests had created additional work for the servants, and many of them were in the kitchens and storerooms and are easily vouched for. The youngest maids, I believe, are not strong enough to inflict such a wound, although the determination of a woman to harm a man who has disgraced her does sometimes astonish even the most experienced of judges. But again, I believe after careful consideration, that all of the house servants can be accounted for.'

'I think of all the servants only Mr Xavier has the kind of brain which could devise a plot to murder, the boldness and strength to do so, and the presence of mind to take advantage of an unexpected chance,' I said. 'But even he cannot be in two places at once.'

Holmes gave me a very curious glance, then after a moment's consideration, carefully drew a line through most of the names on the sheet, including that of Xavier.

'Gorringe has been a feature of the estate for some forty years. He knows the grounds, the waters, the woods, the pathways. If he was at his cottage at the time of the murder, he easily had the opportunity to slip into the woodlands unobserved, commit the murder and return to his duties. Then we have the runners. Those who were ahead of Kingsley were

Prince Rampal, Viscount Northam, Sir Jasper Grey, Baron Brambilla, Chevalier L'Épine, and Luckhurst. Any one of them could have waited hidden in the trees, and circled back unseen. And I cannot positively rule out the two men who followed, Lord Redcar and Sir Hubert Winchip.'

I was impelled to interrupt. 'I hope you do not suspect Luckhurst.'

Holmes offered me a firm stare. 'Can you provide him with an alibi? Can anyone?'

'Well — no.'

'I reserve the right to maintain his name on the list. And now, we come to motive. Let us consider the main suspects one by one. Several, if not all, have a clear motive.'

'I don't think Luckhurst has,' I protested.

'I would tend to agree. His prior meeting with Lady Kingsley before her marriage did not, I think, fire him to such a frenzy of admiration that he determined to stab her unpleasant husband to death.'

Sometimes I was not sure how serious Holmes was, though he did occasionally enjoy a joke, usually at another person's expense. I decided to accept that statement as it stood.

'Mr Gorringe has I am sure learned many secrets in his years of service which he keeps out of loyalty to Lord Redcar. One or several may have given his lordship a reason to dispatch his son-in-law.'

'Lord Redcar, after learning of Kingsley's ill-treatment of his daughter, might well have had an altercation that became violent,' Holmes continued. 'He also wanted at all costs to prevent Kingsley from making his unproven allegations public. He could find the means to fight a mean-spirited will in closed court, but he could not control the vindictive tongue of a living man. And a fight might have easily occurred between Kingsley and Grey. I am sure that Grey would have dispatched his man without a moment's hesitation.'

I found myself picturing Sir Jasper Grey as a gladiator of old in the arena, spearing Kingsley through the abdomen in front of a rapturously cheering crowd.

'We know that Kingsley insulted Prince Rampal's family. He is not by nature or belief a man of violence, and I find it hard to imagine what unusual circumstances might have moved him to revenge. The most unlikely person can sometimes surprise us. To kill for a verbal insult would appear, however, to be an extreme reaction, unless there is some other factor involved about which I know nothing. Something too painful to be spoken of. We know he has a sister.'

'I have just learned that she is shortly due to be married,' I said.

Holmes said nothing but made a written note before he continued speaking.

'Viscount Northam certainly had a powerful motive to murder Kingsley, but we don't yet know if Northam even knew of his true origin, or how much Kingsley actually knew or whether or not he had threatened Northam with revealing it.'

'And there is that rumour that Kingsley is descended from Colonel Keogh,' I said.

'Which we know to be untrue. It is one of those tales that grow with the telling. But Northam might have believed it. And the recent uproar in Oxford after the dramatic presentation would have drawn it strongly to his attention. The Viscounts Northam have certainly not forgotten. Their family motto is "*corrigimus*"; "we rectify".'

'Meaning they will put matters right?'

'Yes, although this might be an indication that the first viscount had already done so to his satisfaction.'

'Both L'Épine and Brambilla found Kingsley's manners insulting, and Brambilla, as a regular visitor to the manor for Lord Redcar's fencing instruction, might well have gathered that Lady Kingsley was unhappy. I have seen him gazing at her portrait, and his wistful expression was quite noticeable.'

'And what of Sir Hubert Winchip? He appears to be sleepy and dull; he may indeed be sleepy and dull, or he might be employing it as a strategy, enabling him to overhear things he might otherwise not know about. Take a look here,' said Holmes, pointing to a page in Burke's. 'I think this entry is trustworthy. Our host's family name was originally Winchip, but in his youth he inherited the minor barony of Redcar on the death of a distant relative and became Lord Redcar, taking that as his surname. He is also Duke of Charlbury, which is a rather more important title since with it comes Charlbury Park. If I am correct, it means that Sir Hubert's father, Ambrose, Lord Redcar's first cousin, was during his lifetime heir presumptive to the dukedom. He would have inherited it had Lord Redcar died without male issue.'

'But we were told he has passed away,' I said.

'We were. This edition of Burke's was published before the birth of Sir Hubert, but it shows there were two brothers and a sister who preceded him. On the father's death, the elder brother would have been heir presumptive. A recent edition would have been more informative, but I must make do with what is here.'

'With Lord Redcar's recent remarriage,' I said, 'doesn't that mean —'

'If the Redcars are ever blessed with a son, the child will be heir to the dukedom, and the Winchips will not inherit. What expectations Winchip might have had on his brother becoming duke, we cannot know. But do you recall what Redcar said to his cousin when we found them resting after the steeplechase had ended?'

'He said he would look after him, or something of the sort.'

'At the time, I thought he referred to Winchip's state of exhaustion, but perhaps it had another meaning. They might have been conversing on family matters. There are facts which I think Lord Redcar has not shared with us. He may think they are unimportant, he may have chosen not to, or perhaps I have just not been asking the right questions. I only speculate, of course. It is all theory, without proof.'

'Do you think the same man who killed Kingsley might also have murdered L'Épine?' I asked. 'Or are they two quite separate crimes?'

'We cannot yet know if they are connected in any way. The solution of the first might lead us to the solution of the second or be of no assistance whatsoever. In the one case we have an abundance of motives and suspects and in the other none at all.'

I had been musing about the death of L'Épine and shared my theories with Holmes. We agreed that Northam's claim to have been the intended victim of the arrow in the woodland was simply a suggestion that he could trace his bloodline back to William the Conqueror, a common conceit of many a nobleman, which could safely be ignored.

Sir Jasper Grey had returned from a run about the parkland and had been exercising on the terrace when the first searchers went to look for L'Épine. Supposing, however, his run had taken him on a path through or on the borders of the wood? Had the archer in the woods been aiming at Sir Jasper Grey but struck the wrong man? If he shot with intent to kill, it was still murder, even he hit the wrong target. If we could place Grey and another man in the woodland at the same time, with L'Épine as the innocent unintended victim, then we would have our killer. It did not escape my attention that it was only the timing of the arrows that narrowly missed me which proved Grey could not have fired them. This did not mean he could not have fired the others.

CHAPTER TWENTY-FOUR

Ever since their first arrival at Charlbury Park, the Oxfordshire police had been extremely diligent in their search for the weapon that had killed Sir Walter Kingsley. The surgeon's report combined with Holmes's observations had given them a clear impression of what they were looking for, but even this had not produced a result. When we next spoke to Inspector Marsh, he was on the verge of admitting defeat.

'I am sorry to say we have had no luck in finding the murder weapon, and I do not think it is here at all,' he told us. 'I am considering the possibility that the killer managed to remove it from the estate entirely by concealing it on one of the carts delivering produce to the manor house as it was leaving. We have interviewed all the delivery men, but of course if they had found the item and sold it, they might not want to admit it. People do collect these things. They like to hang a sword over the fireplace or have one beside the bed in case of burglars. And it may well have been thoroughly cleaned by now. The difficulty is that these swords were made in large numbers, and there are probably many examples, all very similar. I could be looking at the precise weapon right in front of me, and not know it or be able to prove it is the one.'

Holmes acknowledged the inspector's difficulty. He was probably thinking that if the weapon in question was right in front of him, he would both know it and be able to prove it, but he would not have been thanked for saying so. 'Inspector, I have a request to make of you,' he said. 'I have spoken to everyone who might have been involved in the crime, and still others whom I thought could provide me with useful information, with the exception of one person.'

'Oh, and who might that be?'

'Miss Agnes, Lady Kingsley's maid. She may, without realising it, know something that would suggest a motive we have not yet uncovered. I would be grateful if you could bring her to Charlbury Park. You said she was eager to see her mistress again.'

'Lady Kingsley did not ask for her,' said the inspector.

'So I observed,' said Holmes. 'Her mind was undoubtedly confused by the recent tragedy. I am sure she would welcome her loyal servant.'

'I suppose so. The aunt might not allow it, of course. She has no reason to object to Lady Kingsley, but she might want nothing further to do with the family.'

'Perhaps she might accept an inducement?' Holmes suggested. 'You said the aunt was annoyed that Miss Agnes's gown was ruined by her arduous journey after she was so undeservedly dismissed. I am sure that Lord Redcar would be more than happy to arrange for a replacement to be made. You might suggest she brings the old one with her so it can be copied.'

Marsh considered this and nodded. 'I'll see what I can do,' he said.

'I suppose you are no further forward in discovering the killer of Chevalier L'Épine?' I asked.

'Everyone has been questioned and no-one admits to being in the woodland, or can be proven to have been there, at the time he met his death,' said Marsh. 'It's a pity I can't question the squirrels. I'm sure they saw it all.'

When Marsh had departed, I said to Holmes, 'You mentioned to me earlier that there was something to which

Lady Kingsley did not refer, when you spoke to her. I think I now know what it was.'

'Yes, Stamford,' said Holmes, approvingly, 'you are a little slow in your observation, but you are correct. Lady Kingsley did not ask for her maid to be brought to her, although Miss Agnes has been loyal. I would like to know the reason, but I must go carefully. Is there a secret known only to them both that Lady Kingsley does not want revealed? And could it have some relevance to her husband's murder? It may, of course, merely be a vulgar scandal, and I must be prepared to endure that.'

We spent some further time in the library, perusing Holmes's notes without learning anything more. We were pausing in our efforts and considering the refreshment possibilities of a pot of tea when Lord Redcar appeared.

'Ah, Stamford, I am glad I have found you,' he said. 'I don't suppose you would oblige me by looking over Winchip? He doesn't look at all well, and I am thinking of summoning a doctor. I am sorry to say it, but he has been drinking rather heavily recently, and it is not good for him.'

I rose to my feet at once. 'What are his symptoms?' I asked.

'He was staggering rather than walking, and his words were so slurred I could barely make out what he was saying. I am not sure if he understood me. Poor fellow, he has been so unhappy of late.'

'What is Sir Hubert's age?' I asked.

'He is approaching forty.'

I did not say so, but I thought the man looked older.

We accompanied his lordship to his suite, where a bed had been made up for his cousin. Winchip was sitting on the edge of the bed, looking at a tumbler of water in his hand, as if wondering whether it was advisable to drink it.

'How are you feeling now, dear fellow?' asked Redcar solicitously.

'Mm, tired,' murmured Winchip.

'Now, you have the rest of that water. It will do you good,' said Redcar. 'And no more brandy for today.'

'That is good advice,' I said, but I thought it as well to look the man over. Holmes stood by as an observer. His experience with medical examination did not involve the living.

I asked Winchip the usual questions as to his habits. He answered slowly, but I was able to understand him. In common with many men, he admitted to a far smaller usage of alcohol and tobacco than I suspected was actually the case. He did not go so far as to claim that he ate in moderation, as the evidence of his consumption at table had been displayed before my eyes. Concerning symptoms, he claimed only to have felt a little giddy with a slight weakness in the limbs, which had passed off. He did not want a doctor called to him.

I entertained two possibilities. The first was that his indisposition might simply have been produced by overindulgence; the second was that, more seriously, he might have suffered a temporary paralysis following a brief spasm of the blood vessels of the brain. I had no medical books to consult, but a slight drooping at the side of my patient's mouth suggested something more fundamental than the transitory effects of drink. There was nothing I could do for him, as he appeared to be recovering, but I suggested that he should make an appointment with his doctor for a full examination and obtain advice on the best diet for his health.

We left him to rest but requested a consultation with Lord Redcar, and we repaired to his study so as to be more private.

'He does worry me,' said Redcar, after thanking me for my attendance in grateful terms I was sure I did not merit.

'Can you tell us something of his history?' asked Holmes.

'Yes, well, he is the third son of my cousin Ambrose, and I am sorry to say he has never shown any great purpose in life. He idled away his time in college. That was where he took up sports, mainly running, I think, but I always thought it was more for the company and camaraderie of the sporting clubs there. He was never a popular fellow, much given to pessimism, which is never a trait that attracts friends. Over the years, he became less active and sorrier for himself.'

'I assume he is unmarried, or if he is, his wife does not care for him,' said Holmes.

'He has never married,' said Redcar, 'although he has frequently expressed a wish to be.'

'Then his manservant is neglectful,' said Holmes. 'His clothes are well made but poorly maintained.'

'I have often said the fellow should be dismissed, but I don't believe Hubert can be troubled to do so. There is little enough that encourages him to present himself well,' said Redcar.

'You said he was close to his father.'

'Yes, but he passed away seven years ago.'

'And his brothers?'

Redcar uttered a deep sigh. 'Winchip has often said he had a feeling pressing on him that he was doomed to ill-luck. In fact, he sometimes thought the whole family was unlucky. His father, a hale man at sixty, contracted blood poisoning from a scratch and was dead within a week. The older brother died of scarlet fever at the age of eight. The next brother, Archibald, was everything Winchip was not — good looking, a fine athlete, much admired by all. He was married, too, with two charming daughters. I am sure Winchip was envious of him, though he never said as much. Four years ago, he died in a hunting accident.'

'That must have added greatly to your cousin's misery,' I said.

'It did, but then he quite suddenly developed a fresh determination to find a bride. He purchased a new wardrobe, had a man come in to shave him and arrange his hair, wore flowers in his buttonhole, and used the most alarming pomade. And in a few months, he was betrothed to Miss Sarah Kent, a relative of the Eastleighs. I met her once; she was nice-looking, but I can't say I cared for her. He brought her to a family gathering I held here; in fact, it was the one where I announced my forthcoming marriage to my dear Margaret. There were a great many surprised faces there, I can tell you.'

'He is no longer betrothed?' said Holmes.

'No, and he had a fortunate escape, although he didn't think so at the time. Miss Kent asked to be released from her promise, and he had no option but to agree. The last I heard of her she was in a scandalous connection with Sir Jasper Grey. But that was the end of Winchip's matrimonial ambitions, and he has sadly neglected his health and appearance ever since, becoming the man you have met here.'

'When I saw you talking to him at the end of the steeplechase, I thought that he looked unusually dejected,' said Holmes.

'Yes, well, I took the opportunity to have a quiet word on family matters. I needed to set his mind at rest on a few things. I have been exploring the possibility of selling Charlbury Park and establishing a new home in Oxford. I knew he might be upset at the estate leaving the family after so long, but I reassured him that he would not lose anything by it. I want to see him settled and comfortable, and, if it is not too much to hope for, with some purpose in his life. What that might be, I am yet to discover.' Redcar looked at me appealingly. 'Do you think he will recover his health?'

'If he takes my advice and sees his doctor, and then takes his doctor's advice, he may enjoy better health in the future,' I said, trying to sound confident that any of those events would actually take place. I suspected that Winchip would ignore my advice and just resume his present mode of life. 'If you see any change in him, and if the symptoms should recur, then I think you should summon a doctor here at once.'

'I will go and see him, and make sure he has not secreted a bottle of brandy anywhere,' said Redcar. 'And I think I shall arrange for a doctor to call whether he wants me to or not. Thank you, gentlemen.'

After Redcar had departed, Holmes and I returned to the library to talk.

'So now we have a quite different picture of Sir Hubert Winchip's position in life,' said Holmes. 'And one which places him higher on my list of suspects for the murder of Sir Walter Kingsley.'

'How do you arrive at that?' I asked.

'On the death of his married brother four years ago, Winchip became heir presumptive to the dukedom, as his brother did not have male heirs. As he is sixteen years Redcar's junior, he must have had thoughts of one day being elevated to the title. It might well have been on the basis of this expectation that he began to look for a wife, setting himself out as a future duke. He brought his betrothed lady to Charlbury Park, perhaps with the intention of showing her the estate she might one day command as duchess. The relationship cooled rather quickly when his fiancée learned that Redcar was about to marry a much younger wife, with the prospect of an heir who would supplant Winchip. Incidentally, I think I can suggest the identity of Sir Walter Kingsley's secret informant, the author of that poisonous missive concerning the events at the Countess of Eastleigh's ball. Miss Kent. Jealousy and spite were behind that letter. I have not been able to examine the waterlogged remains found in Kingsley's pocket. They may still yield some proof. But we would gain little from it except a powerful determination to have nothing to do with Miss Kent.'

'I think Lord Redcar has been very kind to his cousin,' I said. 'He reassured him that he would always be comfortable, whatever happened.'

'And for many men, that might have been sufficient. For Winchip, I do not know. Consider, what would be the consequence to Sir Hubert Winchip of the death of Sir Walter Kingsley, followed by Lord Redcar being named as the culprit and charged with murder?'

'We know that Winchip was most unhappy at Kingsley's behaviour. He would not mourn the man's loss. If Lord Redcar was found guilty of murder —' I shook my head. 'I can't imagine a peer being hanged.'

'That has not happened for over a hundred years.'

'But he might be confined to prison.'

'Thus extinguishing the likelihood of a male heir, the only obstacle to Winchip advancing to the dukedom should Redcar predecease him. Winchip might even contemplate offering marriage to the widowed Lady Kingsley. We know that he admires her. What we do not know is how clever and how ruthless the man is. He may be exactly as he appears, or he could be a most subtle criminal.'

I grappled with this idea. There are times when I am rather pleased not to be a member of the nobility, and this was one of them.

CHAPTER TWENTY-FIVE

Lady Kingsley's maid, Agnes, was brought to Charlbury by Inspector Marsh on the next day and deposited in the garden, where Holmes and I were to greet her. She was about twenty-five, an agreeable-looking girl of the kind one often sees in the country, robust and well nourished. She was wearing a simple gown that did not fit her well, and might have been borrowed from a larger person, and she clutched a brown paper parcel tied with string. She was apprehensive at first, unsure of why she was being questioned. We sat in a shady spot, and as we talked, I saw the peace, beauty and fragrance of the gardens have their soothing effect.

'Is that your old gown?' asked Holmes, indicating the parcel.

'Yes, sir, I was asked to bring it. The dress I am wearing is my aunt's. The inspector said a new one could be made for me,' she added hopefully.

'And so it shall be. Let me have it and I will deliver it to Mrs Pescott, who will see what can be done.'

Agnes hesitated before she handed over the parcel. 'It is very dirty, I am afraid. My aunt did her best to brush it down.'

'I am sure Mrs Pescott has dealt with worse,' said Holmes, comfortingly.

'She is very kind,' said Agnes. 'And very fond of Lady Kingsley. Nothing is too much trouble for her.'

'Do you often visit Charlbury Park with your mistress?'

'Yes, sometimes she came here with her husband, and when her husband was away, she liked to stay here and keep company with Lady Redcar. He had business in Oxford which engaged him quite often.'

Holmes nodded and chose not to pursue the nature of Sir Walter Kingsley's interests in Oxford.

'Is Lady Kingsley very fond of Charlbury Park?'

'Yes, very. She was born here and was very happy as a child. She and Lord Redcar were almost like brothers, with the kind of sports and games they played.'

'How interesting. What kind of sports and games?'

'Oh, boys' games, really — bows and arrows, and fencing. They used to walk in the woods, pretending they were explorers in a jungle. Of course, she didn't do any of that when she was here with her husband. He wouldn't have liked it at all and would have been very angry with her if she damaged her clothes. He once told her that if she ever tore her gown, she would have to mend it herself, and he wouldn't buy her a new one. When he was here, she was only allowed to walk in the gardens.'

'But when he was not here?' asked Holmes, meaningfully.

Agnes smiled. 'You understand very well, sir. When he was away, she liked to walk in the woods, and I kept her company.'

'I hope she did not tear her gown?'

'No, well — she was very careful not to. Mrs Pescott lent her a wrap. She didn't want to be found out.'

'Do you remember the night of the Countess of Eastleigh's ball?'

'Yes, although I was not there.'

'When your mistress returned, how did she appear to you? Was she happy or unhappy?'

'She was very unhappy, but she would not say why. I thought the master had been unkind to her again.'

Holmes's eyebrow twitched at the word "again." 'I am endeavouring to learn more about Sir Walter Kingsley, what kind of man he was. I am told that he was often unkind to his wife.'

'Yes, sir, I am sorry to say he was.'

'In what way?'

'I think — in every way a man might be. She didn't talk of it often, but I knew of it. I once heard him say he should never have married her, and if she did not try to behave like a lady, he would put her to work in the scullery. But he had no reason to say that; she always behaved very well. He also said —' Agnes took a deep breath. We both remained silent in anticipation. 'He said, "You might think you'll be pleased when I'm gone, but you won't be. You deserve nothing from me, and you'll get nothing." I don't know what he meant by that.'

'And then despite your loyal service, you were dismissed for no reason at all,' said Holmes sympathetically.

'That was a terrible day, sir. A letter came for him. I don't know who sent it or what it said, but it drove him into the worst rage I have ever seen. I am sure he struck her.'

'Did you ever see him strike her?'

'No, that was always behind closed doors. But I helped her dress, and I saw the bruises. Not on her face, where anyone could see them, but on her arms, her shoulders. That dreadful day he called me to him and accused me of passing love notes between Lady Kingsley and another man. It was untrue, of course, but there was no use my denying it — he was so sure he was right. I thought he might strike me, too, but he didn't. If he had, I don't know what I would have done.' As she said this, her hands clenched into fists.

'He never threatened to divorce her?'

'Oh no, he thought that shameful, scandalous.'

'And Lady Kingsley? She cannot have been content to endure such misery. Did she not have good reason to go to law?'

'She did once tell me that unless her husband mended his ways, she would see her father and ask him to help her arrange a separation. She knew she might be left penniless, but I don't think that mattered to her.'

'Did Sir Walter dismiss you on the same day he received the letter?'

'Yes. And he locked my mistress in her room. I was told to collect my few things and go. I told the housekeeper I was going to my aunt's in Lowhampton. I hoped to be taken there, but the master wouldn't allow me anything, not a ride in the trap or even the wages I was owed. I walked as far as I could until it was dark, then I spent the night in a field. The next day I begged a ride on an ironmonger's cart, which was very dirty, and arrived in Lowhampton where my aunt looked after me. I waited there, hoping to hear from Lady Kingsley, and then a policeman came and told me that the master was dead. I asked how he died, but the policeman wouldn't tell me. I thought he might have burst a blood vessel, but if the police have been called — well, I don't like to think.'

I could see that she was hoping to be told, but Holmes simply thanked Agnes and we conducted her to the door of Garden Cottage, where Molly let her in. I was not altogether surprised when Holmes did not deliver Agnes's parcel to Mrs Pescott. We took it to the library and unwrapped it with care, then removed the gown and laid it out along the tabletop. The garment had been well brushed to remove any debris and the worst of the staining, but Holmes brought a lamp to the table and used his glass to make a close examination.

He drew one of his envelopes from his pocket and used his forceps to remove the thread he had found in the woodland, placing it on the white surface of the paper. After careful comparison, he said, 'The colour and thickness of the thread is the same as the fibre used to make the material of this gown. But it is a kind of cloth often used to make servant's clothing.' He carefully cast his glass over the entire garment, missing no detail as he worked. At last, he made an exclamation. 'Yes, here it is, on the sleeve, the place where the fabric caught and the thread was left behind. It came from this garment; I am sure of it.' He returned the thread to its envelope, which he placed in his pocket.

'At least we know how it was left there,' I said.

Holmes did not reply to this but continued his survey. 'Observe these stains on the skirts, Stamford. What do you think?' He handed me the glass and brought the lamp close. The dark brown marks had been subjected to the vigorous brush of Agnes's aunt but traces still remained. 'Blood or rust?' he asked.

'That is hard to determine by eye alone,' I said. 'They are similar in colour, and even in smell. Either is possible. The ride on the ironmonger's cart or skinning a rabbit.'

'I fear so,' said Holmes. 'We would need the facilities of a laboratory to be sure — chemical tests and the microscope. But the amounts remaining on the garment are so small they may not yield any conclusive results. And even if tests do prove the stains to be blood, we cannot declare it to be human; at best, we would know whether or not it was that of a mammal. It is easily explained away.'

The value of this distinction in criminal cases was obvious, and I have often wondered if Holmes's laboratory work was to make a significant contribution to the solution of that puzzle. He was not interested in acclaim, and as he later found, fame could prove to be a burden when heaped upon him. Elucidation was its own reward.

CHAPTER TWENTY-SIX

Once Holmes had completed his examination of the maid's gown, he delivered it to Inspector Marsh, suggesting that it should be inspected by a chemist to see if the stains were blood or rust. Marsh was puzzled by this and protested that Miss Agnes was not in the vicinity of Charlbury Park at the time of the murder. However, Holmes believed that it might be important, if only to eliminate a line of enquiry, and the inspector said he would do what he could.

Inspector Marsh did readily agree to Lord Redcar's request that a doctor should be summoned from Oxford to see Winchip. The family physician, Dr Langley, had recently retired, but his son, Dr Langley Jnr, a gentleman in his forties, was able to visit in his stead.

Langley spent some time with Winchip and questioned me closely afterwards, as I had seen the patient more recently. After some discussion we agreed that Winchip, whom he had found both despondent and irritable, must have suffered an episode of non-permanent paralysis. He described other cases where patients with a similar condition had recovered well in time, and with that promise as encouragement, he had advised Winchip on how to take better care of his health.

Lord Redcar, content that his cousin had received the best attention available, asked Dr Langley if he would call upon Lady Redcar, as her appetite had been poor of late. Langley spent some time in Garden Cottage and returned from this visit in good spirits, having been regaled with tea and sponge cake. He reassured Lord Redcar that his young wife was in excellent health and wanted only regular nourishment and light exercise.

Dr Langley was preparing to take his leave and was bidding me good day when Holmes approached him.

'I would like a word with you, if I may,' said Holmes. 'It is a potentially sensitive matter, and we should speak in private.'

'I understand,' said Langley, with the knowing look of a doctor who is about to be told something his patient wants to keep a deadly secret. 'If you require a personal examination —'

'That will not be necessary,' said Holmes, quickly. 'Let us proceed to the drawing room. Mr Stamford will accompany us. I have asked the butler to ensure we are not disturbed.'

Langley looked mystified but complied with Holmes's request. I too was mystified, but anyone who spends much time with Holmes is obliged to exist in an almost permanent state of astonishment.

'I am making a study of the history of Lord Redcar's line,' said Holmes. 'You can see a number of family portraits in this room. I have uncovered some issues which might be of importance to the family heritage, and these might be clarified by medical advice. You may be able to help me understand, if I have my facts correct.'

'I will do my best,' said Langley. 'But you must appreciate that I cannot divulge anything relating to my patients.'

'This does not relate to a living person, but to Lord Redcar's first wife, who passed away more than twenty years ago.'

'I see.'

'I am about to tell you something in the very strictest confidence, which is why I asked for a private interview.'

'You have my word that I will reveal nothing you tell me without your permission.'

'I have been told,' Holmes continued, 'that a Dr Price was in attendance when Lord Redcar's first wife gave birth to her daughter in this house. Would you believe that some evil-minded person, whom I think has some quarrel with Lord Redcar or is jealous of him, has been spreading the rumour that his daughter, Lady Henrietta Kingsley, is not the daughter of her parents, but was adopted?'

'What a remarkable allegation!' exclaimed Dr Langley.

'And I am quite sure that it was founded not in truth but in malice, which is why I wish to consign it to the oblivion where it should lie. It was a sad circumstance that Lady Redcar passed away only three years after the birth of her daughter,' added Holmes, 'but I understand that she had been in poor health for quite some time. Did you ever meet her?'

'I did not, but my father attended her in her last illness.'

'Not Dr Price?'

'No, I think he must have retired from practice by then.'

'Did your father acquire the practice of Dr Price?'

'Yes, portions of it.'

'This is the lady's portrait,' said Holmes, directing Dr Langley to the painting of the first Lady Redcar.

Langley spent some time studying the picture. 'Portraits are not always truthful, but I can see that she does appear delicate.'

'Perhaps the birth of a child exhausted her strength, which was why she declined,' said Holmes.

'I can hardly comment on that,' said Dr Langley. 'Of course, speaking in general terms, what may follow the birth of a child cannot always be predicted from the general state of health of the mother at that time. Although now you mention it, I recall my father saying —' He stopped.

'Yes?'

Dr Langley looked troubled. 'But I can tell you no more.' He bowed politely. 'And now, gentlemen, I must wish you good day.'

Dr Langley abruptly took his leave.

'How interesting,' said Holmes. 'I fear that is all we are likely to learn from him on that subject, and the rest must only be conjecture.'

After our interview with Dr Langley, Holmes wished to spend some time in the company of his pipe. We walked out to the log seat, where he sat wreathed in smoke. I found a place on a tree stump, which I found had been weathered into an acceptable form. No-one came near us.

'Consider,' said Holmes, as we returned to the manor, 'this delusion of Sir Walter Kingsley that his wife was not of noble blood but adopted from a humble family. It appears to be without foundation. How did it begin? Recall what Mr Gorringe told us, that Kingsley said he had seen a young woman of humble birth and was convinced of a family resemblance. Who could this young woman be? The delusion reached still greater proportions when he discovered that Mrs Stevens, the landlady of the Traveller's Rest, which is hardly a few minutes' walk from here, had been expecting a child not long before Lady Kingsley was born, a child which was never seen. I suggest that the young woman whose appearance prompted his suspicion was none other than one of Mrs Stevens's daughters.'

'That is a very convincing argument.'

'I am, however, as certain as one can be that Lady Kingsley is indeed the daughter of Lord Redcar.'

'Well, we do have the birth certificate.'

'Certificates may tell lies; they may even be forged. No, it was not that which convinced me. Have you observed the expression Lord Redcar adopts when he is determined on a course of action?'

'Yes, his brows and his lip.'

'I have seen the very same expression appear on the face of Lady Kingsley. When she is calm, one might search in vain for a hint of the Redcar line. When she shows determination, the resemblance is plain beyond any doubt. She is without question her father's daughter.'

'Well, that is good to know.'

'She is not, however, the daughter of the first Lady Redcar.'

'I am sorry to say you may be right.'

'According to Mrs Pescott, the first Lady Redcar was always of a delicate constitution, but would this alone preclude her from becoming a mother? Dr Langley's comments suggest that there is more to be learned. I think he may know or suspect more than he is prepared to say. His father might have discovered something in the papers of his predecessor, Dr Price: secrets held at the behest of a noble family — that the mother of Lady Kingsley was not the first Lady Redcar.'

'Then who was the mother? A servant? A mistress?'

'We saw on the birth certificate that the birth was notified to the registrar by Mrs Pescott. There should have been no reason she could not do so on the day after the birth, but it was actually two weeks later. What was the reason for the delay?'

'Oh,' I said. 'And when you asked her if she was present at the birth, she was most adamant that she was. Those two weeks. Is that what you think, Holmes? That she was lying in?'

'There is one more thing I need to do before I can draw this mystery to its conclusion,' said Holmes. 'I really ought to see Mrs Stevens for myself. I wonder if the Traveller's Rest serves a good ale? It would be very refreshing.'

CHAPTER TWENTY-SEVEN

Holmes took care to seek permission from the police for us to leave the estate to make enquiries at the inn, and this was granted, provided that Constable Bennet accompanied us. The constable was naturally curious about the purpose of our visit, and Holmes told him that he was looking for an explanation of some comments Sir Walter Kingsley had made.

'Do you think that would help find his murderer?' asked Bennet dubiously.

'Most probably not, but I never ignore a thread of enquiry, however small it might be. One never knows where it might lead,' said Holmes.

Bennet did not object. After several days spent dragging a rake through the muddy waters of the Charle looking for a short sword, a seat in a country inn was a welcome diversion, even if he was not permitted to sample the ale. He had also taken a prominent part in the examination of the woodland after the death of L'Épine and told us that nothing had been found to assist police enquiries.

The inn was small, but its interior had a homely air, with comfortable oak settles, a well swept floor and tapestry carpets. Although the drinkers refreshing themselves were men in working clothes, one could also imagine a minor country squire finding the surroundings to his taste. There were bunches of dried herbs and flowers freshening the air, and no hint of the smell of stale beer and overcooked food so common in many a London hostelry. Instead, I detected the scent of something appetising baking in an oven.

The inn was, however, well aware of its tragic history. The walls were amply provided with framed engravings of important figures of the past, and there was even a painting, most probably by a local artist, depicting the siege at the old inn. It was tastefully done, with colourful flames leaping from the windows and no hint of the terror within, while Cromwell's soldiers were dark, menacing figures surrounding the building.

Just inside the door was an alcove, and inside it there stood a wooden figure of a man, quite roughly carved, and little more than five feet in height. The face was almost without features, the nose being no more than a bump and the eyes merely colourless pits. There was nothing about it to suggest it was intended to portray a specific individual, rather it was a type of person, a pikeman of the Civil War, which was made apparent by its clothing and accoutrements. It was dressed in rough trousers and a thick coat, and a battered pot helmet was balanced on its head. A pike was in the figure's hand, and since the wooden fingers were unable to clasp it, the staff was tied to the hand with a piece of cord. A leather belt was fastened about the waist, and there hung from it a short scabbard, holding what looked very like a tuck sword.

'Have you seen this sword before?' asked Holmes of Constable Bennet.

'Yes, when the inspector thought the murder weapon might have been taken out of the estate, we visited several local houses, including this one. I asked Mrs Stevens about it, and she said it has been there as long as her family has had the tenancy — that would be some thirty years. As far as she knows it has not been moved in that time, except for occasional cleaning and dusting, and that was last done by one of her daughters over two weeks ago. It has never left the premises, and no-one from the estate, not family, guests, or servants, has been here or touched it. But I did look at it, and I saw nothing suspicious.'

The innkeeper, Mrs Stevens, greeted us as we approached the bar counter. She was a tidy and brisk person, aged about sixty, with silver hair drawn up into a linen cap and a well-rounded face and figure.

'I see you have been admiring our pikeman,' she said with a smile.

'Yes, it is a remarkable piece,' said Holmes. 'Do you know where it came from?'

'When we first had the tenancy, it used to stand outside, but it became so weathered we decided to give it a home indoors, as we were afraid the wood might fall apart in time. It used to be painted with a uniform, but we dressed it up and gave it some old weapons to take into battle. It's been stood there for the past ten years. The inn used to go by the name of The Pikeman, but we wanted it to be more comfortable and welcoming for people on the country roads, so we renamed it The Traveller's Rest.'

A sturdily built young woman arrived from the back of the inn, carrying a basket of herbs and a watering can. She deposited the can by the back door and took the herb basket to another room, which, from the fragrance that emerged from its door as she entered, must have been the kitchen. There was something about her features that resembled Mrs Stevens, suggesting that she was one of the daughters.

'What can I get for you, sirs?' asked Mrs Stevens. 'Constable Bennet,' she added, noticing his striped armband, 'I see you are on duty today.'

'That I am, Mrs Stevens,' said Bennet regretfully, as he might have liked a glass of ale.

Holmes ordered some coffee for our table, and a platter of fresh country bread and butter. 'It must be delicate work, keeping the pikeman in good order for visitors to admire,' he said.

'Oh, it is. One of my daughters attends to that. We like to keep him happy. He stands here to protect us and all our visitors.'

We sat at a well-scrubbed table, waiting for our refreshments. They were brought to us by a slender young woman, who emerged from the kitchen. Mrs Stevens, on directing her to us, called her Susan. Holmes thanked her and complimented her on the care of the antique pikeman. 'I take no credit for that, sir. That is all done by my sister, Emily.' She inclined her head to where the first young woman we had seen had emerged from the kitchen, bringing substantial platters of food to another table. 'To be truthful, he does make me a little nervous, standing there.'

'I understood that he guards the inn,' said Holmes. 'Surely, if that is the case, there is nothing to be afraid of.'

'That may be true, but I have also heard people say that he is haunted by the ghost of a pikeman, and has sometimes been seen walking about at night, searching for his fallen friends.'

'He might be better advised to search in daylight,' said Constable Bennet gruffly.

'He might, but that is not the way of ghosts,' she assured us very seriously. 'They do not like daylight but only come out after dark.'

'Have you seen him?' asked Holmes.

'No, but sometimes I do feel that there is someone here, a spirit, perhaps, looking at me. And when I turn around, there is nothing to see. One of our regular customers said he was on his way home one night and saw the pikeman walking about with the pikestaff in his hands, like he was hoping to fight his enemies.'

'I wonder,' said Holmes, 'would you permit me to take a closer look at the figure?'

'I don't see why not, if it interests you, sir.'

Holmes rose to his feet before she could reconsider and took out his glass, noting all the details of the wooden surface and the old clothing. The feet of the figure were encased in the remains of some aged leather boots, which, Holmes commented, showed no sign of anyone having walked in them for many years.

Taking great care, Holmes passed his glass over the scabbard, grip and crossguard of the tuck sword, nodding with satisfaction as he saw that its design matched the description of the murder weapon we had been seeking. He then gently drew the weapon from its scabbard and made a close examination of the blade, in particular the place where the blade met the crossguard. 'It is kept most beautifully clean,' he said to Susan, who was watching him anxiously. 'And you say your sister looks after it?'

'Yes, sir.'

'Do you recall when it was last cleaned?'

'I think Emily did the regular cleaning about two weeks ago. But there was another maid who came here to stay quite recently, and I think she might have polished it up.'

'Oh,' said Holmes. 'Do you recall the date when that was done?'

Susan gave this question some thought. 'I only know it was the same day as all the gentlemen came to the Park with their carriages.'

'Do you remember the name of this maid?'

'I'm not sure. But she came that morning with a note for my mother.'

'And you saw her polishing the sword?'

'Well, no, I didn't, but I thought she must have done. Mother told me to clean away some cobwebs and when I took the brush to them, I noticed the sword wasn't in its usual place. I was worried at first that it might have been stolen. I knew Emily wouldn't have taken it, but then I thought the maid who came might have been told to do some work to pay for her keep. I looked around for it, but I didn't see it anywhere, so I asked Emily and my mother, and they had nothing to say. Then we all went to look at the pikeman again, and would you believe the sword was there. My mother said it had been there all the time, and I didn't look properly the first time and must have imagined it was gone. Emily said the ghost had cast a spell on me. I don't know what to think. Perhaps that maid was a ghost.'

'And all this happened on the same day that the gentlemen came to the Park?'

'Yes.'

'Did any of the gentlemen come in here?'

'No, they just went past in their carriages.'

'None of the servants from the Park came in?'

'No, just our usual customers.'

'When did you first notice the sword was not there?'

'That afternoon. I couldn't say what time. And then it was back not half an hour later.'

'But, of course, it might have been gone rather longer than that,' said Holmes.

'Yes,' said Susan. 'But I am sure it was there first thing in the morning. That new maid, I saw her admiring it. Do you think it could be haunted? It might have killed people.'

'It might well have done,' agreed Holmes. 'Let me see it in daylight.' He carried the sword to the door and laid it out on a low wall outside. Constable Bennet followed, and Susan scurried after us.

After a while, Holmes said, 'This sword, as we have been told, is kept very clean, but there are often traces to be found not visible to the eye, even with the aid of a glass. I see no obvious blood, but I think that if the crevice where the blade meets the crossguard was scraped with the tip of a scalpel and the results examined under a microscope, they might prove to be dried blood, and mammalian blood which is considerably more recent than 1646. That is not conclusive, of course, although I do not think the sword has been used in the kitchen to prepare rabbits for a pie.'

'I had better take this to the inspector,' said Constable Bennet. 'You are keeping our examiner very busy, Mr Holmes.'

'The other factor,' said Holmes, 'is that the sword was missing from the premises and surreptitiously returned at a time during which the murder of Sir Walter Kingsley took place. And I am not inclined to place the blame on a ghost.'

CHAPTER TWENTY-EIGHT

On our return, Inspector Marsh took prompt action, dispatching Constable Bennet to police headquarters with the suspect weapon, and going to the Traveller's Rest to make some searching enquiries.

Holmes looked for Lord Redcar to give him news of the development, but he was not to be found.

'His lordship has received a letter this morning which has given him some cause for concern, and he has gone to Garden Cottage to discuss its contents,' was all Xavier could tell us. 'And I feel I ought to mention that contrary to the advice of the police, he has asked me to re-open the fencing hall. I am to allow in just one gentleman at a time to practise alone and lock the hall when it is empty.' Xavier was not in a position to disobey Lord Redcar's orders, and I assumed that he had reluctantly complied on the understanding that gentlemen should be free to stab themselves if they so wished.

'I should like to see his lordship, but I will not interrupt him,' said Holmes, and we went to the garden to await him.

'You will have deduced, Stamford,' said Holmes, once we were alone, 'that Mrs Stevens is quite probably a relative of Mrs Pescott. I have studied her features, and there are similarities which are highly suggestive. I am particularly interested in the shape of the ear, which can be very distinctive. I shall one day make a study of the ear and its function in establishing family relations.'

'When Mrs Pescott referred to Mrs Stevens, she did not mention to us that they were related,' I objected.

'Precisely,' Holmes replied. 'And Miss Emily, who is of similar age to Lady Kingsley, might if she was dressed as a lady pass convincingly as a sister or cousin. She is possibly the very person Kingsley saw whom he thought was related to his wife.'

'How might he have met her?'

'You recall when we first came here, we passed by the inn and a young woman was outside watering the flowers? If that was Miss Emily, and Sir Walter glimpsed her, he might well have been led to a conclusion. But now the mystery is clear to me. As Lady Kingsley's true parentage is none of our business, we may lay the question to rest, unless of course it has any relevance to the murder of Sir Walter Kingsley, which I fear it might.'

Holmes was unwilling to say more and so we sat in the shade, ruminating until Lord Redcar emerged from the cottage. He looked troubled, and seeing us waiting there, came to sit with us. Holmes gave him the news about discovering the sword, and his lordship seemed puzzled by it, but said he hoped some solution could be found. 'There may be nothing in it, but I am glad the police are being so thorough,' he said. After a moment, he went on, 'I received a letter this morning which I found very surprising. It is good news in one way, however. You recall I mentioned the will Sir Walter had made in which he left my poor girl without what would have been her right as a widow. I must admit I wondered if he had really made such a horrible document, or only told me he had in order to upset me. I now have confirmation from his solicitor that such a will was actually drawn up, and the terms insisted upon he thought quite disgusting. But then he said that it was a document in draft only. The wording had not been agreed as final, and it remained unsigned. In fact, he had rather hoped that it never would be signed, that it had been drawn up when

Kingsley was in a temper, and he would think better of his folly and make a new, more reasonable will in future. He believes, therefore, that there is a good case to be made that despite his avowed intention, Sir Walter died intestate, and Henrietta will inherit after all. I have just been to tell her about it, and she said that her husband often threatened her with this will, and she believed that it had been drawn up. She could not be sure that he had signed it. She rather thought he had not but was prepared to do so at a moment's notice if he felt he had reason. My poor girl — that she should have had to live with such a brute! How bitterly I regret encouraging her to accept him.'

Redcar drew a kerchief from his pocket and wiped his brow and eyes. When he continued speaking, his voice was harsh and broken. 'I have learned something far worse than that today. Agnes, my daughter's maid, has told me of the violence Henrietta was subjected to. On the day Agnes was dismissed, Sir Walter used my poor daughter badly. He imagined she might be with child by another man, and in a rage he struck her, knocking her to the floor. He then stamped upon her hand, saying she could not now write letters to her friend. Agnes did not witness this dreadful scene, but she has seen the bruises since coming here and attending to her mistress, and says they are considerable. One of them is just here.' He pressed a hand to his abdomen. 'I think you know what that was meant to achieve. Only the strength of whalebone saved my poor child from worse injury. Such a horrible scene would have prompted him to go and sign the will. He was prevented from doing so only by his death.'

There was little we could add to comfort the unhappy father.

'But she is safe, now,' he added.

'And I am sure the police will soon find the murderer in our midst and place him under arrest,' I said.

'I can't imagine what they are waiting for,' said Redcar. 'It has been perfectly obvious to me from the start. It was Grey who killed Kingsley. That scoundrel — no woman is safe with him.'

'But the sword we found,' I protested. 'If it is the murder weapon, Grey was not seen to either take or replace it.'

'Oh, never mind that!' said his lordship, waving away that minor obstacle. 'It might have nothing to do with it. I believe that Grey must have cast his eyes on Henrietta at the ball, as she is a handsome young lady. He addressed her in the manner such rogues do to ensnare their prey, pretending friendship, at least at first. Perhaps that was how she was induced to reveal her sufferings, her husband's threats. But even in her distress, she recognised Grey for what he was and made her escape. Grey must have thought that if he slew Kingsley before the will was signed, my daughter and her fortune would be there for the taking. When Kingsley came here, Grey saw his chance. It is all as clear as day to me now.'

Lord Redcar rose to his feet, seized with a fresh determination, but then suddenly sat down again. 'No — if I tell the police what I suspect and they arrest Grey, they might think my innocent child was part of the plot. But if I stay silent, that blackguard will try to ensnare my daughter. I would rather slaughter him myself!' At those words, his expression suddenly brightened, and an almost beatific clarity came over his features. 'Yes, of course, I shall do what I should have done all along. It is the only way, the noble way.' He rose once more, and this time he strode powerfully back to the house.

CHAPTER TWENTY-NINE

'I'll go with him,' said Holmes. 'Stamford, go to the cottage and see if Lady Redcar can come and speak to her husband. I will do what I can, but it may be that only a feminine entreaty will calm him.'

I ran to the cottage and told Molly of what had transpired, and Holmes's request, then hurried after him.

Redcar was in the manor, going from room to room, loudly demanding to know where Sir Jasper Grey was. Everyone pleaded ignorance, but Grey was discovered soon enough, alone in the fencing hall, practising exercises with a foil.

'Gentlemen!' said Holmes, finding the two protagonists alone together.

Redcar, face to face with his quarry, ignored him. 'And now,' said his lordship, who managed to be both furious and coolly determined at the same time, 'it is time for you to face your reckoning. I challenge you, Sir Jasper Grey, to meet me in mortal combat or to be thought of forever as a coward.'

Grey merely stared at him in astonishment, but Redcar strode over to the chest of fencing uniforms, threw back the lid, took out a gauntlet and cast it at his enemy's feet.

'Grey — do not do this,' said Holmes.

Grey smiled. 'Oh, it would be most impolite not to,' he said and picked up the gauntlet. 'Lord Redcar, I accept your challenge. Please choose your weapon.' Scarcely had he spoken when Redcar, instead of matching his opponent with a foil, seized one of the antique pikes from the display and ran at him, roaring like a thunderstorm. Grey hardly had time to respond, but just managed to deflect the attack with his foil, which, caught by the far heavier weapon, was struck from his hand, and spun away into a corner.

Redcar, allowing no quarter to his unarmed opponent, was preparing another attack. Grey quickly commandeered a pike for himself and wrenched a breastplate from the wall, holding it before him. Redcar evened the odds in the combat by securing a gorget, and the two men faced each other. They were like battling knights of old, with lances and shields; only the horses were wanting. Grey stood his ground, but Redcar cried vengeance and charged. The moment of impact was prodigious, but Grey was able to protect himself with the breastplate, while striking Redcar's gorget with his pike. His lordship was only a little shaken. Both were uninjured and they rounded on each other once again.

On the second run, the main casualties were the pikes, whose ancient wood could no longer stand up to the punishment. Both weapons split apart, and fragments of broken pikestaffs were scattered like the remnants of old broomsticks in a shower of splinters over the floor.

Throwing aside the now useless wood, both men ran to arm themselves with swords snatched from the open displays, and hand-to-hand battle ensued. Redcar lunged, Grey parried, and this time the old weapons held good. As the combatants circled each other, looking for openings, it became obvious that Grey had the advantage. He was taller, stronger, younger, and calmer. Redcar quite obviously wanted to kill his opponent, but Grey simply wanted to stop him from doing so.

The noise of metal on metal had by now attracted a gathering of onlookers to the hall, none of whom dared to try and stop the fight. 'What can we do?' I asked Xavier.

'Nothing. We may fall victim if we come between them,' he said. 'Let it run, and hope they tire before too much damage is done.'

The makeshift shields had now done their work; dented and battered, they were knocked or cast aside. Redcar seized a backplate, and Grey a pot helmet. It was close, intense fighting, but Grey, with longer limbs and dexterity in both arms, was able to use the helmet almost as another sword, to parry and sweep aside Redcar's frantic blows. I saw the arrow wound in his shoulder open and start to bleed, but he seemed not to notice. Redcar was obviously tiring, but then Grey, moving swiftly backwards, stepped upon a piece of broken pikestaff, which rolled and took his foot from under him. Unbalanced, he fell back to the ground, dropping the helmet. Redcar bellowed and went in for the kill, raising his sword for a stabbing blow, but Grey was able to roll aside, and Redcar's sword sank deeply into the floor. It took a few moments for the furious lord to heave the blade free, giving Grey time to recover his feet and weapons. The younger man might easily have disabled his helpless opponent but chose not to, simply steadying his breath.

Once Redcar had freed his sword, the combatants faced each other again, but at that moment, a voice rang out.

'Montague, I beg you to desist!' It was Lady Redcar, who had entered the hall and pushed her way to the forefront. 'For my sake, dear husband, and for that of our unborn child!'

Neither man moved. I took Lady Redcar's arm in case she needed support, but her strength of will held her firm. None of the onlookers dared to speak.

'Go to her,' said Grey. When Redcar hesitated, he added, 'I yield. You have the field.' He threw his sword and the helmet to the floor and made a respectful empty-handed obeisance.

Redcar stared at him for a moment, then he too dropped his weapons and went to his wife.

All the assembled onlookers heaved audible sighs of relief as Redcar tenderly took his wife's hand, his lips trembling, unable to speak for emotion.

'Perhaps,' said Holmes, 'Lady Redcar would like to return to the cottage to rest.'

She smiled. 'I would. Husband, please come with me.'

Lord Redcar, almost in tears of joy, smiled and nodded and began to conduct her from the hall. He then turned to me and beckoned for my company. I hoped my general medical education was equal to the task, but I was of course the nearest thing to a doctor there was to hand.

At Garden Cottage we reassured everyone that all was well, and Lady Redcar simply wished to rest. We accompanied her to her bedroom, which caused me a pang of terror in case I was expected to confirm her ladyship's good news. Fortunately, that did not prove necessary.

'My dear,' said Lord Redcar as his wife reclined prettily on a flowered silk coverlet, 'can you be quite certain? Doctor Langley said nothing about it to me.'

'I asked him to say nothing yet. It is a wife's privilege to give the glad news to her husband, and I wanted to do so myself. But he was quite certain. That happiness will be ours in some six months from now.'

'And you are well?'

'Very well. He said the small incidents of faintness and loss of appetite were quite usual and will soon pass.'

'Is there anything I can do for you? Whatever you might want, you have only to name it. I would go to the ends of the earth to fetch what you ask for.'

'There is a herb tisane which Mrs Pescott knows how to mix and brew. It is so soothing and invigorating.'

'Of course, I will see it is done at once.' Lord Redcar jumped to his feet. 'Mr Stamford, please attend my wife and make sure she is comfortable.' He hurried away.

I made the usual fuss to ensure she was resting properly and took her pulse just to reassure her that I knew what I was doing.

'My husband is so very kind,' she said. 'I do not think his better exists. He may not have told you, but he is planning to sell the estate, which has been in his family many years. He knows I find the manor house too cold and draughty in the winter. He is looking for a town house in Oxford, where we will be more comfortable.'

'Would he sell this cottage as well?' I asked. 'I can see how much it pleases you.'

'The cottage and its garden will be retained as a separate property on their own land, for our use.'

'But the fencing hall? Would he really give that up?'

'He intends to establish a new school of fencing in Oxford, where Baron Brambilla will be chief instructor.' She saw my expression of amazement and uttered a little laugh. 'Oh, I know what people think of my marrying a man so much my senior. They see only a title and Charlbury Park and cannot imagine any other inducement. That is because they do not know him. He is a good man, and I am proud and happy to provide him with the family we both want.'

'He cares very much for his cousin Winchip, also,' I said. 'He has been very kind to him.'

'He has a strong sense of duty, but Sir Hubert is not an easy man to like,' she said. 'He would have expected to inherit the title and estate had Montague not remarried, and the disappointment has not sat well with him, even though my husband has promised to ensure his comfort. The sale of the estate, which Montague was obliged to tell him about, was another blow. I think he was fond of this place and hoped to be lord of it one day.'

'And I was told that his marriage hopes were dashed as well,' I said.

'When he brought Miss Kent here, she glared at me as if she might like to kill me. Her eyes were like knives or arrows.'

'How unpleasant,' I said. 'I am glad I have never met her. Had she been here this last week, throwing arrows with her looks, Inspector Marsh might have arrested her on suspicion of slaying L'Épine.'

Lady Redcar stared at me, and I realised to my horror that I had let something slip. 'Are you saying that Chevalier L'Épine was killed with an arrow?' she exclaimed.

'I — yes — forgive me, Lord Redcar asked that the details were not to be described to the ladies. I should not have told you.'

'When the inspector came here to question us, it was only to ask if we had seen the Chevalier that day, which none of us had. He did not reveal how the poor man had died. I suppose we thought it might have been an accident. He did ask —' she grew thoughtful — 'he asked if we had observed any person behaving in a manner which we thought unusual. Of course, what is unusual in the streets of Oxford might be everyday behaviour in Charlbury Park.'

'Did you see anything?' I asked. 'I mean, something considered quite usual in Charlbury Park which might have attracted some attention in Oxford?'

'As a matter of fact,' she said, 'I did.'

CHAPTER THIRTY

When Lady Redcar revealed to me what she had seen, I was impatient to tell Holmes at once. Fortunately, Mrs Pescott arrived with some refreshments, and I was able to take my leave.

At the manor house, Xavier was supervising the servants in restoring some semblance of order to the fencing hall, which was now closed to everyone not engaged in that work.

Most of the gentlemen were in the drawing room or on the terrace, talking about what had just happened, with Sir Jasper Grey protesting that he had no idea what had precipitated his host to sudden violence. I found Holmes in contemplation, walking near the terrace but not engaging with the other guests.

'I am waiting for more information, which only time can provide,' he said. 'The inspector will let me know if he has learned anything from his enquiries at the Traveller's Rest. I expect that he will be told nothing useful. But I hope to learn the results of the examination of Miss Agnes's gown, and whether the stains upon it are indeed blood, or as she claims them to be, rust. Once I know that, I think I can finally prove who murdered Sir Walter Kingsley.'

'I think I know who killed L'Épine,' I said.

Holmes put away his pipe and listened.

I revealed to him all I had learned from my interview with Lady Redcar, in particular, what she had seen on the day of L'Épine's death: a figure going past the garden gate, walking away from the house in the direction of the woodland, carrying a bow, with a quiver of arrows over his shoulder. It was Sir Hubert Winchip.

'Have you seen him today?' he asked.

'No, he wasn't with the other gentlemen.'

'We must find him,' said Holmes, grimly.

'I am only glad all the weapons are not in his reach,' I said. 'Perhaps he is in his room, sleeping.'

We soon established that Winchip was not in the house, and no-one had seen him recently. With Constable Bennet on his errand to Oxford, and Inspector Marsh asking questions at the inn, there was no police presence on the estate. We were back in the drawing room to see if Winchip had returned there to occupy his favourite armchair when Mr Gorringe appeared on the terrace and peered into the drawing room.

'Excuse me, gentlemen,' he said. 'I don't want to worry you, but has anyone seen my blunderbuss?'

Holmes appealed for calm and went to speak to Gorringe. 'Have you seen Sir Hubert Winchip today?' he asked.

'Yes, he came to speak to me this morning. He asked me what I thought about Lord Redcar selling the estate. I said I didn't know anything about it, but I trusted his lordship to make sure everyone was treated properly. He didn't seem very happy.'

'Did he have the opportunity to take the blunderbuss?'

'He might have done. I was working outside, but my door wasn't locked. He could have gone in and taken it.'

'Is it loaded?'

'No, but there's powder and shot and wadding paper kept close by. I've never let him load it, but he should be able to.'

'What shall we do?' asked Brambilla. 'We have no defence against such a weapon if he chooses to fire it.'

'Perhaps he has gone to shoot harmless squirrels,' said Prince Rampal. 'Gentlemen find that exercise most soothing for reasons I have yet to understand.'

'If he sees a crowd looking for him, he might panic,' said Holmes. 'I shall go quietly and look for him and see what I can do. If any of you chance to see him, keep your distance, and let me know. Mr Gorringe, have a further search for the item in case it has been put down somewhere or returned, and if you find it, please unload it. Stamford, come with me. The man may be hurt.'

'Where shall we look?' I asked.

'He may have retired to the place where he went to fire the arrows,' said Holmes.

'But he had no reason to kill L'Épine, did he?'

'None at all,' said Holmes. 'But he did.'

We were walking to a spot now familiar to me, where there was a little clearing hidden from the house by trees, the place where Brambilla and L'Épine had gone to settle their differences. There on a tree stump sat Sir Hubert Winchip with the blunderbuss held across his lap. He looked startled when he saw us.

Holmes paused at a careful distance. The blunderbuss is not an accurate weapon by any means, as it fires a spread of small shot, but the further one is from it, the better. 'Stamford, stand away from me,' said Holmes, extending one arm to his right. 'Further. Further off. Good. Now, do not come any closer.' He then addressed Sir Hubert. 'A little target practice?' he asked.

'What is it to you?' grunted Sir Hubert.

'Or perhaps you just want to improve your spirits, as you did the other day when you took the bow and arrows out. You did manage to kill one squirrel, but of course you couldn't have known that L'Épine was nearby, as he had kept his little enterprise a secret. You saw a movement, shot your arrow, and found you had mistakenly struck a man. The neck wound prevented L'Épine from crying out, and he bled so prodigiously there was no saving him. Before you could run away the first searchers arrived, and that was when what began as an accident became something else. You had to cover your tracks, and this time you knew you were shooting at men. Grey was injured, Stamford here almost killed. When the others arrived and found L'Épine's body, the distraction gave you the chance to move away unnoticed, your arrows spent. When you encountered Lord Redcar arriving, you were able to convince him that you too had only just come to the scene.'

Winchip said nothing, but I sensed that Holmes had surmised correctly.

'Might I suggest for the sake of safety that you abandon that highly inaccurate weapon and come back to the house?'

Winchip stood up, the blunderbuss held loosely by his side, and just as I thought he was about to surrender the weapon, he raised it and pointed it at us. 'This is my right!' he exclaimed. 'The place I have wanted all my life, and now it has all been taken away on a whim. What am I to do? I was once heir to the title and the land. There was a lady to share it with me. Then nothing. The only time I felt I had power in my hands was when I stood over the body of L'Épine. No-one can take that away.'

'You can't stop both of us,' said Holmes.

I realised that he had judged the probable spread of the shot blast and had ordered me to stand at sufficient distance that only one of us would be in danger if the weapon was fired. It was suddenly clear to me, however, that if Winchip decided to shoot one of us, he would shoot Holmes, as the larger, more dangerous man, leaving me to try and make a capture.

'Holmes,' I whimpered, trying to gather sufficient courage to throw myself in front of him.

'Don't move,' he said, very firmly.

Winchip hesitated, then with a hopeless sigh, put the muzzle of the gun against his chin and pulled the trigger. There was a muffled click, and a spark erupted followed by a puff of dark smoke. That was all. Winchip sank to his knees, moaning, clutching his chin, and dropped the gun. We rushed forward and seized him by the arms.

Other men had been following us, and now that there was no danger, we had assistance to bring the nearly fainting man to the house. Holmes took charge of the blunderbuss.

'How could you tell it wasn't loaded?' I asked.

'It was. I expect he simply poured powder and shot into the barrel,' said Holmes. 'But an old gun such as this also needs powder in the pan. He might not have known that, but even if he had, the carelessness of his handling would probably have dislodged most of it.'

'Probably?'

'Most likely. The little spark we saw must have been residue, not enough to actually fire the weapon.'

Inspector Marsh returned from the Traveller's Rest to find that we had in his absence identified and arrested the murderer of Chevalier L'Épine. Sir Hubert Winchip was taken away in a carriage while Lord Redcar pleaded for his cousin to be treated with care, as he was not in his right mind.

Redcar later admitted that he must have underestimated Winchip's wish for the dukedom and the estate. It was now apparent to him that the news of the proposed sale of Charlbury Park must have rankled and festered in his cousin's troubled brain.

Holmes was able to piece together the events that had led to L'Épine's death. Winchip had decided to quell his anger and frustration by shooting something. He took a bow and arrows and went out into the woods to kill squirrels, birds, and other wildlife, not realising that anyone else would be there. Hearing a movement in the woodland and thinking it was an animal, he had fired an arrow which passed through L'Épine's neck, inflicting a fatal wound.

It was some minutes before Winchip came across the body and saw what he had done. When the first searchers arrived, shouting out for L'Épine, Winchip fired arrows at those nearest to him. By then he hardly cared who he struck or what damage he did. Once out of arrows, he threw the bow, quiver, and gloves into the river, where they floated away. He was able to circle around and avoid the searchers, but on hearing his cousin's voice, he joined him, claiming he had gone out for a stroll after his nap, when he heard the commotion and came to see what was happening.

Mrs Pescott admitted that having been told that Winchip was resting in his room, she had decided not to go and rouse him when the search for L'Épine was called. Given Winchip's usual speed of movement, she could scarcely be blamed for thinking he would not be a useful addition to a search party. Only Lady Redcar had seen him a little earlier, from her cottage window, heading out to the woodlands with the bow and arrows.

CHAPTER THIRTY-ONE

Next day, Inspector Marsh, in a thoroughly bad mood, complained to us that his enquiries at the Traveller's Rest had not been helpful. 'Mrs Stevens and her daughters now seem to think the sword was taken away and then put back again by a maid who might have been a ghost,' he grumbled. 'They don't know her name and can't describe her. If you ask me, they have invented her, and are hiding something. I will give them time to make up more stories which will put them in such knots that it will show up their lies. Then I will go and talk to them again and one of them will finally confess the truth.' He delved in his pocket. 'Oh, and I have a report for you. Some things, at least, are easily decided, such as the results of the tests on Miss Agnes's dress. Not blood, after all — just rust, as she claimed.'

'Despite that disappointment, I would like, with your permission, to speak to Miss Agnes,' said Holmes.

'For what purpose?' asked Marsh.

'I have a theory which I wish to put to the test,' said Holmes. 'I think she may have a great deal to tell us, but the trick will be to encourage her to talk.'

Marsh looked astonished. 'This is somewhat irregular, Mr Holmes, but in view of your service to the police over the L'Épine affair —'

'For which you my take full credit,' said Holmes.

'Ah, well, I am obliged to you. There's many a detective who plays a small part in an investigation and then advertises himself as the man who did it all. Very well, Mr Holmes, but I shall be there to observe and will be obliged to stop anything I don't approve of.'

'And I shall require my associate to take notes,' added Holmes.

Inspector Marsh was able to commandeer Lord Redcar's study for a private interview, and Mrs Pescott brought Miss Agnes to see us and left.

'Now then,' said Holmes to the maid, in a kindly tone of voice, 'there are a number of points I wish to be clear about. I hope you will be able to help me.'

Agnes looked surprised but compliant.

'You have told us that after you were dismissed from Lady Kingsley's service, you undertook the journey to Lowhampton to stay with your aunt. You said you were obliged to go much of the way on foot, and then slept in a field before continuing your travels on the following day. You finally completed the journey by begging a ride on an ironmonger's cart, which accounts for the marks of rust on your gown, which your aunt was at such pains to remove as best she could.'

'Yes, sir, that is the case.'

'The thing is, Miss Agnes, I do not believe your story. The long walk, the night in the field, the ride on the cart. I do not think that any of that actually took place. It was an invention designed to account for the time it took from your dismissal to arriving in Lowhampton, a journey which ought to have been completed far sooner. It was a story told to conceal where you really were and what you were doing there during that time.'

Agnes stared at Holmes. Her mouth gaped open as she uttered little cries.

'Well, what have you to say?' Inspector Marsh demanded. 'If you know the name of this ironmonger who can be your witness, tell us, now.'

Agnes was unable to speak.

'Mr Holmes,' said Marsh, 'that is a serious accusation. If you think that what Agnes has told us was not the truth, then what is the truth?' He turned to her again. 'Now then, Miss, you must be honest with the police. Is there a young man involved? A sweetheart? You would not be the first to admit to such a thing.'

She shook her head wordlessly.

'I believe,' said Holmes, 'that Miss Agnes was sent on an errand by her mistress, Lady Kingsley — a lady whom she has served with loyalty and devotion, and who had suffered greatly at the hands of her brute of a husband. In the short time she was allowed to bid farewell to her mistress, she was told what to do and was provided with the means of doing it. She went to Charlbury Park with a message for Lord Redcar, telling him of his daughter's sad plight and asking him to intervene for her. It was imperative that she enter the estate without being seen. Lady Kingsley did not want to risk word of her plea reaching her husband, since she was afraid of what he might do if he found out. She therefore ordered Miss Agnes to enter secretly, via the one place few persons knew about: the culvert when the waters are low in warm weather. Lady Kingsley, being of an adventurous nature, had made the estate her childhood playground, and I am sure she knew it well. In using the culvert, the dress was stained from passing between the rusted remains of the old iron bars.

'What neither Agnes nor Lady Kingsley knew when planning this adventure was that Lord Redcar was hosting a sporting event. He was not easily found. Perhaps Miss Agnes entered the kitchens and saw the lists of guests and found to her horror that the list included none other than Sir Jasper Grey, the very man her master had suspected of an intrigue with his wife. And then a servant came to say that Sir Walter Kingsley himself had unexpectedly arrived and was due to stay that afternoon. He was even provided with a numbered place in the steeplechase. What was she to do?

'Her saviour was Mrs Pescott, whom she knew and trusted, and who was very fond of Lady Kingsley, almost as a mother to her. Mrs Pescott knew she must protect Agnes and Lady Kingsley from suspicion. She told Agnes to go at once to the Traveller's Rest, where she would be safe and be given transport to Lowhampton. She gave Agnes a note to explain matters to Mrs Stevens. Agnes duly went there, gave Mrs Stevens the note and was told she would have bed and board, and there would be a trap leaving for Lowhampton the next morning. She undertook some cleaning work while she was there, and that was when she saw the sword, and thought of a way she could be of service to her mistress. Agnes took the sword and returned to Charlbury Park unseen. She now knew where her master was likely to be and lay in wait for him. When he appeared, she stabbed him to death. She then washed the sword in the waters of the river Charle, and returned to the inn, where she replaced the sword, hoping it had not been missed. The next morning, she travelled to Lowhampton.'

There was an agonised silence, then Agnes sobbed. 'I didn't do it! I wasn't there!'

'Then where were you?' asked Holmes. 'Only tell us that.' But Agnes continued to sob.

'Can you prove any of this, Mr Holmes?' asked Marsh, dubiously.

'I can prove one thing,' said Holmes. 'You see, Miss Agnes, even a strong young woman like yourself would not be powerful enough to thrust a sword right through a man of Sir Walter's size without it leaving a mark on her. The impact must have been considerable. At the very least I would expect some bruising on your hands from the crossguard of the sword.'

'Then let us see,' said Marsh. 'Miss Agnes, let us examine your hands.'

Agnes, still sniffing, extended her hands and turned them over, first one way and then the other. We all looked carefully. They were not the hands of a pampered lady, but they were free of any injury.

'Well,' said Marsh, 'that is your theory quite exploded, Mr Holmes.'

'I am afraid so,' said Holmes, with a sigh of regret.

'I told you, I wasn't there,' Agnes insisted. 'I don't know anything about it.'

'I agree,' said Holmes. 'You were not there. But your gown was. The question is, who was wearing it?'

Agnes gasped.

'Stamford, as is so often the case, it was you who alerted me to a possibility without realising it.'

'Did I?'

'You observed that Mr Xavier was clever enough to have committed the crime, but as he was in full sight of so many of us when Kingsley was killed, he could not, despite his intelligence, be in two places at once.'

'Well, no-one can,' said Marsh.

'When I made a list of suspects in the murder of Sir Walter Kingsley, I omitted one name from the list, the name of the person with the most powerful and obvious motive to dispatch him, but who could not have done so, as she was under lock and key at the time. Lady Kingsley. She could not be a prisoner at home and at Charlbury Park at the same time.'

'That is right,' I said.

'And yet she could,' said Holmes. 'I suspected the truth some time ago. Why, I wondered, did Lady Kingsley not ask for her maid to be brought to her at Charlbury Park? Was there a secret they shared she did not wish to be revealed? But I could not be certain until I saw Miss Agnes.' He addressed the maid. 'You do not resemble Lady Kingsley, but you are very near to her height, and I estimate that any gown which fits you would fit her also. She asked you to change clothes, and you took her place. You stayed locked in her room, careful not to show your face when meals were brought. Then when she returned, you changed clothes again and travelled to Lowhampton, inventing a story to explain the delay and the marks on the gown. Isn't that what happened?'

Agnes said nothing. She was too full of emotion to speak.

'If I am correct,' said Holmes to Inspector Marsh, 'Agnes is not guilty of any crime, as she could not have known in advance what might occur. She is a loyal servant. It was Lady Kingsley who killed her husband.'

CHAPTER THIRTY-TWO

'I suggest, Inspector, that Lady Kingsley be examined by a doctor for the bruises I would expect to be there had she killed her husband,' said Holmes. 'They have already been described to me, although they were attributed to other causes.'

'But how did she achieve it?' asked Marsh.

'Most of what I described as the actions of Agnes were in fact carried out by Lady Kingsley. She decided to go and see her father, to ask him to protect her from her husband and arrange for a separation. The estate and the woods and grounds are very well known to her. Entering by the culvert she encountered Mrs Pescott, whom she trusts entirely and who would protect her at all costs. Mrs Pescott told her of what was taking place, and the presence of Sir Jasper Grey and the arrival of her husband. The changes in the schedules were being shown to the servants.

'Mrs Pescott urged Lady Kingsley to go to the inn and obtain transport so she could return home, giving her a note for Mrs Stevens. She must have promised to speak privately to Lord Redcar on Lady Kingsley's behalf. And that might have been sufficient, but then Lady Kingsley decided to confront her husband, and knowing his violent nature, she took the short sword with her for protection. Such a blade was easily held out of sight behind her skirts.

'She knew from Mr Xavier's careful plans when the runners would go past and in what order. She confronted her husband. There was an altercation. He ordered her to go home. She refused to go. He said he was about to return home and perhaps — and I think this is in character — he threatened to force her to go with him. And then, and this is the only way to account for the injuries on Lady Kingsley, he lost his temper and tried to seize her. She raised the sword, and he ran onto it with a force that combined the strength of them both, more than she would have been capable of alone. She was standing with her back to a tree, which supported her. The impact was such that her hand was bruised by the crossguard, and the grip was driven against the middle of her body, causing deep bruising. He staggered back, pulling out the sword and cutting his hands as he did so. He then dropped the weapon, tripped on a stone, fell into the river and drowned.

'Lady Kingsley kept her head. She washed the sword and left the wood by the path, taking the tickets with Kingsley's numbers on them, so it would seem that he had left the estate as he intended.

'Returning to the inn, she replaced the sword. Once back home, she changed places with the maid.'

'But wasn't the maid locked up?'

'I am sure that is a detail Lady Kingsley was more than equal to overcoming,' said Holmes. 'The housekeeper, Mrs Crane, may be able to provide enlightenment. I suggest, Inspector, that you go to Lady Kingsley and advise her that you have two theories of what caused her husband's death. One is that Agnes murdered him out of loyalty, the other is that she herself killed him in defence of her own life. I am sure that faced with this choice, she will make the correct one. When she has told you all, I am sure Mrs Pescott will speak in her favour. The housekeeper is entirely innocent in this, acting only for the protection of Lady Kingsley. Mrs Stevens and her family likewise would have had no inkling of Sir Walter's death and are blameless.'

Lady Kingsley was subjected to a long interview with Inspector Marsh, during which a detailed statement was taken. He later told us his findings, praising the widow's self-possession and equanimity under questioning. The facts she admitted were largely as Sherlock Holmes had described. Her husband had not locked her bedroom door himself but ordered Mrs Crane to do so. The room was not usually kept locked, and the key was kept on a board in the housekeeper's office.

Alone in her room, Lady Kingsley had determined that as soon as possible she must go to her father and beg or demand that he take action to bring about a separation. When Agnes came to her door to say her goodbyes, she saw a way to carry out her plan. She told Agnes to ask Mrs Crane for the key so she could say her farewells. The housekeeper was a sympathetic individual and unlocked the door on the condition that Agnes re-locked it before she left, and returned the key to the board.

Lady Kingsley outlined the plan to her maid. Agnes was understandably afraid of what might happen if Sir Walter Kingsley came back and found her there, but her mistress promised that she would ask Lord Redcar to come and rescue her. They changed clothes, then Lady Kingsley, now dressed as her maid, put the key back on the board.

As Holmes had deduced, Lady Kingsley entered Charlbury Park through the culvert, was warned to leave by Mrs Pescott, learned that her husband had arrived, with changes made in the schedules to accommodate him, and was given a note for Mrs Stevens at the inn. Neither Mrs Pescott nor Mrs Stevens knew what Lady Kingsley would do next.

Lady Kingsley told Inspector Marsh that she had never intended to kill her husband. She had gone to speak to him, to tell him that her father was arranging a separation. She had only taken the sword with her to defend herself if her husband was to offer her violence. Her words had enraged him, and he attacked her with murderous determination, running at her, his hands reaching for her throat. In terror of her life, she raised the sword to fend him off, and he ran onto it. In shock and disbelief, he drew out the sword, dropping it onto the riverbank, and stumbled into the river. She was unable to pull him from the water and realised that he was dead. She cleaned the sword as best she could and returned to the inn. She could not explain what had happened to the final two steeplechase tickets and had no recollection of having taken them.

On returning to her home, she was able to retrieve the key without being seen and changed clothes again with Agnes, who replaced it. She told Agnes that Sir Walter was no longer to be feared and she should go to her aunt, making up a story to account for the length of the journey to Lowhampton. She then arranged for a local carrier to take Agnes to her aunt.

Holmes's only reaction, particularly on being told about the tickets, was to raise a sceptical eyebrow, but he made no comment and did not dispute the inspector's acceptance of Lady Kingsley's account.

Inspector Marsh interviewed Mrs Pescott and Mrs Stevens, who, he learned, were sisters. Both admitted that after learning of Sir Walter's death, they had not revealed that Lady Kingsley had been in Charlbury Park at the time as they wanted to protect her from suspicion. Both were quite convinced that she had not been responsible.

Mrs Crane — the Kingsleys' housekeeper, who was also questioned — was a very pleasant and dutiful person. She confirmed the locking up of Lady Kingsley, which she thought disgraceful, and was adamant that she had no idea that Agnes had taken her place.

After consideration of all the evidence, it was eventually decided that Lady Kingsley had acted in defence of her life, and she was not charged with any crime. Those who had protected her were therefore also innocent of crime.

In the days that followed, Lady Kingsley provided her father with an explanation of what had occurred on the night of the Countess of Eastleigh's ball. Upset by her husband's cruel comments and not wanting his company, she had gone out to the terrace to be alone with her thoughts. Sir Jasper Grey had followed her but had only asked after her welfare. Not wishing to spend any time alone with a man, which she knew would arouse her husband's jealous anger, she had returned indoors.

She had not told her husband of the incident, since she knew that he would jump to the conclusion that she had encouraged Sir Jasper's attentions. Not long after the ball, however, she was sent an unsigned note advising her that she had been seen with the notorious rake Sir Jasper Grey and her husband would be informed. Her only recourse was to make sure that her father and Lady Redcar knew of the incident, and that she was innocent of any scandalous behaviour, so they could defend her if it was ever made public. That way, she would be more likely to be believed than if she had stayed silent.

Her husband had long been suspicious that she was interested in Viscount Northam, a man she thoroughly disliked for his boastfulness. She had, out of curiosity, looked into Northam's ancestry, marking the discoveries in her father's library with little slips cut from notepaper, and she had realised that he was most probably descended from humble stock. When paying a visit to a nearby church, she had discovered a record of the marriage of a Robert Fernley, a groom on the Charlbury estate, and a housemaid, which she felt sure was the wedding of Robert Gilmartin. The next time her husband accused her of admiring Northam, she told him of what she had found, and that she despised the viscount for boasting about royal birth but concealing his real origins.

Lord Redcar agreed to accept his daughter's account of what happened at the Countess of Eastleigh's ball, although Holmes was once heard to observe that we would never know the full truth of it. It was rumoured that Sir Jasper Grey never left the company of an attractive woman without asking for a kiss, and in many instances, he received one. Nevertheless, Holmes was content that peace had at last been restored. Sir Jasper's reputation was not enhanced a few weeks later when he eloped with Mrs Fenton, with the alarming result that he became Lady Redcar's stepfather. Lord Redcar's opinion on the matter was not recorded.

Sir Hubert Winchip, who claimed that he only wanted to shoot squirrels and had killed Chevalier L'Épine by accident, was charged with manslaughter and two attempted murders. His trial was listed for the spring assizes, but he was found unfit to plead, and placed in a secure establishment. He died of a brain disease five years later.

Lady Kingsley inherited her husband's estate but never returned to live there. She stayed at Charlbury Park until it was sold and accompanied her father and Lady Redcar to their new townhouse in Oxford, which soon became the centre of the city's busy social calendar. Viscount Northam hoped for an invitation, which he was sure he merited, but never received one.

Lord and Lady Redcar enjoyed a long and happy marriage, which produced three daughters. The dukedom eventually lapsed for lack of a male heir. The last I heard of Charlbury Park, it was in the ownership of a gentleman's sporting club.

Prince Rampal completed his education and went on to have a distinguished career as a diplomat. After a long and patient courtship, he married Lady Kingsley, according her all the respect and deference due to a widow who had dispatched her first husband by running him through with a sword.

When Baron Brambilla opened his new school of fencing in Oxford, Lady Henrietta was one of his first female students. Although there was a room dedicated to the more elegant French style — named in honour of Brambilla's great friend, the lamented Chevalier L'Épine — Henrietta continued to prefer the Italian school, with its fearsome exclamations and direct, vigorous lunges. She was certainly her father's daughter.

HISTORICAL NOTES

In 1877 when this novel is set, the Marquess of Queensberry, aged thirty-three, was a popular supporter of sports, chiefly horseracing, boxing, athletics and cricket, and his reputation for eccentricity had not yet arisen. For a detailed biography, I refer the reader to my *The Marquess of Queensberry: Wilde's Nemesis* (Yale University Press 2013).

Queen Victoria was offered the title 'Empress of India' in 1876 and her accession was celebrated in the Delhi Durbar, held on 1 January 1877.

On 16 February 1841, the 7th Earl of Cardigan (1797–1868) was tried at the House of Lords after fighting a duel with pistols, seriously wounding his opponent. He was charged with shooting at Captain Harvey Garnet Phipps Tuckett with intent to kill, maim or cause grievous injury. There was no doubt that the duel had taken place, and Cardigan boasted of victory, but the defence claimed that witnesses who gave evidence regarding a Captain Harvey Tuckett might have been referring to a different man, and it could not be proved that he was the same man against whom the shot was fired. Cardigan was unanimously acquitted, a decision that was criticised in the press.

It is believed that the modern foot race known as a steeplechase originated in 1860, with a two-mile cross-country race as part of the Oxford University sports in that year.

Charlbury is a village in Oxfordshire whose cricket club was formed in 1874. It is believed that W. G. Grace (1848–1915) is one of the famous cricketers who once played there (source: www.charlburycricketclub.com/about-us).

The rules of cricket have undergone many changes over the years. Boundary scores were first introduced in the 1870s. There were many informal variations, before the rules were updated. Reports of matches in the 1877 sporting press indicate that boundary scores as mentioned in this book were being implemented then.

The company Burke's Peerage Ltd was founded in 1826, when it first published its definitive guide to the genealogy and heraldry of historic families. Burke's *Landed Gentry* (originally Burke's *Commoners*) followed in 1833. Early editions of Burke's *Peerage* were often criticised for inaccuracy, since it appears that the details provided by families were not sufficiently checked before publication. Oxford Professor Edward Augustus Freeman wrote in 1877 that some entries were "purely mythical … deliberate invention … invariably false." (Source: *Contemporary Review*, vol. XXX, p. 12.) More recent editions are scrupulously checked for accuracy.

For the history and practice of fencing in the nineteenth century, I am indebted to a number of sources.

In *Fencing, Boxing and Wrestling*, published by Longmans, Green and Co., of London in 1890, the fencing section is by W. H. Pollock, F. C. Grove and Camille Prevost. Grove's highly readable and often amusingly satirical introduction is strongly recommended (source: www.archive.org/details/fencing1890poll/mode/2up). J. M. Waite's *Lessons in Sabre, Singlestick, Sabre and Bayonet, and Sword*

Feats, (London, Weldon and Co., 1880) suggests that exercises for sabre and singlestick are the same, and includes the apple trick, which I would not encourage anyone to try.

The fencing mask was invented in 1780 by French master Nicolas Texier De La Boëssière, with help from fencer and duellist, Joseph Bologne, Chevalier de Saint-Georges (source: www.olympics.com/ioc/news/fencing-unmasked), but it was not generally adopted for some years.

The light sporting sabre was developed by master fencer Giuseppe Radaelli in the 1870s, but not demonstrated in England until 1893 (source: Malcolm Fare in www.leonpaul.com/blog/the-history-of-sabre-fencing/).

The Vulliamy family of London were clock and watch makers in the eighteenth and nineteenth centuries who enjoyed royal patronage.

The last English peer to be hanged was the fourth Earl Ferrers, executed in 1760 for murdering his steward. He was tried and convicted by his peers.

Evidence given at murder trials reported in 1877 show that it was then possible by examination of stains chemically and under a microscope to determine that they were of blood, but it was not possible to state conclusively that the blood was human.

In 1100, William II, known as William Rufus, son of William the Conqueror, was killed by an arrow while out hunting in the New Forest.

In Chapter 24 it is clear that Sir Hubert Winchip suffered what nowadays would be described as a TIA, a transient ischaemic attack or "mini stroke" caused by a temporary disruption in the blood supply to part of the brain, which often resolves itself in a matter of hours. For an account of how such an event was regarded in the 1870s, I consulted *On Paralysis From Brain Disease in Its Common Forms* by H. Charlton Bastian (New York, D. Appleton and Company, 1875), accessed online via http://www.archive.org/details/onparalysisfrom00bastgoog/. See pp.130–1 in particular.

In the seventeenth century, suicides were traditionally buried at a crossroads, sometimes with a stake through the body. In 1823, an Act of Parliament allowed suicides to be buried in a churchyard, but only at night and without a Christian service. Daylight burials were permitted in 1882 (source: https://www.parliament.uk/about/living-heritage/transformingsociety/private-lives/death-dying/dying-and-death/burying/).

Appropriately, weapons masters Brambilla and L'Épine stare "poniards" at each other. A poniard is a light, thrusting dagger. It is mentioned in Shakespeare's *Much Ado About Nothing*: "She speaks poniards, and every word stabs." (Benedick, Act 2 Scene 1.)

Charlbury Park, the river Charle, St Cuthbert's Church, the village of Lowhampton, and the Dukedom of Charlbury are all fictional.

Holmes did later make a study of the shape of the ear and wrote two monographs on the subject, which he refers to in *The Cardboard Box*.

A NOTE TO THE READER

The timeline of the events in the life of Sherlock Holmes in the canonical fifty-six stories and four novels has occupied, fascinated and sometimes frustrated Holmesian scholars for many years. The most commonly accepted year of Holmes's birth is 1854. He did not meet Dr Watson and occupy 221b Baker Street before 1881.

Almost nothing is known about his early life and very little about his education. I think it is possible that, like Conan Doyle, he spent a year at school on the continent, where he acquired his knowledge of modern languages. He is known to have spent two years at a collegiate university, which means either Oxford or Cambridge, although which one, and what courses he took have never been revealed, but he did not take a degree. The year in which he settled permanently in London is unspecified. His first recorded case is that of 'The Adventure of the *Gloria Scott*', as recounted to Dr Watson, which took place during the university vacation. Holmes had been developing his powers of observation and deduction and was known amongst fellow students for his singular method of analysing problems. At the time this was nothing more to him than an intellectual exercise. During his work on the *Gloria Scott* mystery, however, it was suggested to him that he would make a brilliant detective and that idea took hold and gave him a direction in life.

Holmes realised that he lacked the broad and varied fields of knowledge which would serve as a foundation for his mental skills. The next few years were dedicated to acquiring that knowledge, and in doing so, he created the man who burst upon the literary scene and met Dr Watson in the first Holmes novel, *A Study in Scarlet.*

In my work, I have suggested that Holmes was at university during the years 1873–75, solving the *Gloria Scott* mystery after his second year. Realising that his particular requirements could not be provided by a university course, he did not return, choosing instead to undertake his own studies. He had boxed and fenced at university and while there is no evidence that he devoted dedicated practice to either later on, it is clear that these were skills he retained. His lodgings in London's Montague Street placed him close to the British Museum where he must have spent many hours studying in the library, and he enrolled at St Bartholomew's Medical College for practical courses in chemistry and anatomy.

And that is where my series begins.

Reviews are so important to authors, and if you enjoyed this novel I would be grateful if you could spare a few minutes to post a review on **Amazon** and **Goodreads**. I love hearing from readers, and you can connect with me online, **on Facebook**, **Twitter**, and **Instagram**.

You can also stay up to date with all my news via **my website** and by signing up to **my newsletter**.

Linda Stratmann

2023

lindastratmann.com

Sapere Books is an exciting new publisher of brilliant fiction and popular history.

To find out more about our latest releases and our monthly bargain books visit our website:
saperebooks.com